A Note of Scandal

Nicky Penttila

A

A NOTE OF SCANDAL

To all my teachers

ONE

*We call our fighting men heroes, and how do we show our grati-
tude? They may sit at any corner they wish, holding their bloody
shakos upside down, pleading for alms.*
  —The London Beacon, July 1815

The problem wasn't getting into the wards for injured soldiers, notwithstanding the fearsome head nurse at the entry. The problem was getting out unscathed.

Olivia Delancey could feel the dozen pairs of eyes locking onto her and her fidgety friend Merry as they crossed the threshold into the vaulted space of Ward Four. Olivia's gaze skittered over the forms stirring under dun sheets in cots that lined both long-windowed walls, glancing away from the limbs set at angles of pain in the afternoon shadow, seeking out the second-last man on the right.

A whispered breeze tracked their progress, breaths inhaled and held, then painfully released as the two ladies in city-bred finery passed on by. She held her own breath, as if that would keep the ill smells from making sense.

But worse than the attention were the many pairs of eyes belonging to men so broken they could show no interest at all. Including the one they sought. Lank-haired and listless, Martin Purdy sat propped up, facing away from them, perhaps dozing.

Olivia stopped at the foot of his cot. His left leg and arm thrust from the worn sheet, angry rusted skin puckered and flaking away to expose furious red beneath. She prayed the opiate, laudanum, was enough to deaden his pain.

She shouldn't have brought Merry here, despite her wheedling. The white lie was easy enough. Olivia had only to pretend to be Martin's fiancée and the nurses opened the doors to her, but this dark truth was far too hard to take. But as the girl slipped past to sink to her knees and take up Martin's good right hand, Merry's face shone, as if she viewed some glorious mirage rather than the wreckage Waterloo had left behind.

Martin's lazy dark lashes opened wide, the black of his eyes widening as if to drink her in. "Merry, I told you not to come," he said. His voice carried no trace of the pure tenor that once had soared past the rafters of this very hall.

"If you meant me to stay away, you wouldn't have written you were here." Merry leaned into him, resting her head on his heart, her auburn curls reaching up to his chin.

Carefully, he lifted his bruise-darkened hand, touching her hair as if it were gossamer. With a small sigh and wobbly smile, he suddenly became the man Olivia remembered. The man Merry loved.

Olivia sighed in synchrony, closing her eyes on her tears. Oh, to have someone to love, someone to break the rules for, just to steal a moment together. She had been arranging these meetings for Martin and Merry for years before he shipped out four months ago, and it never grew old.

But without her sight to distract her, the throb of pain coursing through the room was impossible to ignore. Eyes snapping open, she searched for some distraction. The man in the cot beside Martin's must be thirsty, if his rasping breath was any indication. She bustled toward the washstand between the beds and reached for the water pitcher.

"Drink, or should I use the sponge?" She forced herself to look at him to see the answer. Sponge, his lips said, no air behind the word. She turned back.

He could have been her brother.

As she squeezed a slow line of moisture into his mouth, his blue-veined eyelids closed, shutting away the silent scream in his eyes.

"Angel," the soldier rasped, letting loose her hand. Olivia swallowed down her burning shame. It was a pitifully small service, and more to help her own weakness than his. She grimaced a smile and then turned to the high windows a moment to look for her own bit of mercy. Was it really only four years ago that this room had been a grand music hall, and she a wide-eyed debutante nearly faint with excitement at catching her first glimpse of Master Hayden himself?

"It's a fine bed-down here," Martin said to Merry, drawing Olivia back to the present. Merry's lips, nearly puckered from the tight clenching of her jaw, turned down in disbelief.

"Aye, lass. Better than mucky camp bivouac."

That was the truth of war. Not the grand chords and cymbals of the military parades, not the shining buttons of the lieutenants who wanted one last dance before shipping out. Olivia had told some of them no, thinking it too great a sacrifice to her pride to dance with a mere Mister. She welcomed the sharp edge of regret. She deserved it.

What had she done to aid her country, when these men had given their bodies? A mere few hours of stitchery, and poorly done at that. Merry had finished her stockings and gloves for her in exchange for Olivia's correcting her Latin homework.

But she had done one other thing.

"Martin, did you receive my letter?"

"The music? Aye, my lady. Yours was to be the last tune I mustered up."

"Nonsense. You'll be well enough soon. But what did you think?"

A weak smile played across his chapped lips. "You haven't changed. I tinkered it a little, and the grubs right liked it. Took us into Quatre Bras right nicely."

"You all marched to my tune?"

"Fought to it. 'Twas the last lovely sound a fair lot of our boys heard on this earth."

Was it good to be the last thing a young man remembered on this earth?

"Not worth a frown, Miss Olivia." Martin drew the words out. "An inspiration. Even old Nosey asked me about it when I was piled up back of the battlefield."

"Wellington?"

"He said a word and got me this fine accommodation. Better than the hull hospitals out on the river."

Merry snorted as her attention fixed back on them. "Fine accommodation? This room reeks of d—." She stopped short, covering her nose and mouth with her hand. Then she did the same to Martin. "You won't heal here. We need to get you out."

He tilted his head, sliding out from under the gentle mask of her hand. "How do you know 'tisn't me who smells? Better to be hidden among many, here."

"Nonsense." Merry thrust her dimpled chin out as if she were an oversized child. "There must be a way. Livvie will come up with one. Right, Livvie?"

Another two sets of eyes turned toward her. Merry's gaze held hope and expectation, Martin's, doubt under exhaustion.

Olivia felt the familiar angry rumble in her blood. Why must people expect so much from her? Why did they refuse to see her for what she was: a chipped piece of fancy plate, only good for petty schemes and pretty tunes that couldn't be played in public?

But she was a very good schemer, and Martin and Merry deserved her best effort. Hadn't Martin groomed her as a composer? And Merry was more a beloved sister than a friend, standing beside her when the ladies of her consequence would not. For who would ever wish to stand next to the most beautiful girl of the season?

Merry and Martin loved so deeply, lived so fully, they deserved every chance at happiness. Olivia was not meant for love, of course. Her fate had been settled for years. But if she could help them, perhaps a tiny spark of that love might reflect back to her.

She nodded, decision made. "Of course."

The lovers turned back to each other. A shaft of irritation snaked through Olivia's gut. They thought nothing of how it might cost her to help them. Why should they? The first law of love was selfishness.

Pressing on her belly, she pushed the unwanted feeling away. The smells had somehow lessened. She stood and scanned the room slowly, memorizing its sounds and shadows.

England's wounded overfilled its infirmaries and overflowed the hospital ships in the harbors. She should be able to assist a bare one of them. It should be simple, really.

If only she knew how.

Two

This summer, the Baron P--- has no need to frequent the gambling dens, for he is placing his bets on the horse-races for seats in Commons. We raise a tankard to the electoral process.
—The London Register

The last man Will Marsh expected to see at a politician's ale-day was his old Oxford roommate. But Richard Avery leaned against the entry wall at the Swan's Neck Inn in his parade uniform, looking ever more the golden hero.

"Major." Will nodded with mock formality. "Welcome home."

Avery cuffed him on the shoulder, his grin wide, and then hugged him properly. "Still doing your own legwork, I see. Our humble Mr. Mellon rates the attentions of the *Beacon*'s august publisher?"

Will winced, and stepped back, studying his friend. Could

Avery smell his desperation? Surely not. "You look well enough. War becomes you."

"Peace again, now, I fear. And this one will hold." Richard rolled his eyes. "Returned to town last night and here I'm roped into the family campaign. I'm aching for the Continent already."

"A pity. You might give up your inheritance."

"That sharp tongue, I did so miss it. Although your man Bragge was on the ferry over, so it was not a complete drought."

"Wish he were here." Will rather wished he could have afforded the blunt to keep Bragge in Brussels through the diplomatic post-mortem. Nobody could skewer the lordlings of Europe half as well. He ignored the shiver of worry nibbling between his shoulder blades. The paper was still in the black, by a whisker.

"Which one is Mellon?" Scanning the room, Will could not spot the purportedly distinguished member of the House of Commons. Most of the county's menfolk filled the drafty room, drawn by the offer of free ale and the rare opportunity to touch hands with true blue-bloods.

The Baroness and Baron Pettigrew, hosting in favor of their trusty candidate, did not disappoint. Her fiery hair, upswept in the style of her youth, nearly reached the rat-trodden rafters. Pettigrew matched her height with a bicorne hat large enough it might carry a small dog safely. With their high-pitched voices and flourishes of manner, they commanded attention.

Avery pushed Will's shoulder to the left. "There, toward the window. Lecturing that vision in blue silk."

Will saw the woman first. Her delicate elbow was trapped in

a black-furred mitt of a hand, apparently that of Mr. Jeremy Mellon, M.P. He had angled himself as if pushing her toward the muddied wall. As he leered over her, she stood very still. Though she stood in profile to him, Will could tell even her eyes remained still. The weak light from the smoke-fogged window gained luster, passing through the gold-blond ringlets framing her face. All her attention was on Mellon.

"Can you believe that waistcoat?" Avery snorted. "Is it puce?"

Will pulled his gaze away from the lady to take in her companion. "Plum. Latest thing." His gaze flicked back to the lovelier form.

"Drinking in dear Cousin Olivia?" Avery accepted a mug of over-yeasty ale from the passing barkeep.

"Olivia Delancey?"

"The Honorable. And once my intended. Seems I've cocked that up, as well." He sipped the foam off the top of the ale. "Too bad I can't invite you to sup with us tonight. Should be a right circus."

"She hangs so on his words." Will frowned, and then caught himself. She was not the story; that florid piece of political beef beside her was.

"Can't you see? Look at her chin. The edge, there, under her ear." It was pale, but even at a distance he could see a slight tremor. A crack in the chiseled beauty.

"She's ill?"

"White-hot angry, my friend." Will tore his gaze from the porcelain lady to raise an eyebrow at him. "Trust me," Avery said, "she has had that tiny flaw since she was a dandled babe."

"Taken advantage of it, have you?" Will's eyes narrowed, oddly protective. Avery put up his hands in mock surrender.

"Only a very small snake." He grinned. "Down the back of her dress, at a tea party."

"And all she did was set her chin?" Ladies were cold, he knew, but that sounded downright frigid.

"At first. Then the screaming started." Avery pushed into the crowd. "We'd best remove the poor man from danger, don't you think?"

Though the room was small, they made slow progress through the swells of men reeking of sour beef, stale beer, and sweat. Wishing to avoid even the appearance of aggression, so swift a complaint to launch against newsmen, Will allowed Avery to lead. But he did not take his gaze from the lady. Mellon's hand had crept up to her shoulder. Was he pulling her closer?

Will's hand fisted. He might need to punch his quarry before interviewing him.

"Mellon." Avery stepped between the couple, allowing the society jewel to take a step back, arm intact. Will stopped short beside her.

When her attention was elsewhere, her round, full lips dominated her face, the bottom line of the lower lip parallel with the soft oval of her jaw line. But no one would notice the rest of her face, or the fragile cream of her skin, when she turned her gaze on them. Eyes like sapphires, expensive and rare. And crackling with anger.

"Avery. A major now? Felicitations." Mellon latched onto his new prey, pumping Avery's hand up and down as if to draw water. "I know you'll agree with me."

"I have no doubt. What was the question?"

The Diana of Westminster turned her gaze to her cousin. Will forced himself to look away, toward Mellon. His reason for being here.

Then she spoke, and ruined his best efforts.

"Mr. Mellon has been … informing me … of yet another weakness of my sex." Her musical voice dripped honeyed venom. "We cannot create." She flicked an eyebrow at her cousin, sharing an unspoken joke.

"Heaven protect us from the likes of another Caroline Lamb." Mellon's sibilants whistled. "We need good books, not the willful trash that is all women can produce." The final "S" lingered, slithering into a wheeze.

"If she cannot singularly create, at least we all agree woman can pro-create, though that also requires a man," Avery said.

Mellon barked a laugh, playfully punching Avery's shoulder. With effort, Will forced his own hands to relax.

"You take his side?" she said to her cousin. The space between her jaw and her ear pulsed white-red. Her eyes glittered. Why Avery didn't explode into flame, Will had no idea.

"Stand down, Livvie." Avery laughed and raised his arm to grasp hers. She twisted out of his reach, face turning to Will. Her gaze roasted him on the spot.

"Here's Mr. William Marsh, Livvie, publisher of the *Beacon*. Will, Miss Olivia Delancey." Will gave her his best society bow. She neither smiled nor held out her hand. He could not guess what had her so knotted up, but he had to think of something to say. Something about authors?

"You read widely, Miss Delancey?"

"I do." The corners of her lips turned down, but at least sparks did not fly at him. "Even the *Beacon*, on occasion. For the foreign report." She turned her attention back to Avery.

Will's face flushed again. Hers was a common-enough refrain, but still it stung. No one was interested in foreign news now that there was peace. She had stumbled upon the very reason he stood here, deep in these political dregs, rummaging about for a story that would sell. He pulled his gaze away from her, told himself to stop trying to decipher that odd expression, and trained his attention to the man of politics.

Unfortunately, as with the rest of the candidates Will had pursued this past week, Mellon had nothing of interest to say. Another of Miss Delancey's father's gaggle of toad-eaters, the portly Mellon was an empty vessel. Another afternoon that would earn him no readers and no coin.

But though Will's gaze now rested on the man, he still heard a soft hiccup, his Tatiana in cerulean silk trying to get her breath back under control. He smiled, not surprised she could recover quickly. After all, her name, Olivia, did mean peace. Or was it serenity?

The gas-bag politician thought the smile aimed at him, and launched into more of his hackneyed blather. Will let the words slide past his ears, his hearing tuned instead to her slightest movement. It seemed as if everyone in the room had stopped clinking their mugs, talking, even moving. He didn't know how long he stood there, stalking the sounds of her presence.

But Avery had already heard enough. "Such fecundity of

language, Mellon. It is truly a pity the ladies cannot vote for you." He smirked at his cousin. Will turned in time to see her aim another quick knife-slash of a glance at him. His hackles rose.

Mellon had scarcely slowed. "No need for that, none at all. A political nightmare. Not an arena for woman."

"Nor trade, nor the arts." Miss Delancey's soft voice could have cut iron.

"The arts?" Even the man's laugh whistled. "This is where we began. Women may be excellent performers, perhaps adequate craftspeople, but artists? Never."

"And you truly believe that, Mr. Mellon?" She looked down a moment. Her hands knit together.

"We politicians can't afford to lie." He chuckled, looking sideways at Will, implicating him.

Was she trembling?

"Do you know any female artists, Mr. Marsh?"

He did not. He wanted to take her hand, soothe her brow, ease the shards of ice out of her lovely eyes. But Will could not lie, either.

"I'm sorry, ma'am. I know no women who are artistic geniuses. Though I do understand," he said, raising his voice as Mellon wheezily inhaled as if to launch into speech again, "that many lady artists display their work under assumed names. So it may well be the last book I read was written by a woman. *His Lonely Guest*, by Anonymous."

"Penned, but not acknowledged." Her expression changed in an instant. The pulsing slowed, her jaw released. Her eyes softened, crinkling at the corners.

Avery passed a hand in front of her face, but she only blinked. "You're not having one of your ideas, are you, Livvie?"

She blinked again, and then caught Will in her gaze, which now held a different sort of heat. "Would you buy such a work, for your own paper, Mr. Marsh? Your stories are credited to no source."

"They may have no credit, but I know who the correspondents are."

"And are any female?

Mellon's wheezing sounded dangerous, but Will had no ears for it. He suddenly felt he was walking a minefield, alone. "I cannot say."

"See?" Mellon sneezed out. "A wise man, indeed."

"But I would not rule it out." Will tried to read intention in her crystalline eyes and failed. "We do get our best society gossip from ladies."

"From ladies' maids," Avery cut in. "I know of a few."

She continued without acknowledging her cousin. "So, it would not be so large a step to use a lady's own words in print."

Still trying to trace the line of her thinking, Will leaned closer. He inhaled, tasting the warm cinnamon of her breath.

She startled, her gaze jumping to behind his shoulder.

"The lady is not for quoting." Her father, the baron, stood at Will's side, or as close as his mammoth hat would allow. Pettigrew's voice dripped ennui, but the dark eyes hidden in the deep creases of his lids were sharp. "Slumming, Mr. Marsh?"

Will shifted his attention nearly completely. Pettigrew was no lackey. "Heard this would be a contested race this year, your lordship."

"And who, did you hear, was to be the new contestant?" Pettigrew stood in front of his daughter, absorbing all her light. Mellon, cowed by the baron, nodded his regards and slunk toward the baroness, who welcomed him with hearty pantomime.

"I'll not betray a source." The baroness threw her arms wide in mock-surprise, pretending Mellon had goosed her. The crowd about her crowed with laughter.

"Do you have enough for your news-sheet now?" The baron could appear as still as his daughter. Will wondered if his jaw, like hers, could give away his secrets.

Without apparent effort, Pettigrew began to herd him toward the door. Already a quarter-room's length away, Will turned back to the window. Olivia Delancey drew the last of the day's sun from the room's only window about her as she bestowed her quiet attention on an open-faced youth in a baker's smock. The lad looked about to faint.

Pettigrew's pace quickened, and Will reluctantly allowed himself to be escorted out. They passed through the door and into the burnt-orange of a midsummer sunset. Pettigrew rested his long-fingered hand on Will's forearm, signaling him to stop, but did not look at him.

"I hear you reside in this county now. Intending to sell the business?"

"Looking to the future, my lord."

Pettigrew did look at him then. Will couldn't understand the interest in the man's eyes.

"Ever considered a run at politics, Marsh? Might try doing some good rather than always bewailing the bad."

How did he know? Will knew his face betrayed his surprise, for Pettigrew returned an eel of a smile.

"A contest? Not this time. But the next? Might well be."

And more opportunity to wonder at the lovely Olivia Delancey. At least until some society sap trapped her and her jeweled gaze into the velvet coffin of marriage.

THREE

For those left behind – the sweethearts, the young wives, their children – these reconciliations, so long awaited, are that much the sweeter.

—The Beacon

Olivia hadn't seen so much good humor and cheer at a family dinner in years. Cousin Richard could be relied upon to raise their spirits, of course, but their longtime and long-suffering solicitor, Mr. Swizzlewit, also had a few extra guffaws to spare. She missed Merry, who would have made an even six at table, but was hardly surprised when her friend, struggling to keep her composure after the visit with Martin, pleaded sick.

Papa raised his glass toward Richard, on his right. "To Avery, who again courted death in the service of our country."

They drank, Richard deepest. He smacked his lips and set the glass down opposite hers with a hollow clink. "Perhaps the tight-fisted Tories will see it that way, at last." His grin gave his golden face a wolfish cast.

"It was not an unnecessary expense, I'll grant you that." Papa also downed the glass in a single draft. Olivia suspected he had chosen this night for the welcoming-home party because Richard would have imbibed plenty at the alehouse and so would not dent so dearly their depleted wine stores. Still, Papa had had their glasses refilled during the cheese course.

Mr. Swizzlewit, sitting precariously on two of the larger books from the library to make him of a height with the other guests, carefully swerved to gaze at Olivia at his side.

"Here's to more very good news. In the near future."

"Hear, hear," said Richard. He winked at her, and then signaled the servant to pour him more wine.

Swizzlewit, whose feet swung nearly two feet from the floor, smiled so wide his eyes nearly disappeared in the folds of his face. "It has been a long time, Miss Olivia. You have been quite patient, a property you did not have much stock in as a child, if I remember rightly."

"You give me more credit than I deserve." In fact, she was itching to bolt this table and hide in one of the silent rooms upstairs. But that would not solve her problems. She leaned closer to him. "Though I have been waiting for you to enjoy your dinner before asking about something that has been, well, burdening me."

He leaned nearly forty-five degrees to pat his puffy little hand on hers. "Do not fret about the barony. Your father has great prospects. A temporary retrenchment, is all. Quite common, these days." He spoke so softly she knew Richard, across the table, could not hear.

She shook her head. "It isn't that. I have a friend, in need." An image of Martin, bound into that hospital bed, flashed through her mind. Suddenly the wine she'd drunk turned to burnt iodine on her tongue. She must help him.

"A friend." He patted her hand once more, and then pivoted himself up again. "A male friend?"

"A veteran of the wars." She saw him cast a glance across the table. "Not an officer, but infantry."

"Cannon fodder."

"He wishes to marry, and needs a more-secure field."

"You seek him employment?" He frowned. "Can he not do that himself?"

"But I know more people than he, and you know even more. And he still recovers from his wounds. His memories are not as sanguine as my cousin's seem to be."

"Do not judge Avery's memories from his face. His surface has always been gay."

She nodded an apology, keeping her gaze on her cousin. Richard had spent the past hour regaling them with the daily comedy of camp life among the Horse Guard. From what she had read in the papers and heard from Martin Purdy, tragedy was more the order of the day. But a man saw what he wished to see, not particularly what was there.

No, that was not fair. Richard was tailoring the war to his audience. Even Papa, cutthroat enough in Parliament, would not care to hear the gruesome truths of battle.

Swizzlewit watched her, a half-smile on his wizened face. "It's such a pleasure to watch a young woman thinking."

She smiled to match him. He, with the occasional addition

of an equally diminutive Mrs. Swizzlewit, was one of the longest – and strongest – threads holding her life together.

"A young man, college-educated but who has devoted himself primarily to music, needs another form of employment. What do you suggest?"

Head tilted nearly to his shoulder, he gazed at the ceiling. "Literate. Might do well in business."

"What sort of business?"

"There's the rub, my little Livvie. Oy!" Stopped in the middle of straightening his head, he swiped at a wisp of shoulder-length hair trapped in his top coat button. "Mrs. Swizzlewit says I need a hair-cut. I suppose." He shook his pencil straight gray-white locks, vain in his own way. "Your man needs employment because he is poor, I take it? A charity case?"

"He wishes to marry."

"So, not completely bereft." Swizzlewit nodded. Olivia did not correct him, still considering whether to loan Martin money from her own small portion. "What he needs is prospects."

"What sort of prospects?"

"So he can stand before the father and report that he is learning a trade and at such and such a time he will be productive." His eyebrows popped up, and his chin dropped, stretching his rather square face into a rectangle. "Here now. I'll be needing a new clerk soon. Simmons is taking on the office in Plymouth – he's also in the marrying way – and I will need a man to clerk and learn the business here."

"That sounds perfect. He is a careful writer, and keeps his commitments. When do you need him to start?"

"Not so fast, ducks. I'll need to interview the man. And there is the matter of the articles of payment."

She had forgotten that part. Solicitors were not charities. But Martin had little money. Perhaps she could negotiate. "He is a veteran. He has given all for his country. Could you not see yourself—"

"No, I could not. Well, perhaps I could slice a portion from the fee. He would need to pass muster, though. I couldn't have one of those rough-and-readies greeting my clients, could I?"

"He is nothing like that." Olivia poured more wine into his glass. "He was my music and dance teacher. Very fine manners."

"Excellent. For a former teacher of yours, I'll halve the price. A bare thousand pounds."

The bottle slipped from Olivia's hand, falling the last quarter-inch to the table. So much? She schooled her face not to show her doubts, and smiled at him. "Done. When may we call on you?"

"I'm always working, as you know. Work is life." He patted his belly happily. "Just send a note ahead, and I'll come to call on you. Or send the man on his own. No need to observe the formalities." His gaze shifted to Olivia's mother, who was rising from the table. Dismounting could be an awkward moment for the solicitor, but tonight he slid with a boozy grace from the books to the floor.

"My dear Swizzlewit, won't you join us in the parlor?" Mama, who had not changed from the wig she had worn for the political rally, cast a towering shadow over him.

"Alas, I cannot. I have one last meeting tonight, or I would gladly remain in your happy circle." He pulled himself up to bow over her hand.

"A pity. Today should be more than happy." Mama smiled over his head at Richard. "Olivia, perhaps Richard would like to hear that new piece of music? Take him up to the piano room. You may join us for tea afterward."

The marriage proposal. Olivia's back teeth clenched. She had to get Richard to come to the point, Mama had insisted again this afternoon. She thought it Olivia's fault her cousin had not proposed last summer, the first time they'd thought the wars over.

"Splendid idea, Aunt." Richard held out his arm to Olivia. "I've brought you a present from the Continent. The music room is the perfect setting."

This was what she had been waiting for these long years, Olivia told herself as she walked with "her major" upstairs and down the hall to her favorite room. Finally, to leave the nest and start the next stage of her life. She should be giddy with expectation, or at least relief. But her legs moved as if laden with chains, her shoulders tight as if pilloried.

These nerves were just anticipation, surely. She truly did not wish to remain trapped in her parents' domain. Though a lady was equally confined, in her father's home or her husband's. Perhaps it was simply that she did not wish to act in a big scene, pretend to swoon or screech. Just get it over and done, and she would relax.

Richard led her to the loveseat near the unmade fireplace. As she settled down, he stepped over to the chair opposite, reaching for an infant-sized package swaddled in black crepe. A little large for a wedding locket or ring.

"A gift, Livvie. Something you will prefer far more than me." He set the package carefully beside her and untied the cloth wrapping. An instrument, strings, a long black neck leading to a dark-wood bowl.

"A lute?"

"A guitar. *Guitarra*," he said, rolling the Rs. His plait of dark blond hair swung free of his collar as he lifted the guitar free of the wrapping. "Everyone in Spain plays them. I thought of you right away."

He pushed the fabric to the floor and sat beside her on the sofa. "You must sit straight, with a foot up, like this. You mark the note with your left hand on the neck, here," he said, leaning toward her, "and make the rhythm with your right, down here." His handsome, sharp-edged face carried more weight than when they were children together, but his pale, tapered hands were almost the same. She watched his buffed nails as he flicked his right hand down once, sounding a G chord, then touched each string separately. The timbre was warmer than a pianoforte, yellow tones to her piano's bluish ones. And the sound carried longer.

Olivia's fingers itched. "Let me try."

Richard set the guitar in her lap and fetched an odd folding step from among the wrapping. He knelt at her feet, unfolded the step and set it beside her left foot. "Step on this. That gives you the proper angle." He grinned up at her. "The Spanish ladies who play in public have long hems so they won't show their ankles and have the men swooning. You'll need to do that, as well."

"I'll never play in public."

"In private, then." He set his hands on her shoulders, pushing them back, straightening her spine. His left hand took her right, showing her how to place it above the strings at the hole in the instrument's body. She reached around the long part of the guitar the way he had.

23

"Don't press down yet. Open strings, it's G." She grazed the strings with her fingertips, feeling the tension and release in sound. He reached for her left hand, moving her fingers so the tips pushed a string to the wood. "Change just two strings, here and here, and it's A."

Larger than a lute, the guitar sounded richer, deeper. The notes rang through her, as if she were part of the instrument. She could feel her blood pulsing where her belly met the back of the guitar.

"One more finger. D." At her sharp intake of breath, Richard sat back on his heels and smiled. "Thought you'd like it."

"Show me more."

He named the parts of the instrument: the neck, the bridge, the body. "A woman's body, with these curves." Then he showed her how the frets divided notes, the open-note of each string, and how to tune using the ringing harmonics of the fifth fret.

She lifted her fingers to blow on the tips, warm and starting to ache. But she did not want to stop.

"More."

"Don't know much more. But I have a friend back from the Continent who can show you." He ran his hand through those wayward curls, and Olivia saw a difference.

"You're wearing a ring."

He pushed the hand deeper into his hair, holding it behind his neck if to hide it. "Livvie. There's something else." His gaze did not meet hers. The silence grew too long.

"I thought you did not wear them, after that accident when you were riding."

Richard groaned and stood. He paced away from her, to the

fireplace, and kicked a log back deeper into its unlit maw. He turned, his golden face now mottled in reds, his brows furrowed.

Oliva's mind buzzed. Had he inherited a title? But it didn't look like a signet ring, just a plain gold band. Was it a war trophy? A regimental honor? But why would that cause him such distress?

Was it an engagement ring? All the movements in her body stopped dead.

"Don't look at me like that." He blew out a breath, and put his hands on his hips, eyes on the floor. "Zounds if I can think of a way to sweeten it. This is it: I am wed. Her name is Rosa, and she's so lovely it makes my knees knock."

The buzzing returned until it filled the room. Olivia's thoughts seemed to balloon her head. She knew men were unreliable, but Richard had promised – promised – to marry her. It had been assumed all these twelve years and more. He'd all but married her last summer, but never came to the point. Then Napoleon escaped, and any wedding was off, at least until he was caught again. Now it was to be off forever.

As he rubbed his hand across his brow, the ring glinted in the flickering candle light. Spanish women must be more persuasive than the English at getting their men to wear the symbol of their entrapment. They must be better at many things, to steal Richard away from his people. From her.

"Felicitations," she said, the word a glacier.

"Don't be that way. Don't you think this hurts me, as well?" Sighing, he drew closer, sinking onto the sofa beside her. He leaned his shoulders against the back of the furniture, a devil in a god's body, and covered his eyes with his naked hand.

"How could you do this?" She did not regret the harpy's hiss of her voice. "After what we did last summer?"

"Don't worry about that," he said, eyes still shuttered. "No one expects a lady over the age of twenty to be pristine, you know."

How could he say such a thing? Or even think it? Did he truly think so little of her, of what they had done together?

Did he not see her at all?

Under her glare, his golden curls seemed to take on a fiery glaze. This wasn't fair. It wasn't right. He could not do this to her. She wasn't worth much, she knew, but surely more than a piece of flotsam, jettisoned after one sun-filled afternoon of pleasuring. If one could call a patch of awkward grappling and panting pleasure.

He sat there so calm, so unconcerned. From the top of his jack-straw head to the toes of those gleaming Hessians, he was false. A lying, cheating, self-satisfied fool. One best put out of his misery.

Olivia's spine twisted, closing off her air. Her palm screamed where it was smothering the neck of the guitar, and she realized she was standing. A flash of blue in the edge of her vision caught her attention. In the mirror above the mantel, she saw herself, her face a gargoyle's, poised as if readying to hit a high cricket ball, the guitar held aloft and behind like a bat. Or an ax.

If she let her arms go, a smooth curve would take her bat solidly into the crown of his blastedly insouciant head. As if she were watching a play, she saw the body twist just a bit more, reaching the top of the swing.

She stiffened, shocked. Surely the mirror lied. Olivia

Delancey never scowled. She never throttled guitars. And no matter their crimes, she never knocked men's heads off.

When she unclenched her jaw, though, the creature in the reflection did the same. As she loosened her death's-grip on the neck of the guitar, the instrument slid in her double's hands. Its cherried wood caught a flicker of candlelight, spearing it into her eye. She wiped away the liquid it drew.

Enough. She sank back onto the edge of the love seat, face even, back straight. No one could ever say she was not a proper lady. Richard, eyes closed dreaming, seemed unaware of her departure or return.

She passed her fingers along the smooth wood of the guitar. The instrument was far more worthy than the man. "We're all so much used goods," she said, leaning down to pick up its wrapper.

"Don't put it that way."

"I waited for you. Did you have no idea?"

"Of course I did." He punched his hand up in the air, sitting up. He turned to her, his spider's smile full-bore. "Did you think I wanted this to happen? For your father to reject me?"

"His will doesn't matter." The barony was entailed, and nothing Papa nor anyone could do would prevent Richard from inheriting it. Short of murder.

She heard the click-clack of a maid's shoes down the hall and down the stairs, both now bare of the carpet Jaspers had managed to sell last month. All the other doors leading to rooms on this floor were shut, hiding their emptiness. Her music room was the only one on this floor that still had furnishings.

"Papa will only be disappointed that he still has me on his hands to feed and clothe." In truth, her father might welcome this news. If Richard were not married to her, he wouldn't discover the extent of the family's ruin until it did not matter.

Papa seemed always in arrears, and they had made do for so long that Olivia rarely considered it. Nearly everything that wasn't entailed had been sold. Papa wielded a mighty political stick, but could not seem to keep the carrots for himself. Every new position, a rung higher in the pecking order, seemed to cost him more and bring him less.

Resting his forearms on his knees, Richard frowned at her. "Is that all? You'll pick up a beau in no time. They collect about you like moths."

"That was true five years ago. I'm firmly on the shelf now." And rejection by her known suitor would only make her more unattractive.

All Olivia truly had was her music. And that, only because it was secret. She shouldn't have counted on Richard. H was as unreliable as the rest of humanity.

He rubbed at the stubble along his chin. She remembered when she'd thought that sweet. Well, this Rosa could have him, and his inconstancy. Olivia could do better than the likes of him, and would.

Except, perhaps, she couldn't

"Really, Livvie, there's no need for that face. I feel badly enough as it is."

"Of course you don't." She smiled at him to show she didn't care in the least that she'd been stood up after all these years of waiting. Nor that she had shared a piece of her heart and herself she could never get back. But her lower lip trembled.

"You slay me." He crossed his hands over his heart, puppy-dog eyes gazing at the ceiling.

She meant to. As ever, he took far more than he gave. Sharing her body with him had seemed natural at the time. And gracious, she had been all shades of curious. But the deed that sunk many a maiden did not sway her. She preferred a fine brandy and a fresh piece of music to a man's embrace. And no one could take her music away from her.

His pout was merely pretty. But she could not hate him, understanding him so well. He was a man-sized child, all enthusiasms and no sense of responsibility. Perhaps his wife would help him grow. She looked away from him, down at the guitar in its shroud. Poor Rosa. This guitar was likely the more faithful partner.

The room fell silent for a long minute, both of them lost in their thoughts. As when they were in the school-room, Richard moved first.

"Thing is," he continued sheepishly, "she's here. In London." Olivia's surprise must have showed in her face. He nodded as if in emphasis. "We're trying to set up a series of performances for her family. Now that it's safe to cross the Channel again."

"She performs?"

"Guitar and piano. She plays well enough, but her brother and father are the true virtuosi. But she is the only one with her feet on the ground, so she handles all their business affairs. Thing is, the Rinaldis have no reputation here. Yet."

"I see."

"But you, could you help us?" He reached for her hands, and she flinched. But he continued, resting his hands over hers. "It is for the best. You want to learn more about the guitar, and Rosa will teach you, as much as you wish to learn.

If you will merely introduce her to a few of your musical friends."

At the thought of seeing the woman who had stolen her place, allowing her to touch her, even just her fingers, Olivia's stomach knotted. But she did want to know about this ruddy guitar. She wanted to know everything about it. "Sponsors? Or players?"

"Both." He clasped the fingers of her right hand in both of his. "Livvie, they have reams of music that we could reprint here. This is a golden era for song on the Continent. We could introduce scores of composers to England."

"Starting with your in-laws." At least his new relatives weren't shy about their need for funds.

"Who better?" Richard let go her hands and reached for the guitar. Olivia leaned back, out of his way. He gave her his sly-dog smile. "You do like it. And you're tempted."

"I'll consider it." Of course she would help them. Wasn't it her duty to serve others, to turn the other cheek however hard they slapped hers first? At least this time, they could give her something she wanted in return – knowledge. She blew on her fingertips, still humming from the unfamiliar exercise.

"Your fingers will toughen up. Have to keep your nails short on the fret hand, as well." He cupped her hand in his. "You will grow so proficient you'll be able to noodle on the guitar the way you used to at the piano." He sighed. "Back when we were young."

Little he knew.

FOUR

With the drop in wars and yet another rise in the paper tax,
might some publishers consider fleeing their sinking ships? Never
fear: This repository of political truths is on solid ground. But we
hear rumors the morning Beacon *is listing severely.*
    —The Register

A s they entered his office at Printing-House Square, Will
waved Swizzlewit toward the chair by the fireplace.
Though the days scalded bare skin, the evening had
turned cool, and the fire's warmth felt welcome. Though it was
the shortest in the room, the simple armchair was still a bit of a
scramble for his pint-sized solicitor. Will sat on a nearby foot-
stool. "We have your chair on order, but I did not expect to see
you again 'til fall."

Swizzlewit waggled his hands, waving Will's concern away.
"Hear you quaffed with Pettigrew this afternoon."

"Ale only, and thin at that. How low I've sunk, chasing politicians' skirts."

"A noble profession, politics."

"If you're a dog. Speaking of, caught Richard Avery there."

"Now, war seems to have done that young man good." Swizzlewit patted his well-padded midriff. "Dined with the man this evening. Fine fellow." He put his sausage of an index finger to the side of his nose. "In fact, we hope to hear bells ringing soon." He gave Will the slowest wink he'd ever seen.

"A wedding?"

"Keeping it in the family, Avery being the baron's heir and all. They're been promised these ten years, almost."

Richard – and Olivia Delancey? "Impossible." Will's thoughts of dismissal turned to consideration of the pain in his knees, buckling under the pressure of his fists' mighty grip. Letting go his legs, he flexed his fingers, and lifted them to twine behind his head.

No matter to him.

"He's not good enough for her," spilled out before he thought of it.

"Who could be, really? But I digress, and with you nearly at deadline. I'll come right to it. The bank is calling its loan in early."

Will stood in surprise. The lawyer started to rise as well, but Will waved him back down. He paced the room as panic thumbed his windpipe. He could not lose the paper.

"What are they on about?" His voice was reed-thin. "I am four months from discharging the debt. I pay the note, like clockwork, every quarter. It's been three years. Why this sudden change?"

Swizzlewit fumbled with his waistcoat.

"You know the *Beacon* is solvent. We will meet this note, as written. Tell them."

The man seemed to sink into the chair. "I have."

"So why the thumbscrews?"

"It's your board." Swizzlewit rubbed his jaw. "They've requested a reconciliation."

"A what?" He'd never heard the term applied to financial matters.

"They want all outstanding debts cleared, in preparation for a sale of the property."

The blood rushed up to Will's head, screaming past his ears. "To whom?"

"William Cobbett."

The blood drained just as quickly, blind-white anger taking its place. "Cobbett," he spit out. "George would kill us to favor the *Register*."

"Your brother is the chief spokesman for the board." Swizzlewit eyed him warily. "Did you and George have another falling out?"

"Just the one." Five years ago, a rip-all fight that gained Will the paper and lost him his family. Except they were still part of the board that oversaw the print shop and the paper it put out. If they voted as a bloc, they could out-vote him. Especially as they had not invited him to whatever meeting they'd had to cook up this scheme.

He forced himself to remain calm, and failed. "Why didn't he come himself? Sending a lackey like a lily-livered scoundrel." Swizzlewit winced. Will winced in response, wishing he could take back his words. "Not that I ever would consider you a mere lackey."

"I came to see how I could smooth things over between you."

Will dropped to the stool. He didn't have enough in savings to cover the last two loan payments and the shop's other obligations. The paper was losing circulation as war news tapered off. At the current rate of fall-off, he would cover the loan, at its contracted due date, but just barely.

"You know I'm good for this. But I can't pay it now without gutting the business. And how much would that be worth?"

"Looks like Cobbett's seeking a fire sale."

"And my brother plays into his hands." But Will knew George had no love for the firebrand Cobbett. There must be some other reason. But damned if he could think of it. "You handle George's finances, too. Has something changed?"

"I couldn't breach another man's privacy." Will glared at him for a full thirty seconds, and Swizzlewit wilted. "But I could say I've seen no changes. I just don't know."

Will rubbed his face. He would never give up the paper, and his brother knew that. So why was he pushing this hare-brained scheme? He sighed. "Tell George if he wants anything from me, he should come and tell me himself."

Swizzlewit sighed with him, shaking his head. He hopped off the chair and put one of his round hands on Will's knee.

"I can get you another sixty days. But if your board calls for this, I can't hold it off forever. Couldn't you just talk with him?"

"If only it were that simple."

"Going bankrupt is more complicated, by far." Swizzlewit

buttoned his topcoat. "I'll mis-file this for a month, then not get to it for another. That's the best I can do."

"Thanks, man. I will get to the bottom of this." Even if it meant beating the truth out of his feckless elder brother.

Especially if it meant that.

Across the hall from Will's office, the old oaken dining table had gained new luster now that Bragge had returned. The man's salt and pepper curls swirled about his head as he waved Will to a seat at the foot of Will's own table. The *Beacon*'s foreign correspondent, and the chief reason it had the second-highest circulation of the papers in London, had of course taken the seat at the table's head.

"So, old soul, how goes the newspaper war?"

"Fair enough." Will nodded at his sub-editor, Bentley, and poured himself a generous draft of wine. They were just the three, with the theater critic in Bath for the summer festivals. "Better, now you are back."

A look, perhaps of irritation, crossed Bentley's narrow face. Bragge watched his fellow editor and then took a long drag off his cigar. Will wondered again at the tension between them.

They were so different. Bentley a reliable poet, Bragge a vagabond genius. Bentley could marshal an edition together out of hay and horsehair, if he needed to. But Bragge could lead the paper into a new frontier, as well as impress the lords of the realm.

"This is just a way station for me, you know," Bragge said into his smoke.

"War is done." Bentley stabbed at a piece of meat on his plate. "Where will you go now?"

"The news soon will be in the shires, I am thinking. Or in the colonies. Ireland, likely." Bragge coughed deep. "The wife says London is so dull."

"Sorry to hear you say that." Bentley did not look the least sorry. "The city is merely home to the leaders of the new order, in politics and in business."

"A bit Anglo-centered, my lad." Bragge winked at the thin editor, who chomped his meat with a vengeance. "What would Cobbett say?"

"Leave him out of it." Will's voice could have grated metal. Both men's gazes snapped to him. He picked up a roll to butter it and saw his hand was shaking.

Bragge waggled his caterpillar eyebrows at him. "The man has your knickers in a twist?"

"My brother's. George wishes us to leave the publishing business. Sell out. To Cobbett."

Both his listeners sat straight, Bragge having to bring the front two legs of his chair back to earth to do it.

"The Chronicler of the Common Man? Whyever would he want us?"

"He doesn't want us. He wants us dead, with the *Register* scooping up our readers."

"You would not do it?" Bentley pulled on his earlobe, his sharp gaze surveying Will. "Of course you wouldn't."

"We need to maintain circulation." Will forced himself to take a bite of bread, forced himself to chew it a moment before swallowing. "Hold their interest, when all the interesting news has dried up."

36

"We cannot make up the news. We're not a rag, or Cobbett." Bentley chewed on his lower lip nearly as hard as he'd been chewing his meat.

"But we might take up your new 'feature' idea. Tell Bragge what you are up to."

Bentley cleared his throat nervously.

"Come on, man." Bragge chuckled. "You'll need to sell it to the common man harder than to me."

"It's just this. People like to read gossip, right? So tell them a story entire, not just a sentence of titillation. But a true story. A character sketch, not a caricature."

"No dashes?" Gossip items were "blinded," with dashes replacing all but the first letter in a person's name, supposedly preserving some privacy.

"No. Full names." Bentley warmed to his idea. "Or we could still do it anonymously. A chimney sweep, a lady of the manor, a military veteran, or his beloved left behind after he's died on the battlefield."

Bragged puffed on his cigar. Bentley sat frozen, teeth dug into that sorry lip, as the seconds ticked by. Will found he, too, was holding his breath.

"No one will go for it." Bragge took another deep inhale. "It would have to be someone special. Someone with something of the extraordinary about them."

"You mean, the idea is good, just the topics need mending?" Bentley's jaw relaxed, his head sinking onto a propped arm.

"Interesting idea." Bragge returned to his near-supine pose resting on the two back legs of his chair. "But you'd need a better-than-average writer."

"We have you." Bentley could give credit where it was due.

"In your travels, you are sure to find the extraordinary. Will and I can do it here in town."

"Let me think on it."

"Do that." Will nodded to Bentley. "And you. Where is today's leader?"

"In my head."

"Get it on paper. It's ten o'clock already."

Bentley bolted down the last scoop of his stew and took his leave.

"It's grand to be back." Bragge swirled the wine in his cup. "Haven't had Bentley to worry at for months. Can't tell you how I've missed the little bugger."

Will grinned despite himself. "You do look a bit plumper. Wedlock has you thinking of settling down?"

"Heaven forfend." Bragge shuddered. "Whyever would we? And miss the doings of the world?"

"You might well influence the doings of the world. As editor."

"Oh, no. You are not roping me to a desk. Let that slasher of erudite phraseology have it. He'd likely slash at me if I took it, anyway."

"Bentley is too young."

"How old were you when you took the reins? Not yet twenty?"

"That was different. The *Beacon* was a half-penny rag with no reputation and no readers."

"And a decade on, it can move mountains?"

"At least it has readers, and a sterling reputation. A reputation for the truth."

Bragge let the matter lie. In Will's experience, that was the old master's signal for a sleight of hand.

"Your old pal Avery sends his best."

"That cur."

"The often victorious and ever vainglorious. Use him for your new biography. Wring out that last drop of patriotism before the masses forget about the war entirely."

Will snorted.

"Why not? And the man's brought home a treasure. You'll appreciate her, all fiery eyes, flaming hair, and the music." Bragge kissed his fingertips. "*Muy bonita.*"

"He carted his doxy home? Tell the rags, for we won't publish it."

"Shhh. Slander, my man. Take care. She's the missus, don't you know. And the next Baroness Pettigrew." Bragge raised his wine, ruby glinting despite the cheap glass. "That will cause a right ruckus."

This was news, indeed. Will tried to picture Miss Olivia Delancey's reaction to being tossed to the side after a decade of waiting. Would she be crushed, a faced lilac now doomed to a quiet garden? He doubted it. She should be pleased, if only she would see it. Avery was a true friend, but he'd make a piss-poor husband.

Bragge twisted his thumbs into the waistband of his trousers in that odd way Will could not think to reproduce. The action pushed his growing girth up, making him look as if he were with child. He leaned back, his foot on the edge of the table, ready to lecture to the rafters.

"The war is good and done this time, my liege. What are the *Beacon*'s plans for the future?"

Will looked at Bragge, at the candles on the table, out the open door where printer's assistants raced by laden with drapes of dry newsprint.

"Exactly," Bragge said. "You need me out and about, scaring up stories that the citizens will want to read. And young Bentley can work to gather readers into the fold. Or below it. Best place for me is the front lines."

"But what if he is wrong?"

"Then come up with a better plan."

"I had hoped you could think of one."

"I'm a reporter, Marsh, a chronicler. I see the details and sniff out the scandal. I live in the present, and hark back to the sordid past. What you need is a man who looks to the future. A younger man."

"You've made your point, twice over."

"Thank heavens." Bragge's middle sagged back under the waistband, where it belonged. "I was beginning to think I'd have to get you drunk in order to see the folly of your ways. So what will you do about Cobbett?"

"About George." Will drained his glass and poured another. "I suppose I shall have to speak with him."

"Too bad you can't just slug him with a tray of type again."

Will had to agree.

FIVE

The Register *so freely cast aspersions on our commercial integrity, but was not its own publisher promising to shutter the premises a scant five years ago to avoid paying the price for libel?*
—The Beacon

Olivia found her parents sat in their usual post-prandial positions, Mama by the fire worrying a piece of embroidery, Papa by the lamp, journals and papers on the table beside him. Unlike usual, though, they were alone. Mama's fast friend Mrs. Chreme was absent. And Papa turned to look at Olivia as she entered.

"Lost your beau?"

Mama looked up, righting her wig and absently scratching behind her ear. "Cousin Richard?"

"Gone." Olivia shivered, raising goose bumps along her nearly bare arms. She pulled her shawl over her shoulders and took Mrs. Chreme's usual chair, across from Mama.

"He did not propose?" Mama's hands fluttered to a rest over her heart. "We left you alone with him all this time."

Papa shook his paper straight and returned to reading. "You couldn't bring him to it last summer, either."

Olivia frowned, her mind a jumble, one moment relief, the next despair. Chilled now, she had been burning a moment ago.

The paper crinkled again, her father's face appearing above the fold. "Don't frown at me, girl. Out with it."

"He has married already."

The paper floated to the floor. Her parents locked gazes on each other, communicating in that odd, silent way of theirs. Olivia told herself not to feel left out, not to admit that familiar forlorn ache. As usual, her feelings did not listen.

"No." Papa paced to the fireplace, warming his hands a moment above the flames, then turning to walk behind Mama's chair. He leaned down and hugged her shoulders, the rings on his long fingers a necklace. Eyes closed, Mama tilted her hair to the side and leaned her head into his shoulder. She cupped her hands over his.

"At least..." Mama didn't finish the thought aloud.

The minutes ticked by. A log in the fireplace broke in two. Olivia watched their faces, mouths pursing and releasing, eyes darting under their closed lids, trying to read their mind.

Ladies of her acquaintance had often spoken admiringly of her parents' close-knit ways. It did seem a fortunate bond. For them.

For their only child, though, it was dashed lonely. Perhaps, if her baby brother had lived, ensuring the barony would stay in the family, things would have been different.

Probably not. She turned her gaze to the fire to make sure no sparks had jumped to the floor. Mama and Papa both had hearts with room enough for just one.

He straightened, his hands still twined in Mama's. "At least we are safe from Avery's recriminations for a while longer. Now, what to do with you?" His dark eyes surveyed his daughter from top to toe. Mama's watery blue eyes did the same.

"A minister?" she said.

"They go for the dowry. Perhaps someone from the Horse Guard? They are used to buying their property."

"Oh, sweetest," her mother said. Olivia wasn't sure she was speaking to her or to her father. Then Mama leaned forward, reaching out a hand to her. "You know you are not a sack of potatoes to us, so don't be putting on that pretty pout."

"Spuds would do us more good." Papa snorted. "Most girls are out of their parents' hair before they turn twenty. You are nearly half a decade past that now."

Her mother reached across to pat her hand. "It really was unaccountably rude of Richard to lead you on this way. Now you'll be a topic for the harpies, who love broken engagements and old maids in the making." She looked back to her husband. "Perhaps she should stay with Betsy for the season."

"That won't marry her off."

"But it would be less of an expense. If she must weather the storm of gossip, why not do it in the most economical way?"

"Brilliant. That will help us stretch to October. Surely I'll gain the nomination by winter." Papa had counted on that nomination each of the past three sessions of Parliament.

Olivia held up her hands. "But I cannot go to Plymouth. At least, not now. I have responsibilities." She stopped herself, but not soon enough.

"What responsibilities?" Her father pursed his lips.

"I promised my time to a charity project." She continued quickly to avoid having to invent the details and risk giving Merry and Martin's secret away. "But it should not take long. A few weeks, only."

"You should stay for the next national day of thanksgiving, in any case." Papa nodded. "And who knows? A suitor may come out of the woodwork."

"One hasn't yet," Mama said unhelpfully.

"Speaking of the future," Papa said. "We'll have to sell the ruby. Need to cover the ale-days, you know. Unexpected expense."

"But that is my last piece."

"Olivia," Mama said in the slightly less breathy tone she employed to sound scolding. "We all must make sacrifices in this, our time of trouble."

"Selling my ruby." Olivia stubbornly referred to it as hers. "Will it put us back on our feet?"

"Oh, dear, not five rubies could do that. This one will merely keep the wolves from our door for another fortnight."

"And then, what?"

"Your father is due to be named a chancellor to the King." Mama turned shining eyes to him. "That will place us quite well, indeed."

His face flushing, Papa cleared his throat. "It is nearly a done deal. Then, my dears, we shall be rolling in blunt."

Olivia dearly hoped so. A girl of four-and-twenty with good taste and no dowry had a difficult time marrying. And how was she to get the funds she had promised Martin and Merry? Her throat went dry; a spear of ice shivered down her spine.

She shrugged the panic down. She would simply come up with another plan. Soon.

First, though, and as she had so often, Olivia took her leave and retreated to the music room and her reliable pianoforte. She sat before her keyboard, fingers stretching in the habitual scales and warm-up runs. Such mindless tuneful repetition always helped clear her thoughts.

She closed her eyes, head bobbing with the rhythm of the pattering of her fingers. So much had happened today. A new assignment, to help Merry and Martin. An old annoyance, fending off Mr. Mellon. And always, the worries over family funds.

Their temporary retrenchment had lasted five years and counting. Her come-out season, a long six years ago, seemed wildly extravagant now. Twenty new dresses in a single season. She'd had less than a handful of entirely new ones since.

And Richard, and the shock of his announcement. But less shock than relief. Bless the man. The guitar was a delightful gift, one she couldn't wait to master. But his greatest gift was her freedom.

Her fingers switched over to progressive chords, seemingly of their own accord. She pictured him as he was last summer, in the heady haze of the victory celebrations. He had shone, and she felt golden reflected when he accompanied her. It was a glittering gold, though, not deep or rich or lasting. She had barely escaped the noose of a marriage to a man who did not make her soul or her body sing.

Marriage might not always be a torment, though. She might marry someone like that publisher at the ale-house, who at least listened to what she said before discounting it. Her hands moved into minor-chord runs.

That wasn't fair. He had not discounted it all. Just a caveat. And his eyes had told sorrow at any pain he caused.

There was something about the man's smell. She frowned, her fingers slowing a fraction. Sandalwood. Called to mind a late summer day home in Plymouth, at least while the tide was in. The man was a rest for the eyes in that crass, dirty ale-house, as well. Was he a friend of Richard's? Perhaps they would meet again.

She wrinkled her nose. Not likely. Not until the next elections, at the least. Papa's prodigies were primed for re-election. There would be no need for more political soirees.

Politics was said to make a man rich. It did not appear to work for the men of Olivia's acquaintance.

And what to do about Martin? She owed him so much for teaching her all he knew of music. And though her skills now surpassed his, her music would never have gone beyond the walls of this house without him.

Fingers warm, she reached for the marked-up copy of her new piece. Something sounded off in the bass line, and she turned the chord up a seventh to resolve it faster. Too bad no one would ever know it was hers.

Her hands stopped mid-bar.

No one knew the Waterloo march was hers, either. So why not call it Martin's? She could sell it, sell the story of it, and make the money he needed. Now she recognized the shivery wisp of excitement she'd felt at the ale-house. A hint of the answer to their problem.

Fingers starting up again, she started to plot. First, line up

Martin, and Merry for support. Then sell the idea to one of the music journals.

It could work. A number of Hayden's works had sold out their printings last year, even as the country was scrimping its pennies. A rousing march, right now, might well cash in.

Right now.

All thoughts of playing chased out of her mind, she turned and lifted the lid of the seat, pulling out her stores of paper and ink. She'd have to spend half a candle to make clean copies tonight, but it would be worth it.

If it did not sell, she could always take out a loan on the nearly two thousand pounds she was expected to finally inherit on her next birthday. The loan officer did not have to know her father had already told her he'd need it.

But if it did sell, it would be something only she could have done.

Something great.

Six

Marsh's Beacon *says that this publisher made a proposition to government to this effect; that, if the proceedings were dropped, I never would publish another* Register *or any other thing. The charge is basely false. No proposition of any sort was ever made by me, or by my authority, to the Government.*

—The Register

Though Lieutenant Martin Purdy appeared nearly unscathed, just a small dent by his right temple and a slowness along his left side, he was not well. His left side did not follow his orders, or did so maddeningly slowly. He found himself short-tempered and sarcastic, and could storm into a red-hot fury in seconds. Yet when he wanted that excess energy, to help him walk down the steep hospital stairs, for example, he could not summon it up.

Miss Olivia, on the other hand, could weather a raging sea and come out smiling. "Think of it." She beamed that hundred-candle smile at him. "It's a great story. A new march, introduced on the eve of the greatest battle in memory."

"It was the worst battle in memory."

"It was a difficult battle. But here is something good that could come of it."

"A thousand pounds of good?"

"You have no money at all?"

"My military payout is gone to pay for this buggered hospital bed. I beg your pardon."

"It does seem wrong that you must pay to recover from what the army did to you."

Martin was sorry he had even asked for her help. Well, he hadn't asked, had he? It was Merry's fault. Merry and her blasted sweet idea that there could be happy endings.

His head hung heavy on his neck. Miss Olivia's voice seemed to come from down a long tunnel, though he could see her well enough there at the bed down by his feet.

He should thank her for the linen shirt she had brought him. He should feel more grateful, more kindly toward her. It wasn't her fault he had been thrown into hell and then pulled back, a broken man.

But the fact was he couldn't feel much of anything. Even when Merry would visit, every bloody afternoon, his world felt flat. He could feel her touch on his arm, but nothing could touch his heart.

She was wasting her time with him. And Miss Olivia, what in darnation was she getting at talking about music?

"I have written it all out again, clean and neat. All you have to do is get it to a music publisher. We can go together in the carriage. Nurse Schiff says you can go out for short walks."

"She doesn't know anything."

Olivia's frown could burn houses down. Mere men had no hope of withstanding it.

"I'll have to ask Merry about it." He tried to buy himself time with the lie.

She shook her head. "Merry will agree with anything you say. And you know she wants to see you out of this place and on your feet." She smiled at him, only a dozen candles this time but still far too bright.

He hated that. She always brimmed with life, with light. Merry had even more energy. They exhausted him just by their presence. Why would they not just leave him be? He wanted nothing more than to rot here quietly, with his fellow sufferers. Penitents all.

They all should have died on the battlefield, fodder for the victorious generals. If a man did not come home from war rich and covered with glory, he should not come home at all.

Olivia's beautiful face fell. She sank to her knees beside the bed, her gaze full on him. Could she have guessed his thoughts? God help her if she saw his soul.

"Come back." She clasped his hand in hers. "Come back to me, to Merry. There is a lot of living yet."

He couldn't bear to look at her. Those crystal eyes shredded his paltry defenses. "I won't kill myself, if that's what you fear."

She dropped his hand. He saw he had shocked her. "Is it that bad, Martin? Truly?"

He wanted to tell her he was hollow inside. Used up. She would listen to him.

But she would not understand. No one could. Not even him. It was just there.

Nothing.

A soft tap on his hand brought him back to the present.

"I will leave you now. We'll try again tomorrow." She looked up, and the soft lines of tension at the corners of her mouth eased. "Here's Merry."

His beloved was a dusky rose today, her red curls offset by a darker hued dress. Her face, which used to set his heart galloping, was as round and blushing and sweet as ever, and he could see the love in it for him. But he could not feel it.

He hated himself for it. And he hated her, for showing him how he failed her. How every day alive was failure.

He watched the women touch gloved hands and kiss each other's cheeks, gold to auburn. They chatted a moment, surely about him. He wished they would stop. Or rather, that they would continue, elsewhere. But soon enough Merry, a stern set to her rosebud lips, stomped toward him.

"Martin, my love." The soft kiss she placed on his forehead pushed some of the dull ache away. As she sat facing him at the side of the bed, their hips bumped, a comforting weight. But her eyes held the deep brown of determination, and those lips were still set. "Don't dismiss Livvie's idea entirely."

He closed his eyes to keep hers from swaying him.

"Dearest, we have to get you out of here."

"It won't work."

"Certainly not, if you stay abed all day and don't even try." She pushed against his chest, as if to push a cart out of the mud.

"I am weak, Meredith."

"That is only because you won't take any exercise." She tugged his arm, succeeding in getting him to open his eyes. "Why not a walk to the music publisher? What could it hurt?"

How could he explain? The whole thing was impossible.

"Nonsense." She looked around a moment, then back to him. Her gaze locked on his, she slipped the glove off her hand and reached under his untucked shirt.

Her palm on his stomach burned like a brand. He jumped, arms gone to goose pimples.

"Your skin is cool." Her tone was clinical. "No fever." She met his gaze, raised an eyebrow. "Nothing is wrong with you that air and good work can not cure."

"You're a nurse now?"

She winced at his tone. She leaned in, pressing her brand deeper into him. The air of her breath carried traces of coffee. How he missed it.

"Listen to me, Martin Purdy. I will grant you some amount of self-pity. But not at the expense of our future. You go with Livvie, and you help her." She paused. "Or I'll not return."

She pulled her hand away from him and scooted her hips way down to the foot of the bed. Putting on her glove finger by finger, mouth a straight line, she simply stared at him.

A wash of terrible longing flooded his lungs. To lose Merry would gouge a hole in his chest. He tried to stop the tears that formed at the corners of his eyes, but the effort only made him shake, and the tears fell faster.

"Sweetest." Merry was back at his side, a hand on the fabric over his chest, patching back in his heart. With a gloved fingertip, she flicked the tears away. "Don't make me do this."

Swamped by months of emotions in a single moment, he blinked, trying to get his bearings. He was not an empty vessel at all. Something had been bottling him up.

Something that was scared of Merry.

She traced down the side of his hairline with a finger. Sucking in air, he struggled to put the words together.

"I'll go."

She smiled that sunbeam smile, chasing those demonic clouds to the corners of his mind. "Just so."

~

Will loved his brother. But he did not like to see him.

Especially not sitting in the plush chair by the fireplace in his own office. That was his space, his sanctum, and George bloody well knew it.

The eldest, his brother was expert at making Will and his sisters suffer without calling the attention of his parents. He was rarely caught, and never punished.

"Children need to learn to stand up for themselves," their father had said. It was a lesson Will had taken to heart, even after Father was sent to jail for not standing up for himself.

George rose. His stoop was worse, his hair thinner. But the disapproval on his face stood out as strong as ever. Not wanting to be always on the defensive, as it so often seemed when his brother was around, Will spoke first.

"Don't recall you had an appointment, George."

"Come off it." His brother grimaced. "It's important, or I wouldn't be here. You wouldn't have any brandy, would you?"

"No." That earned him a resentful glare, which he welcomed with a bitter warmth.

"I'll come to the point directly. I want – we want – to sell the paper."

"Who?"

"I, of course, and Rebecca. And Catherine."

"You've spoken to Catherine?"

"Written. Haven't received the reply, but I have no doubt what she will say. The first crop in Virginia was not as profitable as they had hoped." George raised an eyebrow. "And they cannot afford to have their money in a failing enterprise such as yours."

Will bit back on his anger. George was baiting him. But spikes of hot fear snickered up his spine. This paper was his life.

"Why now?"

"The war is over. Your circulation is in decline."

"How do you know that?"

George shrugged. He must have a spy in the print-shop, though Will couldn't guess who still felt loyalty to the brother who had nearly collapsed the business a decade ago.

"The drop is not precipitous. The paper makes a tidy profit."

"Which you insist on plowing into new machinery. A steam press! A pair of them. Who ever heard of such profligacy? We none of us has seen any 'profit,' in our pockets, in years."

"The steam press has doubled our profits, net, and it will be paid off in months."

"It has led us near to bankruptcy." George shook his head. "Why must the *Beacon* take the biggest risks?"

"Those who take the biggest risks gain the biggest rewards." Will was sure of this point. "Why do you think we trebled circulation in two years? Why are we the largest daily journal now?"

"Second-largest."

"Cobbett's is not a journal. It is a screed."

George shrugged. "No matter. Father made each of us equal

on the board. It's three to your one on this, Will. We want the paper sold."

"To whom?" Will read the hesitation in George's rheumy eyes. "Cobbett." His voice was laced with venom.

"He came to me." George could not hold Will's gaze and turned his head away. "He wants to run a real newspaper. And he wants to start at the top."

Will snorted. "He wants to shut the paper down, and use the presses to print his 'common man' propaganda. He would break us down for parts."

"Perhaps we deserve to be in parts."

"Only you would say that."

"It isn't my fault I wasn't born a journalist." George turned back to glare at him. "Such a thing didn't exist a generation ago."

"You do appear to have been born for bureaucracy, though, and you found the Patents Office. *Mirabile dictu.*"

"Spare me your Oxford vocabulary. Fat lot of good it's done you in this den." George stopped, unclenched his fists if not his jaw. "This is not why I came."

"Why did you come, brother?" George winced at the final word's sounding more a slur than a token of affection. "Merely to take my temperature?"

"You haven't changed. Just like Father, high-minded to a fault."

Will charged to his feet and lunged toward his brother. George bolted up, eyes blazing, a flash of fear. Startled, Will stopped.

"Mother always warned you about that temper," George said, sidling toward the door without taking his eyes off him.

Will crossed his arms, fists hard, forcing himself to hold back from reaching to throttle his only brother. "Get out. And don't return without a formal statement by the board. With all the signatures present. And send it by courier."

"I'll get it. Katie's will take some time. This isn't just for Cobbett, you know; it's for the family. Your family."

Will unclenched his arms and raised a hand. George scuttled through the door and down the hall.

Katie would never force him to close up shop, unless they were in dire need in Virginia. A letter from her could take weeks or months to cross the sea, depending on the weather.

He was so close, the *Beacon* nearly a thundering success. He would show them how a paper could stay profitable even during peace. All he needed was a bit more time.

And some storms to rage over the Atlantic.

SEVEN

Another impromptu victory parade occurred Sunday afternoon, closing the streets directly on Hyde Park for hours.

—The Register

S ignaling to her boy, Olivia turned toward home, a twenty-minute walk. The sun sizzled, and the air crackled; but a small breeze kept the city comfortable, and her lady's parasol offered some shade. Though she always thought better when she was moving, either in body or on the keyboard, today the motion brought little comfort.

We are not your children, Miss Olivia. Perhaps Martin had intended his face to show kindness, as his voice did. But instead it looked as if he were a victim of rictus, a cadaver's smile.

Along the narrow planks beside the streets, none of the myriad beggars, peddlers, or other riffraff called her attention, and they dared not bar her way. Though her poke bonnet did need new ribbon, she walked unseeing by the windows of shopper's row on Buckham Street. Even the monuments of Westminster, seeming to undulate in the heat, did not pull her from her spinning thoughts.

We are not your children. But without her help, she knew they would fail. Martin would become one of those broken soldiers begging for pennies along the streets. Merry's heart would break, and she would die an old maid. Olivia had to help them. There must be a way.

And if she could find a way to help them, she might find a way to help herself.

Somehow, she found herself in Publisher's Row. The boxy buildings shaded streets more like alleys. Her little tiger tugged at her sleeve, worry on his face. "We won't linger," she told the boy.

But they did. She perused the streaky windows of the publishers and paper-men, papered with caricatures instructional and satirical. She recognized her father in one, a scarecrow feeding pages labeled "Corn Laws" to an overfed Prince Regent.

The windows of the *Beacon* held their share of etchings, and a page that seemed to be of mild interest to a few passers-by, but a large portion was held by the edition of the day. The small lettering and dense paragraphs on the pages forced one man to stand nearly nose-to-glass to read it. Suddenly noticing her, he stepped back, nodding a greeting.

Nodding at him, she sensed her tiger standing close to her side, edging closer.

"Why do you prefer the *Beacon*?" She couldn't help asking.

"Why? Because they pay me! I perform correspondence for them." His already puffed-out chest seemed to expand. Olivia feared for his canary waistcoat.

"Anything of yours in here?" She looked at the day's paper.

"This." He pointed to the top paragraph, the letters twice the size of the others. "It's called the leader." She read it: "The peace talks wrapping up if only the allies could agree on dividing the continent."

She turned back to him, proper admiration in her gaze. "It reads well."

"That's not me, then. I get the facts proper." He squinted at the page. "Looks like Bentley's work, polishing it up."

"Is that why you get no credit?"

He pursed his lips. With his great curls of salt-and-pepper hair and wide-eyed expression, he looked rather like a giant infant, but the strong shoulders suggested otherwise. "Not so much. Scribblers such as myself prefer anonymity, both for safety and to preserve the trust of our sources. Pliers of the newspaper pen may occasionally suffer from the abuse of their professional designation as much as artists on the stage."

"Did not Escott say that?"

"So he did," he said, as if only now realizing where he had taken the line from. "And rightly."

"But don't you want your words to sing?"

"To be sure, ma'am. But we ain't glory-gobblers, like your poets." He swung his arm up as if orating to the doorframe. "We're journeymen, word carpenters if you like."

"You know the proprietor, Mr. Marsh?"

"Of course. It's a small shop." He waggled his caterpillar eyebrows, grinning down at her. "Would you like to meet him?"

"We have met, once. But he is not anonymous."

"The owner can't be. He must take all the grief we pour on him, then add all the grief the government and the public pours on him. And still, on occasion, our Will cracks a smile."

He did the same. "Must be the caricatures he does remind him how."

She smiled in reply, trying to picture the sober Mr. William Marsh laughing. It made him a little too dangerously handsome.

Then the idea struck her.

If the *Beacon*'s press could reproduce drawings, could it not also do music? True, she hadn't ever seen a musical score in a daily journal, but a printer was a printer. Wasn't it?

"Something wrong, ma'am? You didn't like the joke. I am disconsolate." His mouth puckered again, as if he would start bawling at any moment.

"Nothing of the sort, I assure you. But I wonder, does he encourage amateur contributions?"

"To be sure! We all start out as amateurs, do we not? You wish to pitch a story?"

She felt a rush of hope spin up her spine, doused by a cold draft of fear.

"Not to worry. Our Will is a soft touch. Especially for a beautiful woman." The man pushed his curls away from his face with both hands, as if he were wiping away water after a dip in the river. "Let's you and I take him on together."

"Thank you, Mr.—"

"Bragge. John Bragge, at your service." He pulled open the front door and waved her to cross the threshold first. Her hand pressing her heart back into to her chest, she entered the dimly lit room. A long table divided the floor. The wall behind it was a warren of cubbyholes, most filled with neatly folded sheets or rolls of paper. Otherwise, the room was empty.

Mr. Bragge crossed in front of her, walking through the

upraised part of the table that made a walkway to the back. "He'll be in the living area."

She held back. Ladies did not enter men's living areas.

"Perhaps I could speak with him out here."

"Nonsense. Come back to the dining room. There's likely still some tea things. Cook here works wonders in pastry." He patted his belly, which looked large enough to pack away a dozen pastries at a go.

Olivia looked back at her tiger, just entering the room. The boy's eyes were wide, mouth set. He knew they should not be there. She bit her bottom lip. Perhaps this was a bad idea.

"Bring the lad with you. Will won't bite. He's not the least bit mangy."

Olivia gestured for the boy to precede her. They followed Mr. Bragge down a narrow hall. She could see a dining room through the door on the right. On the left, they passed a closed door, then an open one.

This room was half office, half sitting room, and a blizzard of paper. Sheets of newsprint draped over the backs of chairs and tented whatever lay on top of the mantelpiece. A mammoth desk faced the sitting area, loaded with piles of paper in hues from cream to ochre. And among them, reading one of them in fact, was Mr. Marsh.

He looked as comfortable here as in the ale-house, if a bit less formally dressed. His gently weathered face was concentrated on the page. His pursed mouth drew vertical shadows on his cheeks. He had recently shaved.

"*El Jéfe.*" At the sound of his voice, the *Beacon*'s publisher looked up. Mr. Bragge tilted his head toward Olivia, and Mr.

Marsh's gaze flicked to her. The lines in his cheeks disappeared into a smile. He stood, dropping the page on the desk.

"Miss Delancey. An unexpected pleasure."

"Pleasure, nothing. Business." Her guide said it sternly, but his eyes twinkled.

The curve in Mr. Marsh's mouth eased to nearly flat, though his dark gaze held on her. He waved a hand at the two wide-armed chairs facing his desk. "I didn't know you were acquainted with Mr. Bragge."

She let the remark go by, sitting in the chair closest to the door, careful not to disturb the papers aligned across its winged back. The muscles in her abdomen quivered; covering them with her hand, she tried to quiet them. Her boy waited in the hall. If she turned her head, she could see him. He could run for help.

"If you don't feel safe here, ma'am, why did you come? You aren't warm on me, are you?" A quirk in one eyebrow seemed to draw that corner of his mouth up, as well.

Mr. Bragge laughed, the noise originating deep behind that waistcoat. He sat beside her, crossed his ankle over his knee, foot flapping in a secret rhythm.

She bit back a giggle. She could not let this get out of hand. They would not make her feel uncomfortable. Her friends needed her. Olivia squared her shoulders and opened her mouth. The words tumbled over one another.

"Here it is. I have a friend, a veteran, a musician. He has a new piece of music, a march. We wish you to print it in your paper." She took a breath to go on, but he raised his hand, palm out.

"You wish me to buy a piece of your friend's music and print it in my paper?" Two frown lines appeared between Mr. Marsh's brows. "Why not go to a music publisher?"

"Short shelf-life. It's a military theme."

His frown deepened. Before he could interrupt again, she pushed on.

"Martin, that's my friend, he played it on the fields of Waterloo. For his regiment. Wellesley, I mean, Wellington, he praised it and asked that it be played the morning of 15 June."

Mr. Bragge clapped his hands together. "Now that's a story." Out of words, Olivia opened her portfolio and pulled out two of the sheaves of music. She handed one to each man.

Mr. Bragge took his from her hand, eyes on the page. Mr. Marsh's gaze didn't leave her face. The stroke of his finger on hers, against the paper, sent a shiver up her arm.

She let go of the pages, her fingers losing all sense. For a moment, she forgot to breathe. It was as if his predator's gaze sucked all the air from her lungs. Then he let her go, his gaze dropping to the pages.

Nonsense, she berated herself.

"What do you know of music?" Mr. Marsh asked his correspondent.

"Nada."

"Fetch Bentley."

Mr. Bragge hoisted himself to his feet. Olivia watched him leave the room, imagining her last source of safety deserting her.

Mr. Marsh stood, music in hand, and skirted the desk. She forced herself not to pull back, not to flinch, as he crossed within touching distance of her, settling in the seat Bragge had vacated. As he passed, washing-day sprang to her mind, soap and sunshine – and the sharp smell of ink.

He stretched his long dark-trousered legs in front of him, crossing them at the ankles. He crossed his arms in front of the linen of his shirt. She trusted that she had remembered to sand the ink dry so it wouldn't smudge.

"Why the frown?"

"How do you keep your shirts so clean? You must be forever in ink."

The corners beside his eyes crinkled when he smiled. She wondered at the dimple in his chin, and the tiny vertical scar beside it.

"My housekeeper is forever after me to wear those sleeves," he gestured at the desk. She could see no sleeves there. Her gaze turned of its own accord back to him. Though there were three gas lamps lighting the room, she could not tell if his eyes were blue or green.

His smile wasn't exactly straight. Neither was his nose. But in combination, his face had a rugged grace, an odd attraction. And when he smiled, a fierce beauty.

She shook her head. How had her thoughts gone so astray?

A commotion traveled down the hall toward them. Her tiger scooted out of the way. But it was mere noise, Mr. Bragge at parade strength followed by a much thinner man who looked out of temper.

"Miss Delancey, Thomas Bentley."

Mr. Bentley's mouth unhinged, his eyes bulged. "You didn't say it was a lady."

Bragge winked at her. "You wished for a new sort of story. Here it walks in your door, and you complain." He perched on the desk, crushing papers underneath. "Tell him, Miss Delancey."

As she repeated her proposal, more grammatically this time, Mr. Bentley's mouth closed, and then turned down.

"Do you have it in writing?"

"Yes. Here." She pulled the last clean copy of the music from her portfolio and handed it to him. He waited until her arm was fully extended, then reached for it with finger and thumb, as if he were afraid to touch any part that had touched her. Once safely transferred, he draped the sheets over the palm of his other hand.

"But this is music."

She raised an eyebrow.

Bragge muffled a guffaw. Bentley glared at him, then turned back to her.

"I meant do you have a record of Wellington's approval?"

"You mean, a written order?"

"Exactly."

"To play a piece of music?"

"Well..."

"During a military campaign?"

"Put it that way, then. But how can I know—" He stopped.

"Know what?"

"Yes, Bentley." Mr. Bragge reached a hand to the back of his head, ruffling the curls at the nape. "Know what?"

Mr. Bentley cleared his throat, his Adam's apple bobbing. He frowned, thin blond eyebrows nearly meeting, as his gaze swept from his feet to the floor.

"Bentley's right," Mr. Marsh said. "We need to confirm the story is true."

"Since when?" Olivia felt three pairs of eyes snap to her, all rather stony. "Papers write 'we hear' and 'we're told' every day."

"Hear, hear." Bragge circled his hand in the air, like the regent did during parades. "And from far worse sources, let me tell you."

Olivia's chest was hot. They thought her a liar? She clenched her jaw.

"He's just pulling your chain, ma'am. We believe you." Bragge punched Mr. Bentley in the shoulder, nearly toppling him.

"Not necessarily." Mr. Marsh said leaned forward in the chair, closing the space between them. She felt the intensity of his gaze enter her face and rush down to her toes. He was interested. But he was not hooked.

Her thoughts raced, trying to find a new argument. "Why don't you come and meet Martin? He is in a hospital nearby."

"A wounded veteran? Even better." Bragge caught her look of surprise. "Better story, ma'am. Not so well for him, I expect."

"That is why I am here. Because he is ill." She tried to drape her voice with that veneer of dignity that Papa often used.

"Your fiancé?" Will leaned closer. She could not stop herself from scooting back a bit.

"Merely an acquaintance."

"And you are merely a Good Samaritan?" Mr. Bentley had found his voice, though it rather squeaked.

"His fiancée, as you put it, is one of my best friends." How much should she tell them? They would find it all out anyway. They were news-men, after all. But she might color it her way. "The lady's father won't allow them to marry until Martin has established himself. He's trying to sell this music as a start." She stood suddenly, unsure if her knees would hold her. Bentley jumped at least two feet farther from her. Bragge and Mr. Marsh scrambled to their feet. "I can play you the piece. Do you have a piano?"

"A poor one." Mr. Marsh looked toward the dining room. "But the music won't sell us. The story will."

She nodded. Her nerves nearly gone, all Olivia wished was to be out of this room with this trio of inquisitive men, one far too handsome for safety. "Will you meet Martin?"

"Bragge will. And I may join him. Send a note when and where." Will thrust out his hand for her to shake, as if she were a man of business. His touch was iron, yet warm as a coal-fired stove. Their eyes locked.

His gaze seemed to search hers. She prayed he did not see her imposter's soul.

Bragge led her and the boy back to the front of the building.

Out in the street, Olivia had to take a moment to remember in which direction to turn toward home. Soon enough, her mind cleared, and the pumping of her legs cleared her thoughts.

A grin slowly crept onto her face, clearing the cross in her brows. *I did it.*

With Martin's help, she could turn the Doubting Thomases of the *Beacon* into true believers.

Eight

Herein included, in its entirety, slack grammar and toad-eating intact: A letter, over the signature of Mr. Cobbett's solicitor, to the Government. See the original posted in the Beacon*'s display window. We print so you may decide.*

—The Beacon

Martin reminded himself not to grimace as the hack door opened and Miss Olivia Delancey gestured for him to approach. It was too much to hope that she would forget, or find a better use for her time, or a better man to torment with her charity.

He grabbed the handhold white-knuckled, but his bum knee held firm, launching him into the coach. Once seated, his back to the horses and facing the lady, his embarrassment flared sharp and red. Miss Olivia risked much. If she were seen with him, and gossiped about, her reputation would sink. And reputation was that kept the young ladies afloat, it seemed like.

She tapped on the roof, and the driver started them moving. "First stop, Publisher's Row. The two chief music journals are just across the road from each other. Cut-throat competition."

That made him smile.

"Shall we go in together, do you think, Mr. Purdy?"

He looked at the ceiling a moment, frowning. The coach lurched around a corner, and they both grabbed for straps swinging near the ceiling. She shouldn't risk it.

"I should do it alone. A woman is a distraction in business, and you, Miss Delancey, are a distraction in all cases." He formed his mouth into a smile. He trusted it was a smile.

She handed him a portfolio. "Here are clean copies. One has a voice part, but as we don't have any words the publisher might prefer the other one. Do you know what you will say?"

"Merry had me rehearse for an hour this morning. I'll tell the story of the music, then remind him that it has a short shelf life and we should publish now."

The carriage careened again, and she looked out the filthy window.

"Here we are." She slid to the far side of the musty coach. The driver opened the door for him. Before he could go, she reached out and touched his knee to get his attention. She threw one of those hundred-candle smiles up at him.

"Best luck."

From then on, the bad luck ran rampant.

Martin judged the distance to the ground correctly, but his knee did not reach the proper angle in time. He tumbled onto the muck of the city side street, swerving just in time to avoid dashing the portfolio into a pile of horse offal.

He waved off the driver and stood, brushing the dirt off his trousers. Swallowing his heart back into his chest and setting his shoulders, he stepped onto the side-walk, and then through the door of Monsieur LeBoef, proprietor of <u>The Music of Our Times</u>. The man who appeared behind the counter after a few moments' wait looked as if he hailed from the English country-side, not France.

"Monsieur LeBoef?"

He shrugged, rolling hamhock-sized shoulders. "Frenchied the name. Most folks just calls me Beef."

Barely reaching five feet in height, the rotund music-publisher reminded Martin more of a porcine than a bovine. Shaking the image out of his mind, he launched into his prepared text.

Not even twenty seconds into it, Beef raised a hand. "I publish on commission, you know." He must have read Martin's incomprehension on his face, for he continued. "You give me the music, and forty pounds. Fifty if you wish a larger run. Then after I sell fifty pounds' worth, minus printing costs, you starts earning in."

"I pay you to publish?"

"Aye. Of course, you could sell subscriptions in advance. That's how most do it." Beef stared at Martin placidly as he worked the numbers in his head. At a shilling a subscription, he'd need to sell hundreds just to get the thing printed. And it would take weeks. He frowned. It was impossible.

"Hard, aye. But for a man such as you, with a good tale to tell, it should be easy enough."

"Thing is, I need this to print now. The victory celebrations have already started. The first parade is past. It would sell the best now."

Beef pursed his lips, scratching behind his ear. "Yer right. Best be out selling it tonight."

"You won't advance me the fee?"

"I be a man of business, not charity, sir."

Martin cursed the fine linen of his new shirt. He looked too much the gentleman. "Half?"

"None."

Failure. He expected it, but was surprised how sharp it stung. He waved toward the door. "Your competitor, across the way. He gives the same terms?"

"Nay. You might do better by him." Beef nodded vigorously, his hair flopping like a pony's on a fly-infested field. "But his edition dropped today, so there'll be a wait."

"How long?"

"Hard to say. A month, six weeks?" He spat into a spittoon near the wall a man's length away.

Far too long. Further defeat. But Martin could not go out there and tell Miss Olivia so.

The beefy man seemed to read his mind. "Don't wish to disappoint someone? Let me think. A fine cove like you, fallen on hard times." He snapped his fingers, ruddy face alight. "Try Cobbett, down the road a piece."

"A music publisher?"

"A daily. There's speed for you. And if he likes your face, he won't charge you nothing." He spat again. "Mayhap."

Stepping from the reek of wood and oil in the office to the animal smells outside, Martin headed to the coach to tell Miss Olivia the news. She agreed, and he set off down the street to the *Register*'s offices.

This time, the oily smell did not assault him so strongly.

And his heart was not quite in his throat, merely a bit higher than normal in his chest. But when the assistant came back with a barrel-chested, tufted-hair dervish of a man, Martin took a startled step back.

"Purdy. Doesn't sound familiar. Do I know you?" The man and all his wayward parts remained behind the barrier of his counter, but he leaned over it, toward Martin, as if ready to catapult himself over at the slightest invitation.

"M-Martin Purdy, sir. Mr. Cobbett?"

"In the flesh." A tanned hand shot out toward him. It took much of what was left of his stamina to reach out to shake it.

"What manner of handshake is that?" Cobbett shook his head, sending the tufts of gray and black hair on his head swirling. Martin was nearly mesmerized by it.

"I beg your pardon. I have only just left the hospital."

"A veteran of our ill-advised military endeavors? Well, welcome home. What might I do for you?"

"I have, ah, a piece of work."

"A writer?"

"Not exactly. Rather, an artist."

"Caricature? We could use some good ones." He gestured at the wide window beside the door, coated with pages of etchings. "Did you see Nosey or that Blucher on the battlefields? That draws them in. More funds for the cause." Cobbett rubbed his hands energetically. Martin wondered if he could create fire that way.

"No, not caricatures."

The rubbing stopped. "What, then?"

"Music." Cobbett's face fell still. Martin pushed on. "A

rather martial tune. I played it on the field in advance of the skirmish at Waterloo. It made quite the impression."

"And now you wish to impose it on the hard-working common men and women of Britannia?" The man's face, which had started only a shade darker than the gray of his hair, was growing red. His mouth clamped shut, his color continued to boil, up to beet and beyond.

Martin was considering whether he should call for a physician when Cobbett at last opened his mouth. The man took in breath like a bellows.

"Who sent you?"

Martin blinked at the force of his diction. "I beg your pardon?"

"And right to do it, spewing such utter nonsense in my shop. The common man has no time for your Society airs. His place is the field, the shop, the hearth. He doesn't need to have a pianoforte, or a violin, or a rotted 'glee club' to live a decent life."

Martin's head reeled. Who could argue against music? "It is a marching tune, no frills at all."

"A tune is a tune. The common man has no time for it. Someone sent you here. How much did he pay you? I'm walking apoplexy as it is, with the politicians mouthing such utter nonsense this term. And now you." He lunged over the counter, poking Martin hard in the chest.

He rocked back, his knee screeching in pain.

"Get out. Go peddle your elitist propaganda elsewhere."

"Nobody sent me, I promise."

"Tell it to the coroner. Or Mr. George Marsh, if it was him. Or that other one. That's the man. It was him, wasn't it?"

"No, I swear." But Cobbett was rounding the counter, and Martin thought it best to scramble away before that red and white tornado came any closer.

"Go you, and offer it to the *Beacon*," he called out as Martin slipped through the door. "Marsh needs all the help he can get. Buggered elitists, the bunch of 'em."

Martin didn't take another breath until he'd reached the door to the hack. Miss Olivia herself gave him her hand, pulling him inside. "What happened? You look as if you've seen a ghost."

He gasped, inhaling the blessed, if foetid, air. He was safe again, and still breathing. "The man had a fit, wanted to know who sent me to torment him and the common man."

"Cobbett." She clapped a hand to the side of her face. "I should have remembered. The radical."

"The all-out loon." Inhaling deep the damp rankness of the upholstery, he pressed on his fluttering heart. Then he started to cough.

"Always railing about the people aspiring to the middle classes, including their reaching for the objects of their betters. Such as a piano."

"Has no class at all, you ask me."

Olivia sat back in the seat as the coach started up. "The music publisher steered you very wrong. But we cannot give up so easily."

Martin slumped in the seat, running a hand through his too-long hair. They had tried and failed. Simple as that.

But she would not give up, would she? "Why couldn't we publish it ourselves? It would be a better arrangement than Mr. Boeuf offered."

"Le Boeuf." A smile cracked the grim set of his jaw. Then it disappeared. "Need money for that. And I'll not pay usury."

She shrugged, neither agreeing nor disagreeing. "It has not come down to that, yet. There are other publishers."

"Who all will say the same thing." He slumped further, then bounced up as the coach hit a pot-sized hole.

The third time Martin was launched out of his seat, Olivia reached for him. "Come. Sit on this side. I can't afford to damage you. Merry would flay me."

Using the hand-hold, he managed to pivot up and onto the seat beside her without cracking his knee or his head. "Merry was wrong to include you in our little battle. I am not so sure she is right to include me. I *am* sure that you are not to blame if we cannot improve our station."

"I promised I would help you. Both of you." The hack stopped. They exited without difficulty, and Olivia paid the fare. The page acting as her errand-boy hopped off the back of the coach.

"You have made good on that promise. It is not your fault if the market is not satisfied by my appeal. We are not your children, Miss Olivia." He bowed and slowly ascended the stairs to the hospital entrance, closing his eyes to the pain coursing through his body. Though he was eager for its sanctuary, he knew already that rest would bring no relief.

NINE

Who pays the price for Parliament's folly? The Common Man, forced to shoulder the burden of defending the land and now denied his due. If a soldier were to desert the King's Army, he would be shot. What does one do with a Government that deserts its soldiers?

—The Register

When Olivia stepped through the double doors to the hospital's upper wing, her heart sank.

Nearly no one was there, nor were her specially invited guests. And Mr. Bragge would be here in less than fifteen minutes.

The first bed was still filled, a man missing limbs and part of his face. He looked at her with his good eye, though, motioning her to come closer.

"Some water to drink?" she said, reaching for the glass on

the table beside him. He nodded. After a few sips, he tilted his head back. "Downstairs. They are collecting in the inner courtyard."

So that's what Merry had meant about a special showing. Olivia had thought it was merely that Martin would be better dressed.

"Sorry I can't be there," the invalid said.

"You'll be about soon enough. Want me to open the window? Perhaps you'll be able to hear."

He nodded. "If the nurses don't come back and close it."

She hurried back down the stairs. Perhaps it was a bad idea to show Martin hale and hearty. Hadn't she told Mr. Marsh that Martin was dangerously wounded? He would think her a tale-teller. Too late now.

In the arched entry hall, she nearly collided with Meredith. "Oh, Livvie, I thought you'd never arrive."

"Is everything ready?" Merry nodded, too out of breath to speak for a moment. "How did they get the piano out in the courtyard?"

"Better than that. Look." She turned, heading toward the doors to the courtyard. Olivia caught a glimpse of three rows of men in chairs and on benches, and then she heard her name called. By a very masculine voice.

She couldn't stop her hands from patting down her hair as she spun. "Mr. Bragge. And Mr. Marsh, as well. You are prompt."

"Old newspaper habit, ma'am," Bragge said. Today he was wearing a green woolen coat, a muffler spun around his neck. His forehead was quite red. He started unwinding the muffler. As if a release valve, its movement seemed to drain his face of its excess red. She wondered if he knew that triangle of beard on his chin made him resemble the Satan of Salisbury Cathedral.

Mr. Marsh, dressed rather somberly in black coat and trousers, looked about him at the entry. He seemed to be soaking in every detail.

"Not the priciest establishment," he said. Then his eyes rested on her a moment.

Under the warm green of his gaze, Olivia felt quieter, more confident. She could do this. His gaze flickered to the matron who with click-clacking shoes was coming closer. Olivia turned to try to head her off.

"Matron Sneed, these are the men I was telling you of."

"Well, sirs, you certainly have disrupted proceedings here today. I trust it will be worth it to these men, who have given much and gained little, to be set back a day in their convalescence." She glared at Mr. Marsh.

"I thank you, Matron." He bowed. "We are here to tell their stories. Or at least one of them."

"I should hope so," she said, but her tone grew warmer. "You will say how we must make do with nothing? How shameful it is that veterans must pay their own hospital bills when it was the government what asked them to sacrifice themselves?"

"We will surely discuss it." Mr. Marsh nodded at Mr. Bragge, who stepped forward to grasp both the matron's hands in his.

"My dear matron. Sneed, is it? Such hands, so strong." The matron looked torn between snatching her hands back and holding still for another compliment. "We are in debt to you and the many good souls under your management. Your service is exemplary. I salute you!"

He leaned in to plant a kiss on the tops of her hands. Matron Sneed swayed at the shoulders as if she would faint.

"Excellent," Mr. Marsh said. "I did miss you, Bragge. Miss Delancey?"

Olivia signaled toward the courtyard door. She felt his gaze on her as she led them though the doors. For the first time, she wondered if she looked pretty from the back. Then she saw what filled the courtyard, and gasped. She stopped, stock-still. And gasped again, at the touch of a hand.

Mr. Marsh cupped her shoulders, perhaps to stop the rest of him from mowing her down. "I see you prepared a pageant for us," he murmured. Standing in the full July sun, Olivia shivered.

The small courtyard was filled on three sides with men, standing, sitting on chairs or the ground, leaning against the red-brick walls. At least five score, nearly all the ambulatory men in the entire hospital. It must be the barber's day off, for all had at least some stubble on their facts. And they wore an array of uniforms, most barely recognizable as such except for the brass buttons. A few, injured early in their service, wore the familiar tomato-soup red of infantry.

Among them was Martin Purdy. His service had lasted less than three months, and ended painfully. Meredith was beside him, her white gingham with roses a pretty contrast to such undiluted manliness. She pulled his hand to bring him forward. He did not look happy about it.

"Mr. Marsh, Mr. Bragge. This is Martin Purdy, of the 101st. And his – my – friend, Meredith Buckham."

"Of the Hertfordshire Buckhams?" Bragge smiled at her.

"A junior branch."

"Her family is not quite desirous of the match, Mr. Bragge. So if you could keep her name out of any story?"

"Of course." He flicked Merry under the chin with a finger. She nearly giggled. "I know too well how families can be."

"You have quite an orchestra here, Mr. Purdy." Mr. Marsh canvassed the rows of faces. Martin nodded but did not seem like capable of speech. He did not look happy, but did not look unhappy, either. Meredith used her voice for his.

"Yes. We told them you were coming, and why. And they all wanted to do what they could to help."

Martin turned to Merry, who encouraged him with her eyes. "It was Merry's doing. She has made every man in here fall in love with her. Always ready to help. She is sunshine." His words were pretty, but his voice was flat. Merry dimpled up at him as if he had angel's wings.

Mr. Marsh frowned and turned back to Olivia. Bragge pulled out a small notebook, licked the tip of his pencil, and started scribbling.

"Shall we start?" Olivia heard the strain in her voice but did not know why it should be so.

A soldier offered to give up his chair to the men. "We'll stand," Mr. Marsh said, as if she had already kept him here too long.

Martin returned to his place in front of the players. A dozen young men, boys really, positioned their drums between their knees. Behind him, men raised trumpets or bugles to their lips. Martin raised his arm. As he swung it down again, the wall of men exploded into sound.

The noise was near-deafening, the players trained to project across a battlefield, not contain themselves within a courtyard. But then Olivia heard the tune.

Her tune.

It was so changed, with all this brass and rattle. But it was a direct echo of the notes she had played, changed, and re-played in her head and on her keyboard. She was glad she was standing already, for she felt as if her body were made of air and could float away at any moment.

Her tune. And it was good; it sounded good. Her heart was fit to burst, or fly away, or something. She was dizzy, as if drunk.

She held her hands to her cheeks to check her expression. Her grin nearly touched her ears. She nodded in time with the beat, waiting for the key change. Her head tilted in time with the conductor's arm, moving the players into the chorus.

She wanted to dance, to march, to sing. Then she remembered she was not alone.

She looked at the rest of the audience. Mr. Bragge and Matron Sneed gaped happily at the players. Merry had eyes only for Martin. But Mr. Marsh was watching her.

A smile played across his lips. It changed his entire aspect. He still looked as handsome as a fallen angel, but less sardonic, more whole.

Olivia pulled her hands back a bit, pretending she was covering her ears a bit. It didn't dampen the sound, which was coming through her feet as well as the air that touched her ears. She wanted him to like it. She wanted everyone to love it.

The third chorus crashed to a crescendo, and then abruptly the noise fell off. For a moment, no one moved, the silence as stunning as the sound had been. Then a familiar voice broke the still.

"Capital. From the 101st, am I right?" She didn't need to turn to recognize the nasal tone. Arthur, Lord Wellesley, the Duke of Wellington, was unmistakable. Dressed much as Mr. Marsh, but in a better grade of cloth, the victor of Waterloo stood behind them, two of his aides flanking him like shorter shadows.

Olivia tried to move toward him, but her balance was not quite right. Mr. Marsh was quicker.

"My lord Duke, I'm Will Marsh, with the *Beacon*."

"And Mr. Bragge, as well." The hook-nosed duke trained his sharp eyes on Bragge. "Back so soon?"

Bragge shrugged. "You wiped Europe clean. What was left to report?"

Mr. Marsh stepped in again. "You heard this tune at Waterloo?"

"At Quatre Bras." Wellington considered a moment. "The man was new to the regiment. He did a great service that day. A new song for a renewed purpose."

"It turned the battle?"

"Of course not. Music does its job before the fighting. Making the men ready, and willing."

Merry brought Martin to stand before the great man.

"As fine as I remember," the Duke said to Martin, shaking his hand. Martin's eyes, huge brown irises, did not appear to blink.

"We are considering printing the score in the *Beacon*," Bragge told him.

"'Twould be nice to see something patriotic in the papers, for a change."

"We backed your efforts," Mr. Marsh said stiffly. "Unlike others."

"Up to a point." Wellington snapped his fingers. "Here. You should play this tune at the celebration ball. I'll suggest it to the Regent." He waved at the aide on his right, who nodded. "Show the nobs what real music sounds like. Might even want to put words to it." He nodded his approval of the idea, then pulled the matron to the side. She led him away, toward the wards.

Olivia did not think she could breathe, she was so filled with glee. She turned to Mr. Marsh. "Do you believe me now?"

"A wounded composer, a theme to rouse the troops at Waterloo, the appreciation of the Glorious Duke." Mr. Bragge nodded. "Smells like a story to me."

"Composer?" Martin frowned, as if coming out of a dream.

"Excellent," Olivia said, stepping in front of him. She opened her arms to herd the news-men away from the court-yard. "We don't wish to take up more of your time. Is there anything else you need?"

"Just a few details," Bragge said, looking at his notepad.

"I will get them for you. But we must allow the men to rest, as matron says." They were in the entryway now. Martin and Merry lingered behind, doe-eyeing each other. "And Mr. Purdy needs to think of lyrics."

"No worries there," Mr. Bragge said. "I'm sure I have some piece of doggerel lying about. Don't we all? Play it again for me, Mr. Purdy?" But Martin was too far behind to hear him.

Mr. Marsh spoke up. "Bentley will do for you, man. Leave the lovers alone."

Olivia stopped at the top of the stairs to the side-walk. "As you wish. It's your story now. We should discuss remuneration," she said, trying to force her voice into a lower, more business-like register.

"Same as for fiction," he said. "Ten pounds to publish, then a share of every paper sold. And if we reprint, thirty percent of sales."

Olivia frowned. It was better than nothing, or paying to publish as the others would have done. But, she struggled to do the math, they would have to sell tens of thousands of papers to come close to what Martin needed. They needed more.

"What about a second piece of music? If this one does well," she added hastily.

"We'll see." Mr. Marsh, two steps below her, could look directly into her eyes. Olivia wondered at what he saw. "How many other pieces does he have?"

"I can't be sure. At least a few." Three completed, five in fragments.

He must have seen the panic in her eyes. The corner of his mouth turned up. She was looking at his mouth altogether too much for comfort.

"A continuing story sells papers. If this story does well, we can follow with the regent's ball. Then," he shrugged, "who can predict what will catch this town's fancy? Besides scandal, of course."

He tipped his hat to her. Bragge smiled a good-bye, and they walked away together in conversation.

Olivia watched his back until it disappeared in the shade of the bank next door. Her fate felt entwined with his. If he made money on the story, so would she. And Martin.

The *Beacon* would publish the story. Martin might be on his way to success.

And could they truly play for the regent?

TEN

This inspiring story of the wounded veteran who penned the 'Tune that Took On Bonaparte' will continue next Thursday week, when the composer and select military orchestra will perform for the Regent's celebration gala. Paper-renters: Buy your own copy of 'The Tune,' 2d, in time to sing along. Reprints available this afternoon.

—The Beacon

"Are you quite finished with the *Beacon*, father?"

The Baron Pettigrew looked up from his perusal of the back page of that publication. He fixed her with that quizzing stare he used whenever he was trying to suss her out. Apparently unable to divine her purpose, he refolded the paper. He placed it on the table and then pushed it toward her place on his left.

She took it up. She felt him watching her and affected to look bored while perusing the front.

There it was. Her work, in fixed type. She drew the paper closer to her, to be able to soak up every line.

"Something pleases you, Olivia?" Her mother asked, and Olivia realized she might be grinning. She surely felt like grinning.

"I wish I were a correspondent."

Papa harrumphed. "Surely not. A woman?" Mama sighed aloud, drawing his attention. "Dear?"

"Dear, whom do you think feeds the papers all the juiciest gossip? Do you think it is a man?"

"It's not?"

"Of course not."

"Then who?"

"An anonymous lady of the gentry. The very high gentry."

"Not the so-called princess, Sofia?" Pettigrew snorted. The ladies laughed. The image of that lady, nearly deaf and completely unafraid of giving her opinion on everyone and everything, would fill pages of the gossip sheets if its proprietor could ever induce her to talk. Fortunately for the *ton*, he never would succeed.

"So, Livvie, you wish to be the *Beacon*'s secret weapon?" Pettigrew's mouth quirked up at the corner, obviously disbelieving her ability to do such a thing.

Olivia spoke without thinking. "And what if I were?" At her father's equally sudden change of countenance, she quickly added, "Not that I am, of course."

"We make politics, girl. We do not trumpet it."

Pronouncement over, he pulled another paper from his stack. Olivia took up her paper and read her music again. And again. She was on the moon. Over the moon. She had done something popular, something public.

Something permanent.

P anic flashed through Martin Purdy's brainpan when he saw the fat reporter from the *Beacon* barreling toward him. Too late to hide. The hospital's sunny courtyard offered precious little cover.

"Good news, my man. The edition is already into a second printing." He nodded to the gent sitting beside Martin on the planked bench, and stuffed himself in the expanding space between them. "Thought I'd bring you a few early editions in case you slept in this morning."

Martin picked up one of the folded pages, seeing his name in the overlarge paragraph at the top. "Second printing?"

"That means the hawkers sold out the first printing and reported people wanted more. Did it last time for 'Napoleon Escapes Elba,' I hear. I'm Bragge, in case you've forgotten." He leaned over Martin's shoulder to read the paragraph himself. "'Wounded but proud,' that's my line. Bentley wanted to cut it."

"But where's the music?"

"Back page." Martin turned the paper. The top half was taken up with the lines and staves of "The Tune That Took Waterloo."

"I came up with the lyrics, and the title." Bragge sucked on a tooth. "Quite the piece of doggerel, if I do say so."

Martin didn't know what to say. Of course Miss Olivia was

brilliant. The piece was stirring and proper, and anyone listening could hear into her heart, if not her soul. But he had not trusted these printers to even print it. Most of all, he had not trusted himself. He had no illusions about his horrid luck in business. "It's hard to believe it," he said.

"Indeed." Bragge's booming voice dampened the conversations nearby. "Something else. Where should we direct your funds? It's far too much to carry on your person." He gazed at the decidedly shoddy souls all about him. "Especially in London."

"Miss Delancey recommended Swizzlewit."

"Odd little duck. But aren't we all?"

"I'm to article with him."

"A solicitor? Music not remunerative enough?"

"This won't last." Martin lifted the pages.

"Your story? Of course not. Something will overtake it, never fear. But I might be able to spin this web out a bit longer, especially if Miss Delancey succeeds at holding the Duke to his word. We could print a few paragraphs ahead of the regent's *grande fête* as well as after. We might stretch this near a week, barring great fires or the death of royalty."

"You would write about the music again?"

"The music, and more about you, too, man." Bragge clapped a hand on Martin's back as if he were a babe needing burping. "Too early to tell, of course, but this could be a windfall, for all of us. Get you out of this place, assuredly." Nose tilted up, he sniffed at the air, and went stiff. His sneeze claxoned around the tiny courtyard, even rousing sleeping soldiers. "Definitely not conducive to health." He pushed his thick waves of hair back from his forehead, where the force of the sneeze had thrust them. "Say, you don't have another great piece lying around, do you? Make yourself some more coin now, before the high-brows move on to their next new passion."

Coin. The root of all his problems. Merry needed a suitor with blunt. She deserved it for standing by him despite her father's wrath. He owed it to her.

Martin's gaze dropped down to the pages in his hands. They seemed to have grown heavier in the time he held them. He had precious little to do with this success, if success it was. It was Miss Delancey's tune, and his Merry's arrangement of the performance here, that sold the story to the press-men. And he certainly had nothing to add, on paper or in his head. But the lady did; he'd heard some of it.

Could this charade continue to pay true? Should it?

"I may," he heard himself say.

"Excellent. Send word when it's ready. We'll send a courier. Needn't be a march, just something lively." Bragge stood, and the suddenly-lighter bench shifted, pushing Martin's shoulder into the man next to him. Down the line, a half-dozen men similarly displaced crashed into one another.

As the reporter headed toward the exit, the men's complaints grew louder. Martin's reality returned with a crash.

He could not tell any of their voices apart, except by the words they used. He still heard only rhythm. He had no pitch.

How could he possibly write a piece with only percussion?

ELEVEN

Unlike his American cousin, the English working-man has, of late, become a totally different character, with his polished boots, wine at dinner, a servant (and sometimes in livery) to wait at his table, a painted lady for a wife, sons aping the young squires and lords, and a house crammed up with sofas, pianos, and all manner of foolery.

—The Register

O livia was no match for Richard's English Channel-wide grin, especially in the close quarters of a London coach.

"Come, Livvie. Your parents said yes, after all."

Why would they say no, as well-trained to show to advantage – pretty, silent, and docile – as she was. "I fear I'm lost to them."

"Nonsense. You do them credit, more than they know." He shrugged, setting his freshly cut hair spiking in all directions as the carriage turned into a small lane in Cheapside. "We neither of us won the lottery on close relations. Present company excepted, of course."

But her parents were not the cause of the somersaulting in Olivia's belly, or the pinpricks of cold running up her arms, bare under a light shawl.

With the beard he had insisted on keeping, he looked like the most handsome beggar in town. For the dozenth time, she fretted that her outfit, a simple short-sleeved sarcenet in dark blue, would be too fancy, too dowdy, too girlish. Did men concern themselves so with their ornament?

Did William Marsh? The *Beacon*'s publisher had written a businesslike letter reporting sales figures from the paper and the first reprint. The note suggested that already they might expect hundreds of pounds in profit. She dearly hoped so, for Martin's sake.

If he were here tonight, Mr. Marsh would be wearing black. Hides the ink, not to mention feeding into his reputation as a serious publisher. In the three days since their interview, she had learned quite a bit about the man. And her best source was Richard.

"I know Bragge better, of course. Fed him some information. Good information," he said, holding up his hands. "God's truth." Richard's foot tapped impatiently as the coach traveled. He had looked out the window every few moments the quarter-hour of the trip. "I could walk faster than this."

"Mr. Marsh?"

"Right. We were mates at Oxford. My first year. He dropped out after that."

"Grades?"

Richard smiled. "More likely a woman. Or the paper."

"He is married?"

"Haven't heard it if he is. He's wed to the paper, in any case. I'd feel sorry for his wife. Finally." The carriage stopped at a narrow, well-lit townhouse. Richard jumped out the door, pulling the steps out and reaching back to help her down.

"Why?"

"The paper goes out at three, four in the morning. That's a mighty cold night in bed for the lady."

"But typical, for Society." As they ascended the short set of stairs leading to it, the door to the well-lit townhouse opened.

"Not for the lower classes, though. And not for my Rosa. She wouldn't stand for it." His grin was infectious.

"Does she laugh as much as you do?" Olivia's smile did not ease the tension in her abdomen. She did not want to make a bad first impression on the woman who would be Baroness after Papa died.

"See for yourself."

On first glance, it did not appear the woman barreling down the stairs in the townhouse had the ability to smile. Long, roan hair landed on her shoulders and back as she gained the landing. Flowing away from a flawless heart-shaped face, the unbound tresses settled on her shoulders, a graceful mane. Her dark eyes flashing, her red-bow lips pursed, she did not appear to be slowing down as she approached them.

Olivia had to step back to avoid the collision as Rosa threw her arms, and herself, at Richard. He whooped and encircled her with his arms, spinning them both in a half-circle. Their kiss went on so long Olivia had time to unhook her cloak and hand it to a servant and introduce herself to the ruddy, beaming hostess, a Mrs. Reeves, before they came up for air. Had they not seen each other just a few hours earlier?

Richard finally put her wife down on her own feet. One arm wrapped around her waist, he extended the other to Olivia. "Livvie, allow me to introduce my Rosa. Dearest, Miss Olivia Delancey."

"Looks like a starved child." Rosa sneered with her whole face, not just her lovely lips.

"It is a pleasure to make your acquaintance." Olivia heard how prim the words sounded, but she wasn't sure what to do about that. "Richard is so happy. I think it is all thanks to you."

Resting her head in the crook between his shoulder and his ear, Rosa narrowed her eyes at her. If she had had any cracks in her social polish, Olivia would have feared such a gaze would split them wide open. As it was, her puzzlement and hurt over Rosa's behavior was so far from the surface no such probing stare would find it.

The lady's expression seemed to open up. She did not smile, but she stopped scowling. "Reeshard tells me you play the music also."

Olivia nodded slightly, also not smiling. "I love the sound of the guitar he brought home. That is what you play?"

"I play all instruments, but often I dance." She flicked her head, hair swinging over her shoulder. "Why have limits?"

"Will you play tonight?"

For the first time, Rosa's face lost some of its certainty. She looked to Richard.

"Of course," he said. Rosa's shoulders relaxed. Richard took Olivia's hand and led both women up the stair. "We are trying to build an interest in bringing her family here for a tour. Her father is a maestro, and her brother a composer."

"What manner of music?"

"Flamenco. The music of the soul. Of passion." Rosa's gaze behind Richard's back held challenge. "Have you ever felt passion?"

Olivia dropped his hand. She would rather learn from this woman than compete with her for her husband's affection. "Do you have copies of your brother's work? I love to discover new composers."

"He rarely writes his work down." Her shrug caused her hair to undulate like a wave down her back. "We earn money through performance. But here, we are needing more."

The music room was three-quarters filled, but Richard managed to find a divan and chair together. He nodded at a few of the men present. Olivia knew none of the women. She was "slumming," according to her parents. It was too bad that she felt more comfortable here than at the artificial pretense that was Almack's or the other Society chambers she was forced to inhabit. The curious looks of the men and women here were easier to withstand than the daggers of the competitive ladies and rakish men of the ballrooms.

"Don't see your Marsh," he said.

"He's not mine. And there's none of his political targets here, either." But she could picture him fitting in well here. The thought, or Rosa's relative silence, calmed her nerves.

"Did you see Wednesday's edition? Music in a broad-sheet! I asked Mrs. Reeves to invite him." Richard made way for a matron and her maid, and then sat beside Rosa on the divan. "Perhaps he'll do something for us."

"He should, if he is your friend."

"You know precious little of publishing if you believe that, cousin."

As the music started, a violin trio performing a Hayden melody, Olivia watched her new relation. Rosa, clearly bored by such a pedestrian melody, leaned back in the chair, her back actually touching the back of the chair. She twirled a lock of that amazing black-red hair around her finger, and then slipped her other hand under Richard's jacket. He jumped, then chuckled, shaking his head no at her. She frowned, and caught Olivia gazing at her. She raised her thick brows, creasing the olive expanse of her forehead.

Polite clapping followed the end of the violinists' final notes. Mrs. Reeves gestured an invitation to Rosa to take the next part.

"I cannot follow that," she declared, waving her hand in dismissal.

A harpist came next, then a duet. The tenor's performance drew whistles, but earned only a shoulder toss from the Spanish bride. Mrs. Reeves gestured at her again.

"Why not show them how it's done in Spain?" Richard said.

Rosa thrust herself up, but her saunter showed she had grace and poise when she wished to. Her dress, navy like Olivia's, clung to her very feminine form. The men in the audience were suddenly rapt in their attention on the player and the proceedings. Just her sitting down at the piano was enough to cause one man to drop his snifter of brandy. She winked at him.

"To honor my great hosts, I will play an English tune. Perhaps you recognize it?" She brought her hands crashing to the keyboard. No frilly *étude*. Her style of play was so feverish, it took Olivia a few long seconds to recognize the melody, even though it was her own.

But it sounded nothing like Martin's version, or the somber warmth she used when performing it herself. Rosa's focus on the off-notes gave it a sprightlier feel, not so much a march as a prancing on the ground. Or on the heads of romantic competitors.

She could tell when the rest of the audience recognized the piece. A general stirring, then the tenor added the lyric, Mr. Bragge's lyric, to Rosa's music. By the second chorus, half the men were singing. By the end, nearly all the audience had joined in. Their faces fevered, their voices sharp, the tune took on yet another life.

Rosa stretched the last bars with a crashing crescendo, adding an exclamation point to the already strong coda. Slamming the last chord into the keyboard, she stood, as if the crash of sound had pushed her up. The applause started immediately, most of the men on their feet, most of the women seated and stunned.

"So, the English do have some music you like, *señorita*?" A gangly man in the front row teased her.

"A little. With much changes," she said, her gaze straying to Richard and her body following. Her face flushed, she dropped back into her chair. "I need a drink."

Richard jumped up to fetch one. Rosa's gaze dropped from him to Olivia. "He says you know the composer."

Olivia didn't trust that her eyes wouldn't give her away. She watched Richard's back, merely saying, "Yes."

"Does he have more of it? I could build something with it. Something big."

Startled, Olivia's gaze flicked back to the woman, lounging in the chair as she had before. "I will see if I can bring you some."

"Oh, I cannot read it." She frowned at Olivia, as if reading music were a sign of weakness. "You can play it for me. And I will show you the *guitarra*."

"I would love that." The genuine warmth in Olivia's voice seemed to surprise Rosa, who drew her brows down. "It has such a different, such a warm, tone. I would love to hear what can be done with it. What you can do."

"Then I will do it. Richard asked me to, but I could not be sure of you. I said no. But a woman, she can always change her mind." She sat up as Richard approached carrying two glasses. He gave one to her and one to Olivia.

"Ratafia for you, Livvie. For you, my dear, brandy and water." He smiled into Rosa's face. For the first time, Olivia saw Rosa smile. It was like dawn breaking after a stormy night. She could see how Richard could have fallen for her. She was all raw nature, no artifice. Such truth would not work in Olivia's world, but she ached for it.

"I will teach your cousin. We are agreed."

"Excellent." Richard's grin moved from Rosa to Olivia. "You won't be disappointed. My wife is rigorous and exacting, but you will never learn as fast with anyone else."

"I didn't realize speed was important."

"Always, Cousin Livvie. Timing is everything."

It was nearly dark when George Marsh left the accounting office of the Customs House. Will, waiting on the steps outside, had plenty of time to prepare himself.

"Will. How—" His brother paused. "Unexpected."

"Unpleasant, you mean." Will softened the jibe with a crooked smile. "Have to say I'm surprised to catch you at work at eight o'clock."

"The crown's work is never done." George pulled closed the office's outer door, locking it. "Though we are allotted time for sleep." He turned back, towering over Will down the stairs on the side-walk. "Why the social call?"

Will did not rightly know. On the way to an evening of music, he found himself headed here instead. Perhaps it was the memory of Miss Delancey braving the lion's den of a man's office to help a friend. Should he not do something to help a brother? But George's actions threatened his paper. And Will could not wait another month, another day, to do something about it. He had to sort this out with George. Which meant sorting George out. "Buy you a drink?"

"I can drink at home." He stepped down to the planked side-walk. "But I'll walk with you, at least to Printing-House Square."

Neither man said anything for a few minutes. George's steps started to slow, and he puffed a bit keeping up with Will's stride. Could age be creeping up on his elder brother? Or some other burden?

As they turned onto a side street, lit but poorly with the new gas-fed lamps, Will broke into their thoughts.

"Brother, what do you really want?"

George darted a glance at him, but said nothing.

"Is it money? The quarterly profits per member have been steady these past two years."

"But without the ill-advised – the secret – purchase of those presses, profit would have doubled this year. More than doubled."

"I've told you why it had to be a secret. And we're so near the payoff on the note, what difference does three more months make?"

"You can't guarantee circulation now." George was nothing if not persistent. "You may not pay the note. Cobbett thinks you will default."

The bile roiled up to Will's throat, sweeping over the whisper of fear. George's lip turned down, a sneer familiar from childhood. Will tamped down the panic with anger. "If Cobbett truly thought that, he would wait and buy the *Beacon* at fire sale in three months."

Sneer gone, George's brows shot up. Had he not thought of that? Then they clamped back down into his familiar squint. "He told me he wanted to save the family any embarrassment. He had great respect for father." And none for Will, he left unsaid.

"Silver-tongued weasel."

"He supports the common man."

Will didn't jump at the bait. He needed to keep his eye on the problem. He slowed and turned into George's path, forcing him to stop a moment. "He's no true radical. And neither are you. It's something else. You need money?"

"No." But the tic in George's eye gave lie to his words. Will crossed his arms, giving his brother a steady stare. George pushed past him, practically running. His energy flagged before the next intersection. "If you must know, yes. But not me. It's the girls."

"Katherine? Amelia?" What trouble could his sisters be in?

"No. My girls." George fingered a button on his jacket. "They find themselves in love." The button popped off, bounding into the filth of the center of the street. George considered the street a moment, and then decided against it.

"They are so young."

"Apparently not." George sank his hands into the pockets of his vest. "Neither yet sixteen, and both in an interesting way."

"With child? The both?"

"You take my meaning." He drew a hand across his brow, mussing the artfully placed strands over his nearly-bald pate. "We must settle them, and now."

Will almost reached out to take his brother's hands. Bad news, doubled. Who would marry them now? And that would make two more mouths for George to feed, forever. "How much do you need?"

George, as if sensing his brother's intentions, pulled away, nearly into the street. "Nothing. Except what we are owed."

Will felt his anger tip over into words. "The *Beacon* is not to blame for the profligacy of your offspring." The brothers stood rigid. A man passing by them stepped out into the street to avoid crossing the powered lines of their glares.

George flinched, and shame washed over Will. He'd gone too far. "But perhaps I could back a second loan, short-term, just to tide you over."

"I detest money-lenders," George spit out. "Just sell the paper, and be done with it. It is not as if you cared about the *Beacon*. It is merely a weapon you use to slap at me."

"That it is not." Will held himself rigid to avoid punching his brother. Family was a burden, love a battleground. Why should he help a brother who lived only to harm him?

Because he loved him. Because he honored the memory of their father, the first George and the first commercially successful Marsh in their branch. Because he loved and honored their mother, who hated that her sons fought.

"I won't sell. You can't force me until you have Kath's signature, and she'll say no, just like last time."

George walked, draping himself in anger and hauteur as if it were a winter cloak.

"But," Will matched his brother's stride. "I will go to the man who holds my note and see if I can pay the rest over six months. Then I will lend you the money, to be recouped from profits over the next few quarters."

"How much?" George heard the amount, and his face fell. "Can you stretch it over a year? Double the amount."

"Five thousand pounds? I'll try. But if he says no—" Will couldn't finish the thought.

"If he says no, we'll sell." George's voice still carried venom, but Will heard the desperation underneath.

"Going to court would not save you money. Or time."

They had arrived at the *Beacon*'s offices, dark in front but bright as day in the courtyard. The wagons waited in short rows, ready to collect the day's edition and spread it across the city and onto post-coaches to travel the rest of the realm.

"That night I came here, Martha told me not to come home without a promise. She nearly locked me out."

"I seem recall she also found herself in an interesting way before being yoked to you."

George shook his head, eyes on his boots. "But you wish better for your children. You'll see."

Will rather doubted that. He was wed to the paper, and what wife would stand to be a weak second? "Go home now, with your promise."

George clasped Will's hand, his deep-pocketed eyes squinting in the light. "Godspeed."

For the first time in recent memory, his brother left the print-shop without a scowl or a black eye. Friends they might never be, Will thought. But they would forever be brothers.

But damn, where was he to find five thousand pounds?

TWELVE

The morning victory service, in its religious particulars, the memory of the battles lost and won, and the sight of the brave veterans who had survived its carnage, produced in the breast an extraordinary sentiment.

—The Beacon

O nce she saw Martin among the dozens of well-dressed musicians in the performance pit, Olivia allowed herself a hidden sigh of deep relief.

He had not appeared at the rehearsal earlier that afternoon, and he had remained missing through the early evening. She had fought to keep the worry from her mind. He had looked so ill the day before, even his hair limp.

She had no idea why. The music scores were flying off the print-shop's shelves. Mr. Marsh had given them to his gang of street hawkers to peddle, bringing the boys a tidy profit as well. Martin would not be a rich man, but he was no longer poor.

And if they could keep this up a little longer, he might reach past the magical one thousand pounds.

Olivia did not believe he truly needed two thousand. Merry's father must relent, once Martin was embarked on a legal career that promised steady income after a few years. The couple might need to wait to marry, but surely her father would help them along. Merry had said he was shocked and saddened at how out of looks and character she fell when Martin shipped off. There was such a change in her aspect now that her doting papa must have guessed the reason.

But all was still not well. Martin sat at the piano on the right side of the orchestra, balancing the violins on the left. He slumped on the bench, head so low it looked as if he had a striking case of near-sightedness.

Olivia pressed her hands down her simple evening dress and walked down the gargantuan hall to the players. She had assigned herself as his page turner, though such a thing was truly unnecessary. Everyone in the pit knew the tune, and Martin, as its "composer," better than any. All she and the military orchestra leader had done this afternoon was convert the basic pattern into parts for specific players and cast it down two tones for the singers. Soon she would need to go upstairs to the ladies' retiring room and do something more with her hair and ornaments. But first she would discover what had brought Martin so low.

"Have you seen Merry?" she asked as she drew near the piano. Martin slowly raised his head, his dark eyes cloudy.

"Martin! Are you ill?"

"Sleeping, is all." He looked past her, at the orchestra, with a bovine expression. "Merry isn't coming tonight."

"Whyever not?"

"It is her father's birthday. They take such anniversaries very seriously." He shrugged. "Besides, she did not receive an invitation."

"Surely she did." Olivia frowned. "I wrote out the address myself."

"Then it was lost. Or intercepted." His voice was oddly flat, as if he could not care less.

"This is terrible. She should be here. It is your grand introduction to society." She clamped her hands on her hips. "This will set you up, and a few more clever pieces will send you on your way. Didn't you tell me Mr. Bragge might want a third piece?"

Martin looked up at her, his gaze clearing. He tilted his head. "You do not look dressed for a ball, Miss Olivia."

"Soon enough. But Merry." She shook her head. "Her family could listen out in the back, on the lawn. They plan to throw open the windows so the people at the gates and in the park can hear the music."

"Her father's not a one for music. Or crowds." His voice was an aural anvil. "Just as well, at this rate."

Olivia sat down beside him on the bench. "Nonsense. I believe I have heard enough of this Soapy Sombersides talk." She blocked out a dense major chord on the keyboard. "This is a great day. Who would have guessed that a little snip of music would travel from a London drawing room to a Belgian battlefield and then to the house of the Regent himself? Our little war effort."

"Yours, you mean." His shoulders slumped, Martin

reminded her of the performing monkeys on the street, only slower and less clever.

She quickly looked about her to see if anyone was listening, but the other players were deep into their own conversations. "Martin Purdy, I may have written it, but you changed it to a full-fledged march. You brought to the Duke's attention. Your version is the one that turned the tide of the battle."

He cast a baleful look at her.

"Fine, that last part was a bit of an exaggeration," she said, though she expected that would be how the Master of Ceremonies would put it tonight. "But it was you, Martin, who set this all in motion. Take full credit."

"Merry did the bit for the journalists."

"And Merry deserves a prize for that. I couldn't imagine a better staging." She looked around. "Except for this."

He raised his head to look around. Even nearly empty, the great hall, with its parallel columns, outrageous murals and two-storey windows, took one's breath away. Olivia wanted to push those overgrown bangs away from his eyes so he could see the room in truth, but that was best left to Merry. Who should be here.

"I must go change for the party. Will you be all right here?" Rehearsal over, the musicians were leaving the stage. "Perhaps you should take a turn around the park. Clear your head."

Suddenly, her hands were gripped tight. Martin turned tortured eyes to her. Olivia's heart rattled a tattoo. "Promise you'll return for the performance. Promise."

"What is wrong?"

"Just a little problem with my balance," he said sheepishly.

Her eyes automatically went to his ears. Fevers could lead to loss of balance. "Has something happened to your ear?"

"Both. Left is worse." His grip loosened. "Broken ear, broken leg, broken nerves. The leg's what got me out of the service."

"But surely you can play? In the courtyard, I saw you show a man the fingering for the trumpet part."

Martin looked away, down at the keyboard.

"I don't think I shall ever play again."

Will remembered too late that nothing at the Regent's started even remotely on schedule. The celebration extravaganza was to have begun a half-hour ago with speeches and poetry, but not even four dozen people wandered the cavernous pillared hall. The doors had been thrown wide on the public side of Carlton House, and he could see from one end of the long house to the grounds out the last door.

He shouldn't have been able to, if the place was stocked with the thousands promised.

Will wondered if the Prince Regent were even in the building yet. At least out on the lawns, where a giant feast was planned for the city folk, the ale was flowing already. He wandered out the back of the building toward where the action was. His ticket, coated with filigree and safe in his pocket, guaranteed he could again re-enter the halls of Society.

The air was cool for July, but the setting sun still offered some warmth. Along the well-manicured lawn, people of all shades of life strolled and chatted. Some ate and drank, picnic style, near the stately trees. Children squealed at the pony rides and paper boat races on the man-made pond. And, as ever, a gaggle of men crowded the platforms where the ale was being poured.

As he drew nearer, he heard a familiar voice.

"Drink up, my friends! This is what the government has raised your taxes for. Ostentatious frivolity!"

Cobbett had not reached the pinnacle of his tirade. The gray of his wayward hair was still lying flat against his head. Soon, as his language and his body temperature heated up, it would lift and curl. By the end of his ranting, a good half-hour from now, if the past was any guide, his hair would be completely on end, a scarecrow trick that could frighten his audience into dumb silence or rousing cacophony.

With this crowd, Will was betting on cacophony. Either direction was entertainment enough. But it was at least a half-hour off, so Will grabbed a mug of ale and kept walking.

On the garden pathways and along the walls of the garden, men and women were engaging in the time-honored pursuit of one another. He was reminded of a garden, smaller than this one, in Dorset. A blonde, her hair in fancy plaits, her manner enticing and coy. Winking, teasing, paying for good wordplay with a smile and, once, a kiss. Deidre.

A shadow fell over the memory, the shadow of what happened after. After the Lady D, as the papers put it, had taken his heart as her own, she ripped it so gently out of his chest that he did not realize it had gone until she threw it on the ground and stomped it. In public.

"How dare you?" she had said. "A tradesman's son?" And

Will had seen it her way, and felt foolish. He was a practice dummy, a handsome enough dog for her to sharpen her claws on.

He drained half his ale. Just the memory stung, a twinge at the top of his chest. It had been so long ago, true, but it had changed everything. He'd never be fooled by such pretense again.

He had returned to Oxford a changed man, or rather the same man with a changed perspective. He saw how out of place he was, among the top of the upper-crust. Him, with nothing but brains and brawn, no pedigree, no promise. One of the common men Cobbett loved to chide, a gawper with pretensions.

He had given up on school and returned home to London, throwing himself into the family business. Soon enough, George was out, their father able to easily see that Will was the true descendent.

And the paper was Will's, no matter what his father's codicil implied. The senior George had not thought to revise his will, and his sudden death had thrown the paper into chaos. All the siblings were equal partners, with the one running the paper having no greater vote. And one, George, with an axe to grind as big as Westminster Cathedral itself.

Will finished off his draft, wiping his mouth. It did not do to roost in the mistakes of the past. He needed to look to the present, especially if he wanted to hold onto the paper.

Why had Cobbett chosen now, of all times, to make his move? Or was it all George, desperate to head off dual family ruin?

Mug empty, Will turned back to the planks and servers at

the top of the hill. Cobbett's scarecrow hair had climbed up to his ears, sticking out on three sides of his head, a living Punch marionette. He had already reached the "debt is evil but paper money is worse" part of the diatribe.

Will refilled his beer before pushing his way to the front of the crowd of men. "Leave some air for the other speakers, Master Cobbett," he called. "I hear an ale down here calling your name." Some in the crowd laughed, one man said, "Hear, hear."

"Another country heard from. A fellow publisher, but not of the common persuasion." Cobbett's face was red, a stark contrast to the white hair framing his face. "Come up, speak! Tell them how spending their days playing fancy tunes will fill the commonwealth's coffers."

"I would rather tell them to grab another tankard. Looks like the ale may run dry."

His words caused a genial stampede to the service tables, leaving only a handful of stalwarts, or drunkards, in the audience. Cobbett, who preferred his audiences present if not attentive, stomped down the ladder to dismount the stage.

"Marsh." He didn't shake hands, though he did take the tankard of ale Will offered him. "Ahh. The working man's beverage of choice. Tastier than any foreign-brewed lick-kwer."

"Glad to see you still have the energy to rant, Cobbett. The political press isn't working you hard enough, I see. Is that why you are sniffing around the *Beacon*?"

"Beat around the bush, why don't you, Marsh." Cobbett wiped his mouth with the back of his hand. "Truth is, hadn't much thought of it. But your brother said I might get it at fire-sale prices, and I jumped. Easier to corner the market with both a morning and an evening paper."

"Yours is a weekly, man."

"Exactly. Cover the field, is what I say. Sow every field, and reap the reward."

"Sounds like you're missing your farm."

"Ah, a sweet patch of country, that." Cobbett smacked his lips. "The wife's there now. With this over, and news so slow, I may join her for a month or so."

"And rest from improving the lot of the working man?"

"How better to understand it that than to live like one of them? Temporarily, of course."

"It would be more successful than your bid for the *Beacon*." Will tried to keep his voice even. "It's not on the blocks, especially not at fire-sale."

"No need to tell me that. You must have recovered your lost circulation with that stunt last week. Or surpassed it. The Tune that Took Waterloo." Cobbett shook his head, his broom-brush hair flying everywhere. "Crazy idea. Who would have thought it would sell?"

"They're playing it tonight."

"I heard it on the street, on the way over. Even the beggars sing it for their suppers. That's the true test of the market."

"We're running another tomorrow. With this story." Will waved in the direction of the house.

"Don't trust it." Cobbett tilted his head back to catch the last drops of ale. "Something fishy about that report. I feel it in here." He tapped the top of his head with the bottom of the tankard.

Will stood his full six feet one inch, towering over Cobbett's five foot seven. "That story is clean. Like every other we publish."

"Believe that if it suits you." Cobbett gave Will a half-smile. "What am I but sour grapes? That composer came to me first."

"Purdy?"

"Lily-livered twit. I thought someone had sent him to torment me. Who ever heard of running such frippery in a man's newspaper? Nearly tumbled him out of the office." Cobbett grimaced, looking almost sheepish. "Mayhap was a bit rude at him."

Will laughed. "Who did you think sent him?"

"Some young whippersnapper like you." Cobbett winked at him, which made him laugh harder. "More likely, that addled music publisher down the street. The man should go back to his first job. It was a butcher shop before it was a musical emporium, you know."

Will shook his head, still smiling. Cobbett turned to the ale tables.

"See you inside?" he asked Cobbett.

"Never. I'll stay here with the true blue-bloods."

"And their ale. What will you report?"

Cobbett tapped the side of his ruddy nose. "Same as you. But with no unnecessary facts cluttering up the moral. And none of those sweet-smelling ladies, either. Watch your back, man."

Will thought of a particular, do-gooder member of the species, all golden tresses and lofty intentions.

Decidedly dangerous.

Thirteen

Already in its third reprinting, 'The Tune that Took on Water-loo' will surely be familiar to the multitude predicted to be outside Carlton House tonight.

—The Beacon

The first people Olivia saw as she descended the arching staircase to the main floor of Carlton House were her parents, looking as if they had stepped out of a fashion plate from thirty years ago, from powder to patches. Mama waved her oversized handkerchief, signaling Olivia to approach. While all she wanted was to check if Martin had returned to his place at the piano, she knew that here, especially, the formalities must be observed. She curtseyed in front of them, and bent down to buss her mother's cheek.

"Watch the powder, dear."

"You'll find plenty more powder upstairs, Mama. Even for your hair." She managed to somewhat surreptitiously brush stray flakes of it from her mother's shoulder, and then stepped back, the better to inspect her foot-tall tower of hair. "Is that a horse, Mama?"

"Coming out of the surf. Patterned after the fountain at Versailles."

"You, too, Papa. Stepped away from Versailles just this moment."

"I do so love it when we can reprise themes. Everything French is so *en vogue* again." His wig reminded her of the portraits of her grandfathers on the wall of the music room. Perhaps it was the same wig.

They stood just inside the arched entry to the great hall. Olivia squinted past them toward the opposite end where the musicians were installed, but the distance was too great for her to pick out Martin. What had he meant, he could not play? Surely a former music master could overcome a case of nerves. Martin had said his nerves were broken in battle, but surely music was easier than battle.

She had convinced him to step outside, even partake of a mug of ale. Anything to turn his thoughts from failure. Some performers did suffer such fears that they would not perform well in public. But then again, Martin had not said he would not. He'd said he could not.

"We missed you at the cathedral dear." Mama patted her arm. "But Jaspers told us you were helping your charity friends."

Olivia held her tongue. Charity friends, indeed. Both Merry and now Martin were solvent, a far cry from her own family's money troubles.

Her father nodded, scanning the room. Looking for political acquaintances to connect with, she expected. In public, he was always working. "You didn't miss much, m'dear, just the usual blowhard speeches. Did we not hear enough of them last year, the first time we won this blasted war?"

"Language, dear." Mama smiled at the side of his head. "Although the Bishop of Canterbury did signal your father out to praise his fiscal responsibility during the hard times just passed."

"Archbishop, dearest." He squeezed her hand, then moved off toward a judge wearing a similar ages-old wig.

"Of course, archbishop." Mama watched him a moment, sighed happily, and then turned back to her daughter. "Olivia, why you look positively lovely. Who would have thought a peach gown would suit? But it highlights your country-miss hair. You positively glow."

"Thank you, Mama." The compliment touched her deeper than she would care to admit. She did not seek praise, but from her parents it was so rare as to be remarkable.

"You do need a necklace of some sort, though. Such an expanse of skin. I suppose it is the style, but it makes you look positively bare." Mama unwound a twisted silver chain from the collection along her wrist. "Here. This will look well with the silver in your ear-bobs." They moved toward the curtains of the entry, a little hidden from view. Scores of ladies in rustling silks and men in dancing slippers flowed from the side halls into the great rooms. Olivia pushed her artfully draped hair away from her nape to allow her to fasten the clamp. The fine chain carried a teardrop diamond, which fell about halfway from her chin to the neck of her gown.

"'Tis glass, so don't worry if you lose it," Mama whispered. "The clasp is tricky, that's why I keep it in reserve."

Olivia's blush was unbidden. Why must everything remind her of their straitened circumstances? It wasn't as if she were allowed to do anything useful to help. Although, if she took the trusty and discreet Mr. Swizzlewit into her confidence, she might give an anonymous donation to the family fund from the money she was collecting from the sales of her music. From her connection to William Marsh.

As if her thoughts had conjured him, the man himself walked through the open doors to the patio, a room's length away from them. He had dressed the gentleman for the occasion, his jacket a dark gray over snow-white linen, his trousers midnight black. His jet hair was collected in some way in the back, exposing his strong forehead, those sharp eyes and that stern jaw. He walked slowly, as if to accustom his eyes to the candlelight. Then he met her gaze, and stopped.

Olivia's blush grew even warmer. Her hair fell back to her shoulder as the hand stole unbidden to the false jewel, which rose and fell with her labored breath.

"What is it dear?" Mama turned to look. "Handsome. Do we know him? Who is his family?"

A shock of panic raced up her spine. Mama could tell everything.

Olivia found her voice. "He's dangerous, Mama."

"Better and better."

"No. A publisher. The *Beacon*? Papa's man."

"A tradesman." Mama sighed, picking up one of the artfully stray strands of Olivia's coiffure. "Unfortunate." She dropped the strand and looked into Olivia's eyes, commanding her attention. Olivia's other senses remained tuned to the center of the room.

"I am so sorry, dear. We thought it all settled with Richard. Now," she turned, scanning the room as Papa had done, "we must find you someone else."

"Mama." Olivia could think of nothing worse than re-opening that line of inquiry. "Let me attend to it."

"Would you?" Mama's head snapped back to face her. "It would be such a relief. I am afraid I have eyes only for political conquests, not the amorous kind. And you made so clear at your come-out that a political man would not suit."

"Don't worry another moment about it, Mama. I will manage it all." As she always had. "Over there. Do you think they discuss Papa's new position?"

"I do hope so." With Olivia's gentle verbal push, Mama started moving toward her beloved husband, now deep in discussion with two bewigged cronies. Another danger averted, Olivia's heartbeat slowed to normal. And then rocketed at the sound of a masculine voice beside her.

"The Baroness seems to have cornered the market on hair powder." The man himself stood at her shoulder, all energy and strength, his green gaze turned toward her mother. "Leaving you, Miss Delancey, to make do with what nature has adorned you."

"Fashions change, Mr. Marsh. People are steadier." She turned toward him, in part to draw his attention away from mama and her potential to make unconscious mischief. In larger part to drink him in.

Even at close quarters, he was handsome, and that twinkle in his eye showed he knew it. "So they are, ma'am. Let us hope you may always play nature's nymph, as you do so well tonight. Such a flattering arrangement of falling curls." She caught her breath as he reached for her, but he merely took her hand. Awareness shivered up her arm, down her neck. Her whole body seemed instantly alert. Ready.

He raised the gloved hand to his lips. His teasing gaze didn't leave her eyes as he leaned in for the quite proper formal kiss. But the hint of a touch of those generous lips burned through the flimsy material of the glove, searing her hand with his mark.

It was all that was appropriate, yet she felt as if they had sinned on the spot.

The contact appeared to have some affect on him, as well. He paused, then smiled. "Tricky, that winsome smile of yours. I must remember to avoid the ale before our encounters."

"I wouldn't wish to preclude any pleasures of yours. But will not the ale also confound your reporting?"

"Too true." He mock frowned, then grinned at her. It was as if he had washed her in a wave of merriment. She cleared her throat. Without thinking, she touched the bauble at her neck. The movement drew his gaze to her chest. He raised his eyes, and his eyebrows.

"Miss Delancey, are you trying your Society tricks on me?"

She stepped back, confused. Was she?

Pulling her scattered thoughts together, she tried to scare up a safe topic of conversation. "Have you seen Mr. Swizzlewit? He is invited." She gestured toward the open room. He obligingly turned to look. But as she felt her shoulders loosen, her breath return to normal, he chuckled, twisting her back into tongue-tied knots.

She heard a violin tuning. Never had that familiar screech sounded so welcome. She turned back to Mr. Marsh, who had already returned his full attention back to her. "I must attend on Mr. Purdy before the concert begins. You'll excuse me."

"Only if I can have an exclusive interview afterward. With the composer." He winked. "Or his muse."

She could not get away from him fast enough. He seemed to confuse her heart's beating. She worried at her lip, trying to decide whether it was safer for Mr. Marsh to talk with Martin, who might trip up and ruin the story, or with her, who at this rate might well swoon into his arms.

Downright schoolgirlish, she scolded herself, weaving through the people already gathering in the hall. How lowering.

How wonderful. And nothing like with Richard. That had been curiosity, and some lust, true. But it faded on acquaintance. It definitely didn't grow past friendship.

Could she be friends with Mr. Marsh? More than friends?

At the thought, her heart leapt nearly into her throat. She pushed the thought and its attendant feelings firmly down. She needed to concentrate on the performance.

She reached the players, most in their seats, none comfortably. Then she saw Martin, and knew why.

He was lying, knees up, on the piano bench, hidden from the crowd but in full view of the players. Olivia knelt beside his head, tucked into his chest.

"Martin! Are you ill?"

He stirred, lifted his head a fraction. "Miss Delancey?"

"What is it? Sit up, if you can."

She rose, pulling at his available arm, levering him up. He tilted dangerously in the opposite direction, then settled upright on his haunches. He ran both hands into his hair, pushing the long lengths away from his forehead.

"Do you need something to eat? To drink?" Olivia tried to keep the panic out of her voice. She did not know what she would do if he could not perform.

"I had a bite earlier," he whispered, as if he were far away down a well.

"Good," she said bracingly. "So you are ready."

He shook his head slowly, as if it might roll off under a stronger motion. "Not exactly." At the center of the orchestra, the maestro watched them intently.

"What can I do?" She heard the desperation in her voice.

"Look." Martin held his hands over the keyboard in ready position. The right hand looked fine. The left drooped. "I cannot make it do my bidding. For a while, it got better. Then this afternoon, it fell apart again." He dropped his hands into his lap.

Olivia put a hand over her mouth, holding her fear and horror inside. A musician's nightmare, to lose the power of willed motion. But it might be temporary. She must be strong, for him.

"Has this happened before? Are you prone to nerves?"

"It is not nerves. I tried to tell you before." He eyes dripped apology. "This is how it has been since the battle."

"But I watched you play the trumpet."

"You saw me hold it."

But he had not played it, she realized. "Oh, Martin. You should have told me." Her hand clasped the glass of the necklace again. It seemed to be the only strong, steady object in her life.

"How could I? You were so thrilled at this commission."

"Merry knows, doesn't she? That's why she isn't here. Don't look at me like that." His hound-dog eyes were too much for

126

Olivia. A surge of white-hot anger burned from her belly through her arms. She stepped back, in case her hand slapped him of its own accord.

He had set her up.

What could she do? Why could no one be relied upon? This threatened everything they had accomplished. The noise of the gathering crowd blended with the jumble of her thoughts. It would be obvious Martin hadn't written the second piece, or rewritten the march, if he couldn't even play the piano. They would be tarred in the papers, and lose their commissions.

"Miss Delancey?" The maestro stood on the other side of Martin.

Her thoughts raced. If Martin couldn't play, could he do something else? Why would the composer of a piece have to play it, in any case? What could he do? Anything? What to do, where to do, how to do, who to do.

Him.

"Maestro, I was thinking," she said, trying to smile the way she had at Mr. Marsh. "Mr. Purdy here is the man of the hour, is he not? Surely, he shouldn't hide his glory behind this piano, should he?"

"I suppose not," the maestro said, doubt in his voice.

"We should be celebrating him. A man has such a moment only once in his life. Certainly, a man such as Mr. Purdy."

"Too true. I remember my debut." His voice trailed off, and a small smile stole across his lean face. Olivia allowed him to bask in his remembered glory a second longer, and then broke in.

"So, it might be very seemly for you, when the moment was right, to hand the baton to Mr. Purdy. Just for his march, of course." The man opened his mouth to speak, but Olivia, heart still racing, was far faster. "Such a generous idea, maestro. No one will forget your beneficence. How shall we do it? Shall you step to the front, prepare the orchestra? Then, as if you just thought of it this moment, gesture to Mr. Purdy to come forward? Give him the baton?"

She clasped her hands together. "I see it perfectly." She rushed around Martin's back to grasp both of the conductor's hands. "You are an angel. Everyone will say so." The maestro stood slack, mouth agape at Olivia's onslaught of words. "But we'll need a piano player," he managed to squeak out.

"I'll step in. Or sit in, as the case may be." Olivia dimpled at the conductor, who lost the power of speech again. "I won't need a page-turner. I have memorized the score. Copying all those pieces for the players will do that, you know." Using his hands as a fulcrum, she pivoted the maestro's body back to face the orchestra.

"We await your cue. Thank you so much. You have the heart of an angel. Such generosity." With her tiny push at his back, he started shuffling toward his post.

Olivia turned to look down at Martin. His eyes were wide, but no longer like a sad puppy's. More like a terrified puppy.

He should be.

Threading her voice with steel, her whisper carried the sharpest of blades. "You will do this, Martin. It is not difficult. You know how to mark time, and it's a steady tempo. You will stand there, and you will be proud. Do you hear me?"

He nodded, his swallow more like a gulp.

"This is for the best. The regent took your talents, and he should give you something in return. Take advantage."

"It's a lie."

"It is not. You played the piece; it won recognition; it earned its praise. As did you."

Martin seemed to consider her words. Then he straightened his spine and settled his shoulders. "Do I look well enough?"

"Button that jacket, and you're perfect. And when they applaud, do try to look pleased. You deserve this. You do."

On cue, the maestro turned to them, inviting Martin to come take his place. As the man of the hour stepped carefully around the other players to reach the center of the semicircle, Olivia pushed the ornamental potted plants from the side of the piano to directly in front of her and settled on the bench. She was here as the page turner; no one should notice the absence of a player.

She would have to face Mr. Marsh on her own for that interview. Martin would not be able to withstand any questions.

She peeked around a plant out at the sea of faces in the audience. Hundreds. Hundreds or thousands more would hear them from the park, or from the street in front. A happy shiver ran down her spine. Performing her own piece, in front of rooms full of people. She had dreamed of this.

She stretched her strong, steady fingers over the keys. She was fortunate to be young and healthy. She was blessed with the gift of composition. And she would be lucky indeed to get through this night with all her secrets intact.

Fourteen

A young lady of rank, in the warmth of her dancing heart, thus addressed her partner at the Regent's ball, "God bless you – take care and don't tread upon my muslin gown, for you see that I have nothing under it."

—The Register

After the bliss of performance and the cacophony of cheering, stomping, and applause that followed, Olivia allowed herself to breathe easier. The shining horns had drawn whatever small attention was not taken by the composer of the hour, and no one had noticed her. Martin took his bows without frowning once, and took himself off, back to the sanctuary of the hospital, she expected.

She ceded her place to the regent's resident piano artist. He settled himself precisely in place, and then frowned at the other members of the orchestra, who had not yet settled. But as she started to step away, he held up a hand and turned to her.

"Before you go, ma'am. The composer, tell him that the Maestro enjoyed both the sentiment and the composition of the piece."

"The maestro?" Olivia repeated stupidly, looking at the conductor of the orchestra.

"Not him. Maestro Hayden."

He was here? Olivia touched her hand to her cheek, to make sure she was real. Of course he would be here; everyone would come to the peace celebrations. She hadn't allowed herself to think about his hearing her work. Hadn't even allowed herself to dream of it.

Hayden was here.

Her little march was meant to be simple, so even military men could follow it. With the words added, it was right patriotic. If the Maestro had merely nodded after the performance of it, it would sell hundreds of copies. She was sure of it. She closed her eyes to hold the tears back but couldn't mask the unladylike grin. "I'll tell him," she replied.

She slipped behind the orchestra into its ready room, now empty of people. As the music started in, a familiar homage to the Navy, she swung herself in a circle.

She'd done it. Helped a friend, sold her work, and won the praise of the finest living composer in England. She had gambled and won. What could be better?

Noisy with the clink of glassware and the shrieked laughs of a thousand fine-feathered gentry in full revelry, the main floor of the hall pulsed with energy. Olivia passed by gaggles of ladies and their men, greeting some but never lingering.

The end of war had done the unimaginable – brought the *ton* back to the stifling London heat from their cooler countryside manors. She trusted they would leave again soon. It was bad enough to bow and scrape through the endless social season; everyone should have their summers free.

Used to being invisible at these affairs, Olivia had been attracting more notice of late. The "broken engagement" was juicy fodder for gossip, of course. But she had forgotten how people once considered her beautiful; now that she was again on the market, even at her hoary age, she must appear a threat to the most timid of the young ladies. It would explain their narrowed glances and unwelcoming shoulders as she strolled. One girl even changed places with her beau, so Olivia would pass closer by her than him. Well, she could have him. Olivia had far too much on her plate as it was to run about stealing other women's men. Besides, she knew how it felt to be the one who was left.

The politicians had arrayed themselves along the inner wall, nearest the courtyard. She avoided the breadth of them, but could not dodge them all, even with her face abstracted as if she were seeking someone. Plumed in blue and gold, Mr. Mellon stepped into her path.

"Well, Miss Delancey, I hope that performance earlier has convinced you."

Mr. Mellon puffed his canary waistcoat at her. Olivia wondered if it were the only one he owned. It seemed to have ale on it from the last time she'd seen him. The man drank wine tonight.

"I am afraid I don't follow, Mr. Mellon."

"What we talked about during my campaign tea-party. The weakness of the female."

"How has that come to mind tonight?"

"I was telling you as how women, the female of the species,

could never hope to be as creative as the male. No female on this Earth could have penned that stirring new tune."

"The Tune that Took Waterloo?" She could barely contain her surprise, or the quick turndown at the corner of her mouth.

"So martial, so inspirational. So, in a word, male." He shrugged. "It proves my point. Perfectly."

Olivia did let loose a small smile as she struggled to keep her stronger emotions in check. Why could she not simply strike the man, stomp on his over-round belly? Then tell him that piece, that very one, was not only written by a female, but this female. The one with her foot on his gut.

She saved these feelings, too, to savor later, in private. She could not let on their secrets, not with Martin such a live wire of late, and that sharp-eyed Mr. Marsh lurking about.

Not exactly lurking. In fact, she knew exactly where the man was. It was as if she had an antenna especially tuned to him. He was in the back rows, listening to the political men. A sorry lot. She turned to her interlocutor.

"Mr. Mellon. How is it that you are cut loose from the bevy of politicians tonight?"

"I saw you, Miss Delancey, and like a moth I was drawn to your flame. Pity your engagement was called off, but a boon chance for the rest of the field."

He was a moth that could beat its wings forever before she would marry him. A moth that could not tell the difference between fine music and drivel. A moth that could not keep its mouth shut.

"Also, my dear, I did want to point out the errors in your thinking. You have so many beautiful qualities. It is a shame women are so difficult to educate."

Olivia stomped on her own instep to hold her tongue.

"I'm sorry to hear you think so. I trust that doesn't mean you will dislike the next performance."

"Is it a woman? Performing in public? Someone should stop her."

Olivia looked at the floor so he would not see her rolling her eyes. Evidently, he had been drawn to her flame after she performed in front of the crowd. "She is Spanish," she said.

"Loose."

"I should hope not. She is the wife of my cousin, Captain Avery."

"Your replacement? Fascinating." Mellon took her arm without asking permission and pushed aside guests to allow them a clearer view of the stage. Off to the side, Olivia could see Rosa tuning the strings on her guitar.

Her fire-dark hair was not held back at all. Her russet dress was a striking contrast against the red-gold of her instrument and the bronze of her face.

As she strode onto the stage, the front of the room seemed to hush in one movement. She sat on the short bench provided, throwing the case for her guitar down in front of her for a foot stool. The dress must be one of the ones Richard spoke of, specially made for the player, for as she lifted her booted foot to place it on the case, the folds of the dress quickly draped it.

Olivia allowed herself a slight sigh of relief. She had suggested this performance, just a word in the right ears, and she did not wish them to regret their kindness to her. At least Rosa was not tossing all Society's rules of propriety in its face.

Mr. Mellon, staring at the performer, started to sway, leaning in toward Rosa. Olivia wrenched her arm away from him and looked at the others in the audience. Some of the men looked to be needing chairs, for they seemed to have fallen ill. Olivia folded her arms in front of her, cross.

If Rosa's sullen beauty did this to them, how would they react to her gutsy playing?

She soon found out.

The woman started furiously, with a run of arpeggios Olivia could barely follow. The speed of the playing had the player in a study of concentration. Rosa's eyes closed, or were close on her fret-board; it was difficult to tell.

She was a virtuoso, one of those with both the skill to please the ear and showmanship to please the eye. At the end of a particularly vibrant line, she looked up, out at the audience, eyes flashing. Mr. Mellon was not the only man who gasped.

Olivia knew she didn't have that fire in her. For her, playing was more for reflection and discovery than performance. Her music so far did not have the flash of flamenco, either. She frowned, thinking. What if it could?

"Troubles, Miss Delancey?" William Marsh stood on her right, wearing an odd cat-smile, as if he had caught her at something.

Olivia's face mirrored her surprise. She had lost track of him for only a moment, and yet he had snuck all the way up on her. Had he caught her surreptitiously watching him?

"The music does not inspire you?" He gestured at Rosa, but his gaze remained on her.

"It does," she said, trying to pull on her familiar careless-girl mask. "I must ask after her tailor."

"That sentiment isn't worthy of you." He whispered, but he

could have spoken aloud, as little attention as anyone was paying them in the midst of Rosa's aggressive arpeggios. "Jealous?"

Her mask faltered. "I did not mean it so."

"Then how?" He slipped to her other side, effectively cutting her off from Mr. Mellon, who did not seem to notice. Too close. She took a step to the side, turning to face her interlocutor.

"She is part of our family now." Her voice sounded breathy, unsure.

"I heard you arranged this performance." He stepped closer. "That shows a spirit of generosity, despite your words."

"She deserves the opportunity. And it is right to salute Spain."

"Our esteemed ally." He nodded, leaning in. "But perhaps it is difficult, to see a woman who is allowed the freedom to perform, to create? Who can let her hair down in mixed company?"

He looked away from her a moment, gazing at Rosa. Olivia did not dare look away from him. She let out the breath she didn't realize she had been holding. Her mind was addled; she was reacting too strongly to this man, to his words. To his smell, deep and rich. Sandlewood, but hints of the flesh within.

The corner of his mouth turned up. He teased her? The thought cast out her breath again. Her ears had a buzzing in them, unrelated to the passionate rhythm of the guitar.

He could read her. He saw far too much. She reached out to touch him, no, to push him away. He turned at her movement, stepping into the path of her hand.

A thrill of power coursed through her arm. It filled her

center with energy of an unfamiliar sort. Unable to stop herself, she jumped. Then quickly looked around to see if anyone saw.

She could never make a scene. Not here in public. She took another step back, pulling her hands tightly behind her, as if they were tied.

Step by step, they sidled to the side of the great room. Toward the shadows.

"Are you disappointed your fiancé found someone else?"

"It isn't that." She was not quite sure she could call up a vision of Richard at the moment. Her awareness was centered on the man in front of her.

They passed the seven-foot-high sterling candelabra and into the shadows, far from the crowd. Olivia would not have believed she could feel so alone in the midst of a gala. Alone, but for one other.

"Avery's wife is quite beautiful. And talented."

He stepped closer. She felt the fabric of the curtain behind her. No more room to maneuver.

"But no match for you."

He reached out, his hand grazing the slope of her jaw. It felt like she imagined a caress would feel.

It was a caress.

Sighing, she tilted the side of her face into his hand. Warm and firm, its strength seemed to soak into her skin. He had roughness on the tips of his fingers. Calluses. Her fingers must feel that way now, too, on her left hand. From the guitar.

She closed her eyes, savoring the moment. The passion of the music seared the air, painting her skin with extra sensation, releasing her busy mind from its binds.

With a flurry of notes and crescendo of sound, Rosa finished the piece. The whole room was silent a moment, still. Then crashed into a thunder of applause, even stomping. The effect was startling, and as loud as it had been for Olivia's march. Although the march had had applause from the fields and the street, while Rosa's guitar did not carry that far.

In the shadows, whatever spell it had on her broke. Olivia's head snapped away from his hand.

He pulled his hand away, fisted it, put it in his pocket. His eyes seemed to hold a summer storm in them, blue-green swirl. His jaw clenched, released.

"Beg your pardon, ma'am."

"Olivia," she said. She didn't know why, but as he had read her thoughts, her feelings, at the least he could use her name. "In private."

"Will." His gaze flicked to the crowd, then back to her. "I like your idea of private." He took a step back from her. He couldn't leave now.

"Wait. Rosa – Mrs. Avery – is scheduled to play two pieces."

"As you wish." He stepped to her side. At least he was not crowding her, but she found she missed the sight of him. She did not miss his presence, though. It shone off him in waves, a sizzle of sandalwood, strength, and skin. Familiar, but not at all restful.

Rosa pushed her mane of hair back, showing her gorgeous neck, free of ornament. Olivia touched the false pendant that hung around her neck.

"Ornament suits you." He leaned in. This time, she did not wish to move away. "Simple, elegant ornament. And how does your hair stay up? I see no pins?"

"So you are not omniscient, then. I feel at least a dozen

poking my scalp." She turned away from the stage to look full at him. His eyes had cleared. Now they were a dark green, reminding her of a cat. The tiger in the London zoo. But here, uncaged.

"And me considered so observant." He shook his head, his frown false regret, his gaze not leaving hers. "Must we be silent during the piece?"

"Only if you wish. It is a premiere."

He nodded. "So must be appropriately appreciated." He winked. "Olivia."

His teasing startled her into a smile. He matched it, a grin that would make an old woman ache with pleasure.

Rosa started, a stirring downward arpeggio that made Olivia unaccountably irritated. Reluctantly, she turned back to the stage.

Without thinking, she took a half-step back, closer to the side of the man near her. He was nodding with the music, which rounded in on itself with the same tantalizing rhythms as the first song. She started to nod, gently, as a well-bred lady might in a foreign land. This manner of music was never heard here. It stirred her blood, as the man beside her stirred her mind, her senses.

He brushed his hip against hers, then away, in rhythm with the music. And again. Each time it was as if he released butter-flies hidden in her loins. Sparks of tiny joy, secret pleasure.

Then his hand skimmed her rear, and she nearly swooned. Before she could turn to administer a set-down, his hand had nestled between hers, still crossed in the back.

Olivia hesitated mid-turn. No one could see their hands,

behind her back as they were. He held still, watching the stage, waiting for her reaction.

She turned back to the stage. He started his swaying again, small changes in position, touching different points on her palms, her fingers, the tips. Each a pinprick of awareness, of pleasure.

She slid her fingers of one hand deeper into his. With the other she brought out her fan, snapping it open near her hip and waving it upward, cooling her overheated skin.

"Send a little of that air this way." His whisper tickled the curl near her ear, setting off sparks that reached her neck. She heard a rushing. Her own blood, speeding at treble time.

He leaned in, blowing a breath along her exposed collarbone. Too much sensation. Too much.

She tilted the fan toward him. Its mild pressure appeared to be enough to push away his lips. Fortunate, as she was near to melting here and now.

This was nothing like it had been with Richard. They had shared their bodies, in the summer between the war, expecting to be man and wife soon. But her skin had never felt so alive, so full of wonder. And with a stranger, who did not feel a stranger at all.

Though she could not hear it so well as before, she swayed with the music, matching him. Their hands slid across her backside, and she found did not mind at all. She wanted to tease him. She did it more, and felt his arm stiffen, his hand clench then release.

Then the clapping started up again, and the spell was over. With regret, Olivia unclasped her hand from his. She dropped her fan on its string and politely applauded her cousin's wife. Will, after a moment, did the same.

She spotted Mr. Mellon barreling toward her. Her spirits returned to earth.

"The man is quite insistent. Should I ask him some difficult questions on the Corn Laws? The web-sters? Ah, there's the smile."

She held it even as Mr. Mellon reached him, puffing and rosy cheeked.

"Splendid girl! And tempting as Eve's apple, I do say." His gaze turned back to the stage.

"She is the wife of my cousin," Olivia said, trying to sound stern. She heard the faint giggle in the undertone, though. Will raised a brow at her, which set off inner hysterics. She clamped her mouth shut, lowered her own brows and stared directly at Mr. Mellon, who recoiled.

"To be sure. Off limits, of course. But all the more chance to gain her acquaintance. Would you do me the pleasure, Miss Delancey?"

At such a direct request, Olivia could only nod assent. She turned her gaze back to Will, who looked as collected cool as an autumn day. Only his eyes still sparkled, that odd blue-green she was growing to favor.

"Accompany us, Mr. Marsh? Right up your paper's alley, another musical prodigy."

Will took Olivia's hand and bowed over it. "Sadly, no. I must search out the exchequer before he is too far into his cups." Letting loose her hand, he traced the nail of his thumb on her palm. Exquisite torture. "A pleasure, as always, Miss Delancey."

Olivia's gaze followed him through the crowd until Mr.

Mellon stepped directly into her field of vision. "Haven't you heard? Bibble at last may step down. Your father is on the short list for the position."

"Exchequer?" She frowned. "Is not that to do with finance?"

"He holds the purse strings for the country."

"Heaven help us." Olivia felt a bit faint.

"I feel sure it will." Mellon patted her hand, and placed it at his elbow. "The lovely Rosa?"

It took a good five minutes to get within touch of their target. Mr. Mellon spoke little in the meantime, though Olivia noticed he did make noise. An odd wheezing rose from his lungs, and his breaths seemed to catch for a moment, then let go. But he was smiling, nodding genially to those about him, as if he were having the time of his life.

Rosa sat on the edge of the stage, as if she needed her feet free to kick unruly people away. None were unruly, though, and all save Olivia were men. Rosa lifted her arms, pulling her hair off her shoulders and tying it in a loose knot in the back. Mr. Mellon's wheezing worsened.

"Cousin Olivia." She smiled, a wolf's grin. "You have brought me a new friend?"

Olivia stepped aside to allow Mr. Mellon closer to Rosa, and her swinging boots. She saw Richard far to the back of the stage, ingratiating himself to the maestro. Already the impresario. "This is Mr. Mellon, a political friend of the family. Mr. Mellon, Mrs. Richard Avery."

"Charmed, to be sure," the man whispered, his round face red and beaming. Then he toppled to the floor, in a dead faint. The men around him took a step back, leaving it to Olivia to try to catch him or at least keep his head from cracking against the floor. This she did, but barely.

Rosa jumped to the floor, her boots clacking beside Olivia's kneeling form. "That often happens while I am playing, but never when I am just sitting still." She crouched beside Olivia and placed her hand on his chest.

Mr. Mellon's great belly heaved. He breathed, at least. But there was no way she would be able to move him to one of the couches at the wall. He might be trampled here.

Rosa stood. "Who will help me with my overactive admirer? Who has the most muscles?"

The younger men, those not yet strapped into corsets, pushed and shoved toward her, falling over themselves like puppies to tell her of their prowess. For all their effort, they offered precious little help to the prone man at their feet.

"Step aside. I'll get him."

The puppies froze in their tracks at the sound of authority in Will's voice. He bent on one knee at Mr. Mellon's side, surveying the carcass. "Top heavy, or do you think the bulk of the weight in the middle?" He raised both eyebrows at her.

Before she could form the words to chide him, he'd slid an arm under the man's shoulders and the other under his knees and heaved the both of them aloft. "Where to?"

"Benches to the side of the stage, here." The young men scattered, then reforming their circle around Rosa. "Can you carry him all alone?"

Will grunted, shifting Mellon's dead weight in his arms. "He's a big fish. But no more than a rake of papers wet from the press." Rousting a couple deep in conversation, he deposited Mr. Mellon into a reclining seat on the bench. Olivia sat beside him, chafing at his now-chill hands. "Water? Or something stronger?"

"Water. And thank you."

"Wouldn't do to lose a member of your father's cabal." But his gaze told her he didn't do it only for the Crown.

"I thought you leaned Whig."

He stood, surveying the crowd. "Your sister-in-law is talking with the master of ceremonies."

"Perhaps he should call for Mr. Mellon's coach."

"I'll see to it."

A long two minutes later, Mr. Mellon stirred. Olivia dropped his hand but helped push his shoulder into an upright position. A servant brought a tumbler of water. Mr. Mellon swigged it, and almost gagged.

"Thought it was whiskey. Just as well." The red had faded from his face, and his breathing was no longer as labored. "How long was I out?"

"A minute. Perhaps more."

"Getting worse, then." He turned to gaze at the commotion near the stage. "Ah, the lovely Mrs. Avery. Do you think I made an impression on her?"

Olivia merely nodded.

"We should entice her to our political rallies. Think of the votes!"

She could think only of another body to entice. She shivered, the rules of deportment warring with the wants of her body.

FIFTEEN

"A parade, a party, and be done with it," the populace may say,
but peace may not mend our hearts—nor our coin purses at the
speed we all might wish.
    —The Beacon

M artin managed to get out of that hell-hole of a gala and across the city to Merry's father's house by eleven o'clock. He trusted they were not early-to-bed people.

Mr. Buckham ran a reputable trade in haberdashery. Under normal circumstances, the daughter of such a man would never have met such a man as Martin Purdy.

But Mr. Buckham was owed a great deal of money by the Baron Pettigrew. As a manner of interest payment, though no one would call it that, his daughter was allowed to spend the occasional afternoon with the Baron's daughter, learning how to behave as the upper-crust did. Merry had proved quite the hit with Miss Olivia, and a true friendship had grown.

Thus it was that Miss Delancey's music-master made the acquaintance of the haberdasher's youngest child. Soon, Miss Merry appeared in the music room every week at lesson-time. Not long after, it was decided that she should have some instruction in the musical arts as well, and Martin had been introduced into the close-knit Buckham household.

And, not six months later, permanently ejected. Mr. Buckham did not think it seemly for his little angel to be warm on an itinerant music master with barely two crowns to rub together.

All they had to fall back on was the clandestine meetings still occurring at Miss Olivia's. She was not gaining any instruction, but as her father was so slow to pay wages, it did not much matter. Miss Olivia merely played what she would for the space of an hour, and Martin and Merry spent the time together.

Merry herself came to the door, the flush on her face highlighting the red highlights in her hair. "I thought you would never come. He is already done with brandy." She pulled off his cloak, her shawl slipping down her arm. She saw his admiring glance. "Daddy's favorite dress." She curtseyed, dimpling, then playfully pushed him backward. "Come!"

He trusted she had read her father correctly. This could go badly indeed.

"Papa!" She led the way into the cozy sitting room. "Look who has come to wish you joy on your birthday." She turned, smiling at him in a desperate sort of way. Two of her sisters, the other unmarried ones, sat to the side of their mother. Her father sat in the coziest chair, by himself, by the fire.

Martin wished he had insisted the barber cut his hair.

"Congratulations, Mr. Buckham." The man had Merry's eyes, but his own square face and scowling lips. Martin wiped his hand on his trousers, then extended it. Mr. Buckham took it, and four female voices were heard to sigh.

"I suppose you're here to apologize."

"Ah, yes. I am very sorry I had the misfortune to, ah—"

"Steal my little girl's affection." Buckham's voice rose an octave. Martin was glad he wasn't one of the man's clerks.

"Right. Most inappropriate. Especially as she stole mine first."

The room seemed to gasp. Buckham bolted to a stiff backed sitting position. "What do you mean, sirrah?"

"I mean no disrespect. None at all." He looked up at Merry, who had crossed to behind her father's chair. She knelt to his side, putting her hand on his arm. Buckham leaned back in his chair. "I merely wish to ask for your daughter's hand in marriage."

"Blasphemer! Ingrate!" Even Merry's hand could not soothe him now.

"Papa! Give him a moment, please. Everything has changed."

Buckham grunted. "Explain yourself, then. If you can."

"May I sit?"

"No."

"Well, I have just returned from performing in front of the Regent himself at Carlton House."

"It was the celebration gala, papa." Merry's voice dripped with pride. "The early portion, of course."

"My fortunes are not so failing as when I asked for this same privilege a year past." Martin trusted his knees could hold him another few minutes. This was so important. He must not fail. "I have money in the bank, and am recently articled to a Buckham Street – sorry, Burton Street – solicitor. In two years' time, with good effort, I should be able to hang out my own shingle."

"Or join in the lawyer's own practice." Merry patted down the length of her father's arm. "He has prospects now, papa."

"How much is this lawyer taking you for?"

"One thousand pounds."

"And you have it?" The man's chimney-sweep eyebrows rose as he stared down his nose at Martin.

"Yes. Well, nearly."

"From banditry during the war?"

"No, sir. From selling musical scores. The song that was played tonight."

"The song taking Waterloo?" Merry's mother, a rounder version of his beloved, piped in.

"Just so. It's earned me eight hundred and counting. I account I need at least nineteen hundred total, for living as well as learning."

"Unless he can stay with us." Merry's voice took on an unpleasant wheedling sound. "Above the store-room."

"That room is for the clerk of the store-room, you know that." Her father pulled his great gorilla hand, furred with white now, and placed it over Merry's dainty one. "Meredith, think on this. This, this, musician. He can't even remember to shave every day. This is the one you want?"

"Have I changed my mind all this time, even once?" Merry smiled as he shook his head slowly.

"I admit, it shocked me. You always seemed to get over

disappointments so quickly. But not this time." He looked up at Will, his rheumy eyes bright. "Sit down, young man, before you topple."

Martin sank gratefully into the seat opposite, at least until he encountered the pin cushion tucked on the side. He rolled a bit to the side to pull it out. Merry's closest sister, Agnes, squeaked and jumped up to fetch it from his hand.

"You'll get used to that," Buckham said. "Now, man, are you serious of intention? Solid of purpose? Could you keep tallies of the stores-room while you learn your new trade?"

Martin held his wildly beating heart back. "Yes, sir."

"Then I suppose I can let you have the room, the job. And my Merry." Buckham took Merry's hand, which had stilled under his, and handed it across the short space to Martin. Her eyes shone blue as the sky at him, her mouth a welcoming smile.

"Welcome to the family, Mr. Purdy. Let us hope you deserve it."

Martin let his heart fly freely. Even through the fog his thoughts always were in these days, his joy was clean and clear. This is what he wanted, what he had always wanted.

It would not matter that sometimes he could not feel his left side, that sometimes his hand would not do what he told it to. He held his quill with his right hand.

Merry's expression matched his mood. They grinned at each other as if they had won the biggest prize in Christendom.

As they had.

Olivia stretched, fingers grazing the headboard of her bed, toes nearly at the end, feeling the silk of her nightrail, the smooth linen of the bedding, the slight scratch of the goose down underneath. Was this what it means to be a woman? To feel somehow more alive, more awake to sensation, even when drowsing?

That Mr. Marsh – Will – had unwittingly aroused a sleeping giantess. His feather touch, his humor, and his eyes that saw deep inside her and found her beautiful. A man who could appreciate women, as well as good writing and Whig politics. A man with more to think about than the twisting of his cravat. A man who could be the muse for a more passionate style of music.

If only he had a title, even an honorary one. Without it, he could be only a man of her acquaintance. Papa would never let them marry, even if she could bend this Will to her desire. But surely he could figure in her dreams.

She laughed aloud, startling the silence of her chamber. She felt beautiful. Desirable. Her mind was all colors, all sounds. She closed her eyes as a trill of notes started gathering at the edge of her consciousness. As she dropped into sleep, she smiled.

She felt a new composition coming on.

SIXTEEN

A young military gentleman of family but ill fortune lost £7,000 on Sunday Morning at a gaming house in the neighborhood of Pall Mall.

—The Register

"I s that the *Beacon*?" Breakfast plate in hand, Olivia stopped at her father's shoulder to have a closer look, but the typeface was wrong.

"*The Register.*"

"How can you read that rag?"

"I beg your pardon." Her father turned from the paper and gave her a hard stare that followed her until she was seated.

She was not swayed. "You do remember that it was the *Register* which reported peace back in February and was forced to retract its statement next day."

"As were the others. An honest mistake."

"One the *Beacon* did not make. And it was the *Beacon* that reported peace, in truth, a day before Home Office announced it."

"Oh, you love the *Beacon*, do you? The rag that finds music more important than politics?"

"Malicious criticism." Olivia heard the rise in her voice.

"Children, behave," her mother cut in. "Pettigrew receives those and many other papers, as you both well know. Now, Olivia, tell me whom you saw last night. I spent the evening with the political men, as usual."

"Not now, love." Pettigrew folded the paper and dropped it to the table. "First we have business to discuss."

"What sort of business?"

Papa waited for the maid to finish at the sideboard and leave the room. "We need to retrench," he said. "And you, Olivia, must take better care whom you are seen with. That Rosa may be fine enough for Richard, but we need not extend her any courtesy. She'll not be invited here," he said with a sniff, which only made him sneeze. Powder from his wig settled on the table.

"And that publisher," Mama said. "The handsome." She paused at a look from her husband. "I mean, completely disreputable looking one."

"Mr. Marsh merely asked after you, Papa. Is your appointment imminent?"

"Sadly, no. Bibble simply will not step down. Or die." He let out a great belch. "I may expire before that doddering infant does."

"He did sound closer to it than ever at the gala, though, dearest." Mama handed a cut strawberry out to him. He bit into its center, met her glance, and inhaled the rest. "You can be the exchequer of my heart," she said. "Any time."

Olivia concentrated on buttering her bread.

Papa cleared his throat. "Back to business. Olivia, as you have nothing pressing, you will travel to the house in Plymouth. Take inventory of what can be sold, and ask Aunt Betsy to help you contact the marketers."

"We're selling the house?"

"Of course not. It's entailed. Just everything in it."

"Aunt Betsy, as well?"

"None of your cheek. She will do well with a room or two. I am sure that is all she uses now anyway."

"Why must I go? You don't usually trust me with these details."

Her parents shared a glance. Olivia suspected they thought they were guilty of something. She could not guess what.

"Put simply, we are short of funds. Even with the money you'll at last come into from your grandmother on your next birthday, we will not cover the expenses for this quarter. It's only 300 pounds per annum, after all."

Mama nodded vigorously. Fortunately for their eggs, she had not powdered yet. "Besides, you got us such a good price on the master bedroom furniture. We trust you to use your market magic on the furnishings in Plymouth, as well."

"Could Jaspers accompany me? He did the actual selling."

"No, we need him here," Mama waved a hand dismissively. "Papa might be called up at any moment. We need to be prepared to entertain."

They would be hard-pressed to entertain more than a half-dozen here, Olivia thought. Only three rooms remained furnished on the main floor, including her closet of a music room. Only two public rooms remained so upstairs. They did not even have a spare bed any longer.

"Of course, I will go." It would ease the monotony of her days, if nothing else. And Aunt Betsy was her favorite relative. "But I must return in next week."

"Whatever for?" Mama was feeding Papa again.

"For Miss Buckham's engagement dinner."

"Miss Buckham? That charming red-head?" Papa was momentarily distracted. "Wondered why we hadn't seen her in so long." Mama frowned at him, and he hastily said, "Girl ate far too much."

"Can you not befriend girls of your own station?"

"They all have children and husbands. And we do not encourage repeat calls." Olivia shrugged. "It's Miss Buckham or Mrs. Avery."

"Heavens, let it be Miss Buckham." Papa put a hand to his chest. "Or whatever her new name is. I thought I would positively faint when Avery's bride showed her ankle in public."

"Mr. Mellon did faint."

"He is right as rain now. But it shows that woman is a viper. Avoid her, Olivia. We cannot cut her, more's the pity. But we needn't invite her into our bosoms."

Mama clapped. "Excellent play on words, dear heart." She stood, reaching for Papa's hand. "We're attending a private soiree at Carlton House tonight. So we won't be able to see you off tomorrow morning." Embracing, they walked toward the hall.

Papa turned back. "Send us an accounting before you finalize the sales, won't you?"

Retrench. How Olivia despised the word. Especially as it seemed to apply to her alone.

She dropped back into her chair, pulling the bowl with the remainder of the strawberries close to her. She would eat every one, not saving the four her Papa liked to have in the afternoon with his tea.

Perhaps then they would think of her.

Bragge barreled into Will's office, dropping into a chair that would now forever smell of wet horsehair.

"You could have taken off your cloak. That's an antique chair."

"What? Sorry, sorry. Why would you keep anything of value in a place like this?"

Will rubbed his forehead. "Why, indeed?"

"Don't distract me. I have news!" Bragge sat up in the chair, raising a soggy arm above his head. "A scoop. No, truly, listen up." He scooted forward in the chair, glancing to the door.

"No one is here." Will tried to sound patient. Bragge's boyish enthusiasm was growing tiresome. Will was starting to see the wisdom in allowing quiet, if sullen, Bentley the helm of the *Beacon*. Bentley respected the importance of the paper. And he respected the property of others.

"Right then, this is it." Bragge paused in his stage-whispering. "Napoleon is coming to England."

Will paused to make sure he had heard correctly. "That can't be true."

"God's teeth." Bragge shook his shaggy head. "Heard it from

a merchant captain. The Terror of Europe surrendered to the captain of the *Bellerophon*. They're in our waters now. On their way to Plymouth."

"What will they do in Plymouth?"

"The captain wasn't rightly sure. If the port gives him safe passage, he'd be a refugee. A prince."

"Impossible."

"But a good story." Bragge propped his hands on his knees. "Somebody from the *Beacon* needs to go to Plymouth. Before the coaches are all filled."

"Go."

"I'm needed to ferret out that financial mess over at Lords."

"Then Bentley. I'll have to wake him up. He can catch the late coach."

Bragge smiled speculatively. "Still afraid of the water? Do your interviews on land."

"That has nothing to do with it." Though they both knew it did. Will would not give such a scoop to anyone otherwise. Except Bragge, the man who "owned" it.

"Perhaps I can sweeten the deal. I also hear news that a certain lovely lady, too, is on her way to Plymouth." Will frowned, not understanding. "A certain blond goddess, who loves the musicians. Traveling without her parents, I hear."

"To Plymouth?"

"Family has a place in the center of town." Bragge shrugged. "The source isn't as good as the emperor's. But I would trust it."

"Why would she go alone?" Will bristled. "And why do you think I would care in the first place?"

"As to the second part, I have no idea." Bragge rolled his eyes. "Perhaps the mooning, or was it the personal attention to certain stories. Over-attention, as Bentley put it. Or perhaps it was the rumors of certain attentions paid, when no one was looking, except, perhaps, the lone *Beacon* employee actually performing his function."

"So you saw me."

"And I distracted the papa long enough that he did not see you. Say thank you, Bragge."

Will was silent. Then he bowed his head.

Bragge followed suit with his customary flourish. "She's nothing like Deidre."

"How do you know? And how do you know of Deidre?"

Bragge sighed mightily. "We newsprint hacks know all, and we don't tell even a half of it." He lurched to his feet, rivulets of water rolling onto the floor. "And now, from the goodness of my bleeding-ink heart, I hand you my scoop. Do not blow it, *mon capitaine*. Come back happy." He saluted and went out again into the rain.

Will watched the man's progress across the square. Bragge stopped and talked with a small boy, the carter he worked for, a servant having a smoke, and the lead press-man, all before he reached the door to the paper's offices. Small wonder he had all the intelligence the city had to offer.

Will rubbed his chin. He needed to shave. He needed to pack.

He needed to get over this feeling.

He ran the hand through his hair, gripping tightly at the nape of his neck. He closed his eyes, to better feel the pain.

He could not want another lady. Not after the last time. He could not afford it. He did not wish it.

But oh, he did.

His dropped his hands back into his lap. The pads of his fingers remembered the curve of her chin, the smooth cream of her skin. The strength of her fingers gripping his in secret.

Behind closed lids, his eyes traced the dip where her shoulder met her neck. The liquid gold of her dress. The hard amethyst of her eyes softening when she smiled. Glowing when she smiled at him.

Enough. He launched himself up and out of his chair. The pacing was familiar, even his tabby recognized the pattern, jumping onto the back of a chair and observing him warily. But this time, every time lately, the movement would not tame his thoughts or his feelings.

He wanted her, all her creamy skin exposed to him, with its hidden pockets of rosiness. Would she be a blonde underneath, as well?

This was just his body talking, he reasoned. It had been too long without female succor. But he had never had it this bad. And the thought of sating his passion on another female held no appeal. It had to be her, or no one.

So it would be no one. He could not afford another debacle with a peer's daughter. Once was bad enough. His paper had a reputation to uphold. A mistake in affection in youth was one thing; an inappropriate liaison when he was nearing thirty was another.

To forget Deidre and her mocking laugh, he had left college and rejoined the family business. And he'd done well. He had built a modern country home, away from the grime of Printing-House Square. A gift for Mother, who had enjoyed the last years of her life there, it now stood empty.

He needed someone.

Will stopped his pacing, facing out the window to the square. The rain was letting up, a few stray strands of sun filtering into the courtyard.

After he paid the final note on the presses, Will would hand over the reins. Bentley was ready to run the day-to-day, and if he wasn't he needed the practice. Will would spend more time at home, in Berkshire. He would practice being a squire, perhaps meddle in shire politics.

He might marry. A sweet country girl. Not a temptress in silks and satins. Not the most beautiful woman he had ever seen. Certainly not someone who could attract his hands without even his mind noticing.

They were reaching out now, toward the window, as if she were there, her gently rounded ass tempting.

He gripped the window's sill instead. Gritting his teeth, he heard the church bell toll the noon hour. He rested his forehead on the cool glass. The cool spread down his neck, a wash of rationality.

He had an appointment with his lawyer.

A note to settle.

And a lady to forget.

SEVENTEEN

In Paris, the Corsican Tyrant is spoken of in the journals, and in the debates, without any share of that respect which was but lately attached to his name. After his former abdication he was invariably termed the "Emperor," but now he is called nothing but "Napoleon."

—The Beacon

Will found Swizzlewit seated, per usual, behind his massive oak desk. His chair set at its lowest height, he sat upon three large law-books, his feet resting on the seat. Looking up, his wizened cherub face cracked a grin. He waved Will in.

"Glad to see you. You've seen the receipts?" He nodded. "You can pay that note anytime now, with naught a care for cash flow. Brilliant idea, that march."

Will cantilevered gingerly in the guest chair, also spun down to its lowest level. His knees came dangerously close to his chin as he sat. "Good. Is it enough to cover a loan as well? I wish to buy out my brother's interest. At once, if possible."

Swizzlewit drew the *Beacon*'s ledger from his collection on the giant desk. He propped it up on a lectern, settled his reading glasses across his nose and stared at the pages.

"How well is the second installment selling? Sweet melody, that one."

"Perhaps two-thirds the first."

"And you have another?"

"Promised."

"Not guaranteed." The lawyer pursed his lips, his gaze traveling down the column. He leaned over to grab a pencil and paper, scribbling some figures. "You can do one or the other. Not both."

"Not unless I have another boom circulation."

"At least one." He tilted his head at Will speculatively. "If you buy George out, will the note hold?"

"The pressure to sell will ease. But I do not wish to default, or even come near it." He shuddered. It was a man of business's nightmare, not making that last payment and losing everything.

Swizzlewit removed his glasses. "Then I suggest this. Pay the note as agreed. Pay your brother one-third, with promises for the rest over the next two quarters."

"He needs it sooner."

"Then I recommend you scare yourself up another scoop."

Scoops were as rare as rain during sunshine. But if the Napoleon extra could pull in readers, it might do as well.

The bell over the door rang. Another client. Will started to rise, but Swizzlewit waved him back down.

"Come in, come in a moment." Swizzlewit waved a rounded arm at the doorway. Will saw the brown traveling skirt first, then the face above it. Fire burned, and then ice rolled down his spine.

Olivia Delancey and her undersized manservant.

He was not ready to see her yet. Not prepared. Not strong enough to let her go. But he must stick to his purpose. George needed funds, and the paper needed to cover the note for those steam presses.

She stepped through the door, smiling at the lawyer. He knew the moment she saw him. Her eyes registered her surprise, widening. Her smile grew even warmer.

Swizzlewit rubbed his hands busily. "Such a surprise to see you here this morning. It isn't often done, you know, a woman seeing a man in his office. But we're nearly family, you must understand, Mr. Marsh."

"Mr. Marsh, good day. I did not expect to see you again so soon."

"Nor I." His voice was sharp. A fraction of the warmth in her face faded. He ignored the frisson of guilt in his gut.

"Right." The lawyer filled the silence. "You are posthaste for Plymouth, right, my dear?"

"Yes." The light faded further from her eyes, her posture grew more rigid. "A family matter."

"No one is ill, I trust? Your Aunt Betsy?"

"No, nothing like that." She pulled her mouth into a small smile, but Will could tell it had not altered the cloud over her mood. "Are you going to Plymouth as well, Mr. Marsh, or is Mr. Bragge already on his way?"

He sat up, suddenly alert. "Why would I?"

"To see Napoleon, of course. It was all the talk at the stable yard. I could hardly hire a seat on the stagecoach; they were all spoken for."

"Will here might give you a ride." His lawyer cast him a knowing glance.

"Unfortunately no," he said, earning a double raised eyebrow from Swizzlewit. "I'm not going."

"Is it not a, how do you say, a first?"

"A scoop. But not if everybody has already heard of it." His churlishness surprised him.

She pursed her lips, thinking. "But not everybody has seen it. Perhaps you should send your caricaturist."

"Will is his own artist."

Now Olivia raised her brows. "Both a writer and an artist?"

He brushed aside her compliment. "Drafting, not artistry. Perhaps I'll go tomorrow. When the roads are clearer."

"It is a clear day today. Tomorrow carries no guarantee, and even more bodies will be traveling to Plymouth, once they read about it in the papers."

Will grunted, unwilling to give her the satisfaction of being correct. "I will make do."

Olivia's gaze was on him. He felt as uncomfortable as if tiny ants were running up his leg and into his conscience. He grimaced at her. "Do you have the next piece for me?" He nearly snarled.

Her eyebrows shot up, as if startled into action, then crashed back down to meet the glare that settled in her eyes. "Yes, sir, I have it copied out, but I must show the pages to Martin first to be sure they are correct."

Will shrugged. "Today, then?"

"Of course," she said. "I leave today." As you are not, she left unsaid. She pulled up straighter, if that was possible. She took a step back, toward the door, and shifted her attention to Swizzlewit. "I am sorry, sir," she said. Her eyes were bright. Were those tears threatening?

"Nonsense, my dear. Simmons in front has your bank draft. Be sure to deposit it as soon you arrive." Swizzlewit saluted her. "Bon voyage, and say hello to the Corsican menace for me."

Will watched her go, the brown of her travel coat spinning behind her. He felt like a cur. A cur that had been set free.

"So." Swizzlewit gave him an appraising glance. "Were it I whom a beautiful lady looked at so warmly, and smiled at so brightly, I should not be in such a hurry to crush her tender spirits."

"Never you mind."

Swizzlewit snapped the *Beacon*'s ledger shut and moved it back to its spot on the bookshelf behind him.

"Never mind, Swizzlewit."

"Or perhaps I thought I could not, must not, aspire to such an exalted vision of loveliness."

"That's enough."

He turned back to face Will. "Or perhaps I would fear that such a lady could only want me to toy with. A plaything, a game."

That was far past enough. Will stood, seething. "I don't need to remind you I can take my business elsewhere."

"Ah." The lawyer leaned back, folding his hands across the rounding of his belly. "I see."

The man saw nothing. Will smashed his hat upon his head, nodded brusquely, and stomped toward the door.

"Give your brother my best," the lawyer called after him.

Will only grunted. Leave George out of it. And as for Olivia Delancey, she was not in it in the first place.

~

What a churlish specimen of a man. Olivia stomped her foot, safely hidden beneath the folds of her dark traveling skirt.

So he did not wish to ride with her, fine. So be it. But did he have to be so rude?

Poor Mr. Swizzlewit, to have to work with such a two-faced character. Olivia peered down the street. She had an hour and a half before she had to meet the coach. Enough time to peruse the lending library, say farewell to Merry and Martin, and give Martin the new score to hand in to Will. Mr. Marsh, if you please.

Olivia knew she was frowning, but she did not care. She had to admit, his attitude stung. But it was only to be expected. She had allowed the moments of intimacy they had shared at the gala. Give a man a line, and he'll sink you.

Her booted feet took her at uncommon speed through the streets, her tiger, Jaspers's youngest boy, racing to keep up. Clouds threatened, but the rain had petered out. Good travel weather. For some.

And why was it her place to serve as the family man of business, anyway? Only because she was good at it, and she was good at it only because she could pay attention for more than ten consecutive seconds.

No, that was not fair. But blast it all, none of this was fair. It did not seem to bother her most days, because most days she could still work around all the impediments and obstacles. And the truth was, she realized as she strode up the steps to the hospital, most days she just did not care.

But today was not most days, and she did care. She cared about a man, what he thought of her, whether he thought of her. Whether he dreamed of her, as she had of him.

He could not be as casually cruel as all that, could he? She so rarely was wrong about people.

The nurse on duty directed her to the courtyard. Martin and Merry sat at one of the picnic tables, holding hands, smiling infantile smiles at each other.

Olivia held back a moment. They were not the people she was vexed with. They were the people she wanted to help. And she was helping them, it would appear.

Martin awoke from his trance first. "Miss Olivia! I leave tomorrow."

"Your head is all clear now?"

"Not exactly." Martin shaved every day now, but his care had not reached to the shaggy head of hair on his head. "The surgeon says it needs time. A second to destroy, and months to heal."

"But Martin will start as Papa's warehouse chief tomorrow," Merry spared a moment to glance at Olivia, then turned her attention back in happy full to Martin.

"That is good news. And with Mr. Swizzlewit by month's end."

"If the money holds out."

Olivia bit her tongue, hard. Could he not sound the least bit hopeful? It wasn't as if he were doing any of the heavy lifting.

"Speaking of music money, could you carry this new score to

the *Beacon* for me? I leave on the four o'clock coach, and I fear I won't make it on time."

"New score?" Merry frowned.

"Yes. I was copying it out."

"Martin, you dog! You do have a lot of energy, despite what you say." Merry pushed at his shoulder, a light tap that still set him rocking side to side.

"Must I?" He gave Olivia his biggest puppy-dog eyes. "Merry can stay only another half-hour."

"Walk with her. It will extend your time. Her family's home is along the same path."

Martin closed his eyes, as if the thought of such exertion exhausted him. Olivia felt the now-familiar surge of anger. Why must everyone be against her? They would help take her money, but help her? Never.

"If you go now, Livvie, you will make it." Merry smiled into her beloved's eyes. It was easy to see whom she preferred.

Olivia turned on her heel, storming out. As if they would even notice. Would a tantrum count against her if no one witnessed it?

Not when she was a child, and not now. Why had she expected life would change when she became an adult?

It seemed she had acted – had, in fact, been – an adult since she was eight years of age. Yet the people around her, her friends, especially her parents, were allowed to remain children. And like Will – Mr. bloody Marsh – were allowed to throw tantrums that she then had to soothe away.

Enough. Let them all do without her for a while. She was for Plymouth. On her own. She would enjoy the spectacle of seeing the man who brought Europe to her knees now safely in English custody. She would not even offer to send a correspondent's letter to the *Beacon*. What did she owe that partisan rag?

She would hand the sheaves of music over to the clerk, assuming he even had a clerk, and be on her way. Will Marsh could stew. Martin and Merry could stew. And her wastrel parents, who seemed to forget they even had a daughter until they needed her to do something unpleasant, well, they could stew longest of all.

Eighteen

The cruelty of this person is written in characters of blood in almost every country in Europe, and in the contiguous angles of Africa and Asia which he visited; and nothing can more strongly evince the universal conviction of his low, perfidious craft, than the opinion which is beginning to get abroad, that, even after his capture had been officially announced, both in France and England, he might yet have found means to escape.

—The Register

As soon as that lovely brown skirt swirled out the door, Will knew he had made a gargantuan mistake. He walked back from Swizzlewit's to the *Beacon* in a black mood, angrier at himself then he had been in quite some time.

Most days, he followed his own compass, confident he was doing what was right. But sometimes his compass would lose its magnetism, or would run up against a powerful magnet, and lead him astray. Truth was, it did not matter if Olivia Delancey was a fine lady. It should not matter that he felt some, nay, a great deal of, physical interest in her.

She was a client, a contributor to the paper, and outside of Bragge her efforts had done more to increase circulation these past weeks than those of anyone else. He owed it to the *Beacon* to be cordial to her, polite at worst. His recollected rudeness was what was making him so irritable. It must be.

He rubbed at his tired eyes. He had spoken harshly to a gentlewoman. What would his mother have said?

His father would have said well done. Best to catch them up before they bring you down. George Senior was an expert, and he had earned his expertise in the hardest of ways.

When a fetching young thing had come bearing the latest incendiary paragraph from the opposition, his father had run it, word for word. Unfortunately, the Royals had found it too much, and sued for slander.

His opposition cronies, the ones who paid him to always be ready to post the occasional paragraph addition to his daily report, did not come to his rescue. For following orders and keeping his sources secret, his father had gone to jail. Will had learned that lesson well. Don't trust ladies bearing foreign gifts.

But wasn't it the callow, slanderous politicians who were to blame, not the lovely young thing who had brought the note? Somehow the two were confounded in Will's mind.

He pounded the tall bench in the *Beacon*'s public room, startling a pile of today's edition and scattering some of last week's musical reprint.

He was not his father. Not weak, not in the pocket of any political or Royal manager. Not at the mercy of his emotions.

His *Beacon* took no bribes, not for placement, nor favor, nor information. Will procured his own foreign papers through the mails and had them translated at his own expense. He had learned during the war how the Home Office could muddy the pool translations. *Beacon* readers got the truth, or the truth as far as the Continental journals would go.

He couldn't stay here in the store. He started pacing up and down the narrow hall. When would Bragge appear and put him out of his misery?

The door squeaked five times that hour. Three people to buy music, one to place an advertisement for domestic help. And then, when his nerves were at their rawest, Miss Olivia Delancey.

Her face was pond-still; then she saw him, and the look shifted to translucent glass. But he could read her now, and what he saw surprised him.

She was angry, too. Livid, as far as a pale, well-bred English lady could be. What had put a bee in her bonnet?

"Here is your copy," she said, doing away with any attempt at pleasantry. She set the pages on the counter and turned away, not even looking at him. The pulse in her jaw stood out like a thunderstorm under her bonnet. She was going to walk out that door without even looking at him.

He tipped the hinged part of the table up to get to her side of the room. It fell with a crash behind him, startling her into a slow, but not a stop. She had her hand on the door handle by the time he reached her. He put his hand over hers, and pushed it off the latch.

"A moment, Miss Delancey."

She stepped away from him, but she was still in his house, so he considered that a small victory. And she looked at him, blue eyes blazing. "I think you have wasted enough of my time today. Or did you forget some criticism or put-down you would like to add to the collection?"

He still held her hand. She pulled it down, forcefully tearing it from his grip. He couldn't let her go. He grabbed onto her shoulder, slippery under layers of cloak.

"Take your hands off me, sir." Her lips were straight lines, her jaw line white with anger.

"Wait," he said, raising both his hands to the sides of his head. "You wish to box my ears? Then do it."

"You dare me?" She frowned her perfect brown eyebrows down at him.

Their gazes locked for long moments. He had no idea what she saw in his eyes, but hers, ringed with smudges from lack of sleep, seemed to swirl. Anger, pain, determination, dozens of other bits he could not yet recognize. Nearly mesmerized by the changes in her irises, he did not register that she had taken a step forward.

But he felt the smack on the side of his head. He winced. She had taken him at his word. And she hit hard, lady or no.

"Good." She frowned at him. But he could see her eyes were not as frazzled with emotion. Her breathing was regular. "It does feel better."

"What happened? A fight with your composer?"

"Not exactly." She shrugged. "Just...everything."

"One of those days."

She shot him a dagger of a gaze, then shrugged again. "You did your part."

"That is why I stopped you." Will placed his right hand on

his heart. "Miss Delancey, Miss Olivia, I wish to apologize for my earlier behavior. I have excuses plenty, but no reason."

Her mouth dropped open, a sweet circle. He felt a surge of need to plunder it. He shoved the ache back into the farthest wall of his heart. That was not what she needed now.

"No one ever apologizes to me. And means it. Not even Richard."

Will moved his hand from his heart to hers, then down to grasp her gloved hand. "Well, he is an idiot. As his college roommate, I can attest to that."

"You roomed with him?"

"Only for a year."

"Was he one of Mr. Bragge's secret sources? During the war?"

"If I told you, it wouldn't be secret, would it?"

"I might tell you one of my secrets." She gave him an oddly timid smile, as if she were unsure of her allure.

"A false promise. You have no secrets from me."

"No?"

"Not with that expressive mouth. And those eyes." He stroked her chin. "And that jaw line."

She leaned into his touch. "Can you be sure?"

"As sure as I am of anything. I knew you were hopping mad when you came in here, and it was not all about me."

"True." She lifted her head away, just a fraction, from his hand. "But you didn't seem to know you'd stung me in Mr. Swizzlewit's office."

"I did know. But what you may not have known was that our solicitor had given me the worst of news, and I was angry with the world and ready to lash out. Unfortunately for you, and for me."

"For you?"

"Most assuredly. For I knew it meant that later I would have to humble myself abjectly and plead for forgiveness."

"You did not need to."

"I did. You see, Miss Olivia Delancey, your good opinion means much to me, it turns out. I did not feel right after you left, not until I saw you walk through my door."

"Such flattery."

He shrugged. "Truth. We don't go much in for lying here."

It was her turn to put her hand over her heart. "I thank you for your kind apology. It is accepted. Now may I do something for you?"

He could imagine many things she could do. Likely none of them were what she was thinking of. "What?"

"Come to Plymouth. I know the town well, and can guide you. We might even arrange to row out and meet the ship in harbor. A first."

"A scoop."

"Meet me at our house at Manor Gardens above Union Street. I'll get you your story."

How could he say no? "Deal. And a finder's fee." He took her jaw in his hand again, thumb over her cheekbone, and pulled her gently toward him. He brushed his lips against hers. The barest whisper of a touch, but it pushed all the thunderclouds from his mind, making way for the sweet warmth of spring sun.

Then she pressed back, and the sun grew hotter. His hips moved of their own accord closer to hers, possessive. Her hand on his chest, over his heart, seared him, marking him as hers.

Footsteps sounded in the hallway, and they pulled away. Her gaze was softly intent, as if she were trying to read his mind. He prayed she could not. He had no wish to frighten her, with her garnet eyes and temporarily dovish manner.

"Until tomorrow, then." She turned toward the door.

He leaned past her to push it open. She accepted the closeness, and did not look back as she left. He closed the door on a sigh.

"Consorting with the help?"

Bragge. Will turned away from the window, much as he wanted to follow her progress down the street. The confounded man was at the counter. How long had he been there?

"Dinnae fash yourself, as Bentley's forebears would say. I saw nothing, I can claim nothing. Except." His grin was wide. "The lady enjoys performing her own errands. Quite unusual. Quite."

He picked up the music, started humming.

"Is that the new tune?"

"No idea. I'm the percussionist, you know. But I did hear something out of tune today." He shuffled the pages back in line. "Very nice hand. For a man."

"Miss Delancey copies them out for him."

"Yes, but where does he come up with the originals? Such as this one?"

"I don't follow."

"Martin Purdy can't play the piano at the moment. He has a palsied hand."

"And Beethoven is deaf. Your point?"

"Nothing, yet. Only suspicion. Admittedly, stirred up by your friend Cobbett."

"A poor loser."

"As may be. But were I you, I might ask my lady-friend what she has seen. Perhaps she could describe the maestro's method of composition. His fiancée apparently cannot."

"She is not my lady-friend."

"More's the pity. Would she prefer an older man? With, shall we say, a great deal of worldly experience?" Bragge roared, the noise grating on Will's ears. "You should see your face. 'Glower' paints it too pretty."

"Give me those pages."

"No, no. I'll just porter these on to the printers. You look like you could use a drink. Or a jump in the rainwater barrel." He turned and headed down the hall.

"You could be replaced," Will said sourly. Bragge raised a hand above his head, waving Will's spume away.

Why not go to Plymouth? He could easily do the reporting, and a cartoon, a good caricature, would move more papers.

And the paper, he reminded himself sternly, was all he could afford to care about.

NINETEEN

Captain Sartorius, of the Slaney frigate, arrived yesterday with dispatches from Captain Maitland of the Bellerophon, confirming Bonaparte's surrender and conveyance to England. He is at our doorstep.

—The Beacon

Aunt Betsy, as tidy and proper as always, welcomed Olivia with a generous hug and a delicately raised eyebrow. "'Tis always good to see you, dearest, but I fear your trip has been in vain. I received your father's letter only yesterday, or I would have sent my own return post. He must have forgotten."

"Forgotten?" Olivia set her satchel on the hall steps and followed her aunt into the front sitting room.

"He instructed me to sell the furnishings already. The 'excess' furnishings, he termed it." She sniffed daintily. "All that remains is two bedrooms' worth, and a spare cot. Then this room, the study, and half the dining room. And the servants' furnishings; those wouldn't have brought much anyway."

"The piano?" Her voice squeaked.

"Of course not. It still guards the solarium. I did manage to keep two of the mustiest chairs in that room, as well." She looked about her. "Everything down to the walls. Even the curtains, in some of the rooms. You would be surprised how much curtains can fetch."

"So we've leached all we can from this property." Olivia leaned back into the soft cushions of what she suspected was the only sofa in the house.

"Aye. I am grateful it is not my family's history I am dispensing with." Her aunt shuddered. "What will Avery think when he discovers the truth?"

"Knowing him, he'll think it all a great jest. It means fewer servants to pay, as well."

"But his wife?"

"She will have more to say about it. Oh, Aunt Betsy, she is the woman I wish I were."

"Dearest, you are one of the finest young people I know."

"But Rosa Avery. She is not afraid to show her talent. She faces down those who would tell her she is inappropriate."

"And she has won the hand of your fiancé." Her aunt gave her a steady stare.

"That is less important. No, truly, I am glad I do not have to marry Richard. I discover my appreciation of him grows in proportion to the distance I keep between us."

Betsy tittered, then laughed out loud, though behind her neatly gloved hand. "I did miss you, Livvie. But I do wish you were happier with your lot. And what prospects have you? Is there another man?"

Olivia felt the blush creeping up her neck.

"Ho! I see how the wind blows. Is he pining away now that you have absented yourself from town?"

"He may come here, in fact."

"All the better. We need some fresh blood here. He is fascinated with our newest hostage?"

"Napoleon has arrived?"

"On the *Bellerophon*. A ship of the line, anchored a quarter-league out. Apparently, he takes the air at five o'clock on the nose. The boatmen are earning small fortunes taking the folk out to try to get a glimpse of him."

"Have you done it?"

"Me? I am far too proper. But with you here, I do feel a bit frisky. Perhaps we can do it together?"

"At least we know how to swim."

"If only we could throw these whalebones back in the sea. Whoever devised corsets for women should be drowned."

"I will look into it. Perhaps we may go tomorrow."

"Rain tomorrow. Besides, first I must parade you in front of all our acquaintances. Next day, perhaps."

"He'll stay another day?"

"Indefinitely, the wags say. At least through the week-end. Perhaps your young man may join us. As a safety precaution."

Aunt Betsy winked.

After a series of downpours, stuck coaches, and, finally, one stubborn nag of a horse, Will entered the port town of Plymouth a full two days later. The usually bustling city felt empty, odd since the innkeeper back in Exeter had warned that all the inns here were filled to capacity. Everyone must be at the docks. Will shivered in the sweltering heat.

He'd be late to Napoleon's party in the Bay, but it had seemed idiocy to turn back. Will had to hope that no other publisher had thought to commission a caricature of the little general. Illustrations were rare enough still to attract readers.

He could not tell which of the tall-masted ships in harbor was the *Bellerophon*. Again, Will thought how fortunate he was to have lined up a native guide. Surely a woman who grew up port-side would know how to recognize a ship. And how to help him describe it.

Suzie pony, as the innkeeper called the beast, headed toward the town's center of her own accord, the path likely very familiar. He would need Olivia's help to find lodging as well. The innkeeper told him Plymouth was "filled to the gills with folk, all agog to see the monster," Napoleon. He would offer Will lodging at the inn, but could not guarantee it. "Never had so many bodies. Packed to the rafters."

Though he heard nothing but the fulsome wind skirling along his wide-brimmed hat as he crested a hill, Will could see the bustling show at dock-side. Down the hill, at Manor Gardens, Will patted Suzie's neck to stop. She tipped her shoulder as he stepped out of the saddle, hastening his descent. She stood docile enough as he stepped up to the green door and reached for the knocker.

A woman who looked to be Olivia's aunt herself answered at Will's knock.

"We had given you up. Not all of us, of course." Will could see traces of Olivia in her aunt's spirit and energy, though he was not sure she was her direct relation. "No time to waste, young man."

"Will. William Marsh, ma'am."

"Exactly. Set your things down just inside here. My man will see to the horse. She goes to Cobbler's on Front."

Will set down his small saddlebag as the trim woman disappeared around a near corner. She reappeared a moment later, tying the ribbons of an overbrimmed bonnet. He hurried to pull out his pouch with his sketch pad and small note-book and pencils. She was already down the short stairs and on the sidewalk waiting.

"Just pull the door closed. Nothing more to steal here." She waited for him to reach the sidewalk, then turned and proceeded to race down the hill.

"Livvie has rented a skiff just for us. The boatman promised to wait until the last moment. Which has nearly passed, if I read the sun aright."

"These things are like clockwork?"

"Aye. Leave before four-fifteen. The man himself likes to take the air starting at five. And he, for one, has a very precise pocket-watch." She cast him a sidelong glance.

Will did not mind walking, or even running, after so long in the saddle. But it was an affront to his manhood to huff and puff and then see that Olivia's aunt was not the least winded in this pell-mell flight.

"Livvie tells me you are a writer?"

"Publisher. Of the *Beacon*."

"Adequate foreign report, I find. Less lately."

"My chief correspondent has returned home."

"But it is you come to report on the little general?" She paused at the bump of a small hill, not to rest but to scan the extensive docks. A small smile passed her usually pursed lips. "Not a job for your correspondent?"

"We all like to keep our hand in," Will said.

"And our eyes on the prize. There," she pointed to the left. "Beside the fire-boat. I will take you down, and my man will take me home in the coach. Then he will return for you when we see the boats returning."

"No need to bother. I think we can find our way back." He did not see the woman, but the boat was hard to miss, with its red detailing and ropes and hoses. There must be five hundred people scurrying about that piece of dock. Most were far too close to the edges, hovering over unreasonably small rowing boats. Will's stomach lurched.

"Not a man of the sea, are you, Mr. Marsh?" A note of humor graced Aunt Delancey's iron voice.

"No, ma'am." Will hated water. He was trying not to think of getting in a tiny boat. He held his thoughts on Olivia, on not embarrassing himself in front of her.

"After a rough ride like you will have, you will appreciate a smooth ride home."

The smells of fish, oil, and salt hit him when they were nearly up to the wooden part, the docks. Will had somehow missed that stage in nearly every boy's life where ships and everything nautical became obsession. London's docks were as filthy as the River Thames; no one thought to frolic in them. He was far from his safe ground here.

The sprightly woman gave his hand a squeeze, surprising him. "Not to worry. Olivia is an old hand at the tiller. She'll keep you upright and dry."

"There you are." Olivia's face mixed relief and pleasure, which pleased him far too much. Her golden curls were forced into a plait down her back and held down by a straw-formed bonnet that would have looked more appropriate on the head of a French seaman. Quickly coiling a length of thick rope, eyes flashing full of purpose, she was health, youth, and beauty personified.

But she stood by a boat not even twelve feet in length.

He exhaled and focused again on the lady. Her blue and white striped costume was faded and a few years from current fashion, but far more practical than the bows and tiny parasols he saw on ladies further down the dock. Odd how seeing the turn of her ankle, too often hidden, caused his stomach to lurch. Or perhaps it was the water roiling behind her.

"Let me hand you down."

"Take care, Livvie. You have got a lubber on your hands."

"Yes, Auntie." Olivia's voice sounded both obedient and exasperated. She reached for his hand, squeezing it. Will was washed with a wave of comfort. "What do you grin at?"

He caught a glimpse of her cornflower-cast eyes under that hat, and then she turned to toss the coil off the dock, into the tiny boat. He took the now-free hand and raised it to his lips, trying to leach some of that confidence for himself.

She grinned. "It is mild seas today, and we will stay in the bay. The biggest danger today, I fear, will not be the sea but the other boats."

"I feel so much better," Will said. She squeezed his hand. Did she think he didn't notice she was pulling him toward the water? "Here's Tommy. Just reach for his hand."

Easier said than done. Unwilling to let go of her hand, he nearly pulled her into the narrow islet of water between the dock and the boat. His feet more or less on sturdy planking, he looked back, suddenly realizing the danger he had put her in. His heart leapt into his throat. Had he killed her?

Olivia still had one foot on the dock, and seemed to kick it out, converting a headlong tumble into the grimy bay into a barreling jump into Will's shoulder. Off-balance, he tried not to fall out of the narrow craft, managing to sit, quite firmly, on a wooden bench that spanned the middle.

And she laughed, damn her.

"Not the most graceful embarkation. At least we're all so late that no one will pay attention to us."

Will crossed his arms in front of his chest. He would not be teased. Especially not in this dangerously rocking situation. Olivia did not appear to notice. She pointed to her aunt to unwrap the last rope holding them to the dock, then caught it and wrapped it up into a neat pile.

"You'll want to move, guv." The oak tree named Tommy bore down on him. "Lessen you want to do the rowing."

It was the first Will had noticed the giant wings of oars to either side. Not sure how to get up in a confounded boat, he put his palms on the seat and pushed. Fortunately, Tommy was ready for this, as well. He caught Will well before he would have tumbled onto his face. He also did not remark on it, which earned him Will's gratitude. No doubt, the tree expected far more entertaining pratfalls in the near future.

Olivia, walking as if she was on dry land and not a rocking ocean, made it to the back bench of the craft in three steps. She turned and seated herself with a dainty air. Then she saw him.

"Come." She held her arm out, though he was a good yard or two away from her. "You can keep hold of the side like you are. Just go hand over hand." She demonstrated in miniature, her hands crossing each other on the planking.

She made it sound so simple, he thought as he lifted one hand to cross it over the other. Then he saw the water, bobbing up and down, and froze.

He did not know how long he stood there, three points connecting to the wood of the boat. The water was huge, and dark, and deep. The wind brushed the moan in his mouth away before he could hear the sound.

This was the end of him.

"Will." Her voice was in his ear. "Tommy needs more room for the oars."

Her hand was on his, on the wood. The other grasped his crazy-waving hand, covering it on its way to cross its mate.

Will took a side-step toward the back bench.

She picked up his hand, the one that had a moment ago felt nailed to the railing, and crossed it over the other. They took another step. And another, and they had reached the bench.

Will sank down on it, keeping a hand on the railing.

He might yet live.

TWENTY

He has been allowed to take on board carriages and horses, but admission was denied to about fifty cavalry, from whom he had the impudence to require accommodation. A creature—who ought to be greeted with a gallows as soon as he lands—to think of an attendance of fifty horsemen!

—The Register

P ain shot through Martin's good leg as he sat down before his potential employer. Who knew chairs could perch so low?

"Trouble, Mr. Purdy?" Mr. Swizzlewit only now was ascending the three-step wooden stair to his own chair, topped with books to make its seat even with Martin's chest. He'd not heard the crack fatal to his kneecap. Martin struggled to mask the grimace on his face. Luckily, the solicitor did not stare at him directly on seating himself.

"So, Mr. Purdy. You wish to join those who pursue justice?"

Swizzlewit interlaced his puffed fingers, resting them across his balloon of a belly. He looked like an overgrown elf, and nothing like Martin's picture of a successful solicitor.

He pushed himself straighter on the low chair, ignoring the cries of his knee. At least he still felt something down there. "You are very generous, sir, to grant me this opportunity."

Swizzlewit flicked his hand up as if to wave away the compliment. "No need to toady. Olivia has sung your praises, and I am sold. This is merely to help us get better acquainted."

Martin's shoulders eased inside the too-fine man's shirt and simple cravat. Again, a leg up from Miss Olivia. The charade with the paper was a small price to pay for all she had done for him. "Thank you, sir. What is the position, exactly?"

"It is whatever I say it is. Talking with clients, waiting outside and inside courtrooms across the city, and reading and writing the law. The ideal is that you will know the ins and outs of this racket by the time you've spent three years as my shadow. As my legs, if you will."

Martin's gaze automatically dropped from the man's face to his too short calves. He winced at the unintentional rudeness, but Swizzlewit waved that away as well.

"Common reaction. I must stop employing that metaphor, apt as it may be." He tilted forward and pulled a piece of paper from the stack at the corner of his desk. Dipping a common quill in ink, he started scratching words. "Martin Purdy. Original profession: Instructor in musical arts?"

"Music and dance."

"Any scandals attached?"

He sat up straighter. "None."

"No broken young-girls' hearts?"

"I trust not. Most of my pupils were boys."

"Good." The scratching stopped, and Swizzlewit looked up, fixing him with a kindly stare. "Now, may I ask, how you are set up?"

"You mean, where am I living?"

"Yes, among other things. I mean, what is your position in personal life?" He held up his hands. "I do not mean to pry, but to obtain an advocate's license you must prove you are an upright fellow. I must swear to it, as well. So, you see, I must ask."

"Mayfair. I live above a warehouse owned by the Buckhams. In exchange for lodging I oversee the warehouse. It is easy enough, and won't interfere with my work for you."

Swizzlewit nodded. "I know of Mr. Buckham. Their good will toward you speaks well of you."

"I hope so. I am engaged to their youngest, Merry."

"Felicitations! A married man is a stable man. When is the consummation, if I might call it that?"

"None set. We must wait for me to establish myself."

Swizzlewit nodded, tapping the feathered end of the quill against his lower lip. "Wise of old Mr. Buckham. We'll have to see how quickly we can bring you up to speed. Now, how do you know the Honorable Miss Delancey?"

Martin cleared his throat. Looking away from the clear gaze of his employer, he troubled a button on his coat. "I tutored Miss Delancey on the piano."

"Right, I remember. The music master who carted himself off to war."

He shrugged. "Buckham wouldn't let us marry."

"A common tale. But what has changed now? Your attachment to me?"

"Aye. And the funds that ensured it." The young man let go the button, resting his hands back on his knees. "I have better prospects now. One the father finds easier to comprehend than music-making."

"Miss Delancey has loaned you the funds?" Swizzlewit frowned. "I don't recall her having such a sum available."

"No. I sold a bit of music. We sold it together, actually. And it has brought in some coin." Martin stared his hands. If he concentrated, he could stop the left one from shaking.

"The March that Saved Waterloo?" Martin nodded, head drooping a bit more. He forced himself to meet Swizzlewit's gaze. The solicitor pursed his lips, frowning. "You must be very proud."

"It is a fine piece of music. Though not to Mr. Buckham."

"I see. So you are giving up music?"

"My injuries prevent my playing."

"But surely not your composition? It could be a lucrative side occupation. I expect you'll wish to grow a family. You'll need all the funds you can get, believe me."

"That's played out," he said, slapping his hand on his knee for emphasis.

Something in Swizzlewit's aspect changed. His gaze grew colder, sharper. Such a look surely drew shivers from any opposing witnesses.

"Has Miss Delancey involved you in some scheme?"

"Scheme?" Martin prayed he could not see the truth in his eyes or hear it in his voice.

Swizzlewit snorted daintily. "She's my god-daughter, you

know. I've seen a full two decades of her schemes. What did she rope you into, boy?"

"Miss Delancey has been nothing but kindness to me. I told her as I played the tune on the field, and she came up with the idea to sell it."

Silence and a raised eyebrow said the jig was up. "I expect she did." Swizzlewit tilted his head to the side. "She didn't write the ditty, did she?"

"She told the publisher I wrote it, and convinced me I had a hand in rearranging it."

"Just like Livvie. This might not be good." Swizzlewit rubbed his chin. "Thing is, you need to be seen as upright. Upstanding. No scandals, no gossip."

"I cannot control gossip." Martin heard the sullen taint in his words. Loose talk had lost him more than one commission.

Swizzlewit nodded. "Olivia won't let it get that far. And I know she's persuasive. I've got a slobbering hound dog at home to prove it. Brute is as high as my shoulder already yet thinks he's still a puppy. But from now, my boy, you keep your head down and your nose clean."

"Straight and narrow. She sold you a dog?"

"Not a dog, a 'rescue.' Called me a hero." Swizzlewit rolled his eyes. "A real schemer, that girl, but always to the good. We trust."

Martin realized he had a small smile on his face. He liked this solicitor, and the idea of becoming one himself.

"You'll start Monday?"

In the teapot of a boat, Olivia, still holding Will's left hand, swung past him to sit on his left. She did not poke fun at him; she said nothing at all. She simply held his sweaty hand in both of hers.

He might die of gratitude.

"You want to keep your eyes on the horizon, the edge between sea and sky." She gestured toward the wide ocean. "Or at least out to where the big ships are anchored. It helps to keep your bearings."

"How long will it take?"

"Not long." He was surprised she understood him, his voice but a croak. She absently petted his hand as if she had a cat on her lap, or some such. Will did not want to draw attention to it. Then she might pull away, and that would be worse. He pulled his eyes from the boards in the floor, past the knees and the rhythmically moving arms of Tommy. The man's stony gaze carried over their shoulders.

Will followed the motion of an oar up, out, and into the water. His stomach lurched, and he pulled his gaze to the horizon, where the edge of the nearly black water met the blue of a sun-soaked sky.

That was better. The boat, with his stomach and all the rest of him, continued its churning and yawing through the waves, but Will could see that it was merely the boat, and not the world, that was amiss.

And now he could see they were part of a floating parade. At least two dozen similar craft were pulling or sailing in the same direction.

"All of us are going to see Napoleon?"

"This is the last dregs." Olivia squeezed his hand. She had

not forgotten they were connected. "I watched at least an hundred small craft take off from the docks." While she was waiting for him to arrive, she did not say. "Most are small, though not as small as we are. But there are a few tug-boats and two-masters making taxi trips. It is quite the windfall for our sailors."

"And we will all jostle for the same position?"

"One side is preferred, yes. But the sea is quite large. And your vision is good, right?"

"How will Tommy know where to seat us?"

"We went out yesterday."

His gaze snapped back to her. "Just you two?"

"Oh, no." She held her hat with her free hand, gazing out at the horizon. "Aunt Betsy came with us. She thought four might be too many today."

"In the thunderstorm?"

"Only a sprinkle here. And we were fully prepared. Water-proofs, all the rest."

"Your aunt, as well?"

"You've met her. Would you tell her no? Or would she listen? There's a reason she and my father do not live together."

Her gaze turned fully to him, the now-familiar warmth with it. "We expected you yesterday. Did the *Beacon* keep you?"

"Bentley has that well in hand." In fact, the man was overeager to show Will how well he could run the presses in his absence. "The storms delayed the stage from Bath."

Olivia nodded. "You're late, but don't worry. From what I've seen, the journalists from London ride in and out in a day. That can't be enough time to learn the truth of the matter."

She turned back to the sea. "Yesterday we took the less-

popular side and could see why it was so. The emperor –
former emperor – does pace from side to side, but he spends
the most time on the side of the ship from which you can see
the land."

"So he's not pining for France."

"Apparently not. What do you think will happen to him?"

Will shrugged, which moved his held hand along her thigh.
His stomach lurched again, but not because he'd stopped
watching the horizon.

Testing, he pushed his hand deeper into her skirt. Olivia's
gaze did not waver. He glanced up at Tommy the Tree. The man
had his eye on a boat to their right, veering toward them.
Tommy expertly dipped away from danger. To distract him
from their peril, Will stretched his fingers into the fabric,
pushing until the tips felt what must be her body.

She did not look down, but the muscle under his touch
tensed. The hand on top of his relaxed, as if to allow his hand
more leverage. As the boat tilted, her hip slid into his.

He looked away and smiled. The lady in the wayward boat
beside them, all frills and pink parasol, smiled back.

Will continued his stealthy approach, hoping Olivia's
shoulder would follow her hip. The lady in the near-boat seemed
to drop a yard beneath them.

Then the swell of wave hit them. Will's hand gripping the
railing remained still, but the rest of him seemed to arc around
it. He was off the seat and on tip-toes, staring rigidly at his hand,
willing it to hold fast.

Then the wave passed. He landed heavily on his hip. Olivia's
shoulder dug into him as she fell, then slid down to the seat
again.

"Blasted hard to see with all this traffic out here." Tommy spat, adding liquid to an already too powerful sea.

Will was panting as if he had run a mile with a murderer behind him. But again, she was laughing.

"Hard to be a swain in a rocking boat." She punched his arm gently. Her smile eased his racing heart.

He shrugged, an apologetic grin at his lips. "Tough for this lubber." He looked back out at the sea.

"Have you truly never been on the water?"

"Nor in it. Except bath-houses." He turned back to her, as balanced and poised on the sea as she was in her father's home. "I thought Napoleon must be on land by now."

"We are all afraid of the sea. That is what makes us careful." She grasped his upper arm leaning into him. "But does it not make you feel alive? Part of something far bigger than one's self. Something gigantic."

"Terrible and wonderful?"

"Exactly. Look."

They had reached the edges of the crowd. A patchwork of boats and ships crowded about the HMS *Bellerophon*, with her two great guard ships on either flank.

"Do you know much of the ships of the line?"

"I remember the *Bellerophon* from Trafalgar."

"And the Battle of the Nile before." Olivia said. "I especially appreciate its designation as one of the Arrogant class. Perfect for its guest."

"May I use that in my reporting?"

"Of course." Her eyes sparkled, reflecting the glints from the peaks of the ribbons of waves. "As background, only. Not for quoting."

Tommy was doing a yeoman job maneuvering them between the outlying boats, but Will could see it would get far more difficult soon.

"Are people standing up in those front boats?"

"Yes. They are so close together people tie them tight. Then you can walk from one to another."

"*You* can."

She laughed. The sound eased his mind. "I just may. A few of the boats are floating eateries. A ride like this can make a girl thirsty. And we may see someone I know."

Again, Will was reminded that she had grown up here. He needed her help, in more ways than just saving him from spewing his lunch into the ocean. "Thank you."

She pushed him away playfully. "Thank me later. You have work to do."

Nearby was the HMS *Ville de Paris*, the flagship of Admiral Lord Keith. Keith had ordered the *Bellerophon*'s Captain Maitland not to allow anyone on board, not even the usual traders in foodstuffs and supplies. The guard ships kept the curious from coming directly alongside the ship, but did not bother the flotilla of look-seers.

The scene reminded Will of a holiday in one of the city's parks, with the ladies and gentlemen tourists parading in their finery, while the locals were clad more wisely in seaworthy linens. Colorful parasols bobbed all along the front line of the flotilla, while the back rows contained mainly men uproariously happy with themselves and the sport. These men were not even looking for Bonaparte, simply getting drunk with the rest of the crowd.

He could pick out the food stands now. Ladies in kerchiefs and aprons would lean out to another boat, handing out the vittles and pulling in the money; then the boat would move on and another take its place.

Tommy paused, turning to Olivia.

"Do you think the left, Tommy?"

"Aye. We will take the flank." He eyed Will. "Miss Olivia said you'll be doing a drawing?" Will nodded. "Best to get where you can see the most at once then."

Many of the boats they passed looked over-full to Will. His heart quailed for the men seated on the railings. Olivia saw the direction of his gaze.

"The water is on the calm side, believe it or not. They will be fine, if a bit waterlogged. Watch out!"

A bigger boat, four sails punched out like big bellies full with wind, bore down on them. Its nose within a yard of them, it pivoted smartly, spewing spray in their direction. "They won't be the only ones," Will said, glad he had not yet pulled out his sketch pad. Three young fops leaned over the rear railing of the sailboat, hooting.

"Whose yacht is that, Tommy?"

"The admiral's. See the flag up top? Don't know the company, though."

Will did know one of the company in the next boat they passed. Stowed among a dozen men and gentlemen was Cobbett, his untamed hair even wilder in the wind. They passed so near, Cobbett could lean over and talk.

"No scoop for the *Beacon*, boy!" His gaze lit on Olivia, but there was no recognition in his face. *Good.* Will did not wish to share.

As Tommy pulled ahead of Cobbett's overloaded boat, the older man waved a salute. Will waved back. The *Times* was probably here, too, and the smaller papers. But none had caricaturists on staff.

"Have you heard of any journalists here?"

"Is that who that was?"

"William Cobbett."

"The Common Man?" Olivia turned to better look at Cobbett. "Then everyone must be here. I know there is at least one of the Academy artists, a man who works in oils."

"He won't be drawing for the press."

"You wish to be the only paper with art?"

"It would set us apart."

"Not to mention sell on its own. Double-duty, like the music."

Will nodded.

"Did you listen to the new piece? It carries a nautical theme."

"How timely."

"Just so."

As they came within one hundred yards of the *Bellerophon*, they had to draw nearer the gun boat as well. The open portholes loomed. Will did not think the cannons were loaded, but they looked deadly just the same.

Now he could just see the deck of the ship. Only a half-dozen men were visible, three in the stripes of the merchant marine. The others were in full dress naval blues, their epaulets dusky gold, their sashes bright red.

Two more finely dressed officers appeared on the deck, which set the crowds in the boats astir on the skirling water. Then the man himself appeared.

Unaccompanied, his bicorne hat drawn low on his head,

Napoleon paced away from the crowd. Then, to their shouts of delight, he paced toward them.

He, too, wore his finest uniform, although little of it could be seen under the brown great-coat he wore over it. Will noted the lack of a sword. All the officers wore those impractical tall boots, shiny as on parade day.

"He was alone yesterday, as well." Olivia shaded her eyes under her bonnet. "They say he still wears his spurs, but I can't see it. It would harm the deck."

The scourge of Europe turned away from his conquerors, and paced about the middle of the deck for a span.

"He remains amidships," Olivia said. "It can't be much exercise."

The crowd expressed its displeasure at the loss of its view. Calls of "This way, Boney!" and "Here's a cracker!" drew laughs if not the man himself.

"Yesterday, we serenaded him with one of the sailor's songs." Tommy spat again. "Today's crowd isn't sailors, though. Look at all the women. And those idiots."

The sailboat that had nearly overturned them was now threatening a boat that looked to be a floating family outing.

"He's pulling sail too hard." Olivia stood up, arms out, as if she could push the rowboat out of harm's way. The larger boat, listing at thirty degrees and building a wave of its own that could swamp a boat, swerved away from the rowboat, merely drenching the family. But the sailboat didn't right itself, but tipped further toward the water. Two of the gentlemen riding the back railing slipped into the sea.

The slip righted itself, but was already three lengths away from its former passengers. Another rowboat, farther away than the family's boat, started rowing toward them. The children threw what looked like apples or tomatoes at the heads of the men in the drink.

"Serves them right." Tommy's hard-oak face had flushed. "Damned careless."

The calls for Bonaparte were rhythmic, a chant. Then they turned into song.

Purdy's song.

Will, counting the cannon holes to get it right on his sketch, did not recognize it until he heard Bragge's over-the-top line, "the Corsican devil tamed, the empire restored." He turned to rib Olivia about it, and stopped short.

She was standing again, hips automatically moving with the current. Hands clasped to her chest, she was not singing. Tears rolled down her face.

He watched her a moment, unsure what to do. He did not wish to unbalance her. He glanced at Tommy, who shrugged his bewilderment as well.

Bonaparte seemed to respond to this call. He turned and marched back to their side of the ship. Will sketched furiously, marking in as much detail as possible. How the man's collar reached nearly to his ears, the deep sockets of his eyes. How his shoulders seemed to thrust back, perhaps to balance the fulsome roundness of his belly. The hint of red on his cuffs under that giant coat.

How the British officers gave him wide berth, yet followed his every move with their eyes. How they wore their full complement of weaponry, while he appeared unarmed.

The ex-emperor courteously allowed him a full ten minutes to memorize every detail. Green coat, red collar and cuffs, gold epaulettes. Five of those minutes Napoleon spent staring out at his audience through what looked to be an opera glass.

Too soon, the Corsican sat down, presumably to write. Though they waited another fifteen minutes, he did not reappear. Will sketched the family in the boat beside him, noting the colors of the sails on the boats and a top hat passing by in the water beside their boat.

The wind was coming up. He sketched the placement of the ships, and the variety of boats. Already the closest-in ones were turning to return to land.

Olivia gestured at a couple in a nearby rowboat, the lady barely able to contain her billowing oversize bonnet, the gentleman looking about to rise aloft in his straw hat as wide as his shoulders. The pair had their arms aloft, trying to tame their headgear, their movements rocking the rest of the boat and its four other passengers. Perfect for caricature. Will sketched the boat, then its occupants. He worked fast, but not fast enough.

The gentleman, spinning toward their boat during one of his dervish dances, saw Will and divined what he was up to. He called to them, waving both his arms as if warding them away from a crash. Will had just a bit more to do, the curve of the lady's arm flowing into her neck and the line of her back, a deep arch due to her voluminous chest.

It wasn't until he had fixed the line to his satisfaction that he noticed the boat was nearer than before. The man was waving at his oarsmen to go faster.

"Best be leaving." Tommy reached back with one oar. The boat started to turn, too slow.

"Ogler! Cheap peeker!" The man's high-pitched voice carried well even in the wind. "Give me those pages!" The boat was nearly upon them. Then a swell in the waves favored them, and slowed Tommy's progress.

The scarecrow of a man, hat flapping, started swinging his umbrella like a pump handle at Will. But he misjudged the distance, the weapon flailing harmlessly two feet from their boat.

"Stand off!" Olivia leaned on the rail between Will and Tommy. "This is open water."

"Nonsense." The man turned away, looking for another weapon, no doubt. He found it. The end of an oar came swooping sideways at them. Tommy was in no danger, but Olivia was directly in its path. Will stood, reaching both his hands in front of her. She ducked out of the way.

The oar swung into Will's hands. He grabbed hold and tugged.

"Are you all right?" He looked down. Olivia was on the floor of the boat. Laughing.

Will started to join her, but choked off his laugh as he felt an answering tug. The straw hat was over the water, the man's head still attached to it though his feet were still in the boat. His weight was pushing the oar into the water.

The wash of a returning wave rolled his attacker back to standing in an arc of splashing water. The jerk on Will's hands pulled him out of precarious balance. He took a step back, the back of his knee bending over the rail of the boat.

His first thought was that he had never seen Olivia's eyes go so wide. His next was that he had forgotten to keep hold of the boat. Then all was cold, wet panic.

TWENTY-ONE

The seamen of the Bellerophon gave a current accounting of the movements of Napoleon to the ever-present gawkers in the boats. They wrote in chalk on a board, exhibited on a stand at the edge of the deck: "At breakfast."—"In the cabin with Captain Maitland."—"Writing with his officers."—"Going to dinner."—"Coming up on deck."—&c.

—The Beacon

The world was slate, then blue, then dark again. He could not breathe. His heart seemed to be filling his lungs with blood.

His mind blurred. He couldn't remember his name. So cold. Stop scrambling.

"Stop scrambling!"

A voice.

Olivia.

His realized arms and legs were flailing of their own accord. Scrambling, really. He stopped them.

One hand still held the oar. A wooden oar. So it would float. It was above his head. Which meant that the top of the water must be up.

He put the other hand on the oar and pulled up like on a chinning bar. His face felt a breeze. It must be in the air. He opened his eyes.

He was a boat-length away from Olivia. Tommy stood beside her, another oar in his hand. They kept going up and down in his sight, as if they were playing jump-rope. He laid his head on the oar.

Olivia lifted her arm. She was waving him in. But he was too tired. He had to catch his breath. The cold was not so painful now. Nice, even.

"No! Give me that oar!" She held out her arm.

Bossy wench.

He tried to move the oar toward her. A wave helped him.

At full stretch, she reached for it. Just outside her reach. She leaned farther. She would fall in.

No, Tommy had her. And she had Will. She pulled the oar, and he swung in a lazy semicircle, mimicking the swing of that oar in the air. Swimming was like mathematics. He always fell asleep in maths class.

His shoulder hit something hard. The boat. Then a hand gripped the back of his coat and the top of his trousers. Tommy hauled him up, depositing him, dripping, at the bottom of the boat. He picked up the oar and heaved it away.

"There's your oar. Now get away from us if you know what's good for you."

"Sorry, Tommy." Will could see the other boat, its steward touching a cap at them. The crazed scarecrow man seemed to have vanished, perhaps pushed to the bowels of the boat. "I'll send the sailors after you."

"See that you do." Tommy looked down at Will. "Feel the cold?"

"Not much." Although come to think of it, he did feel the warmth of hands on his shoulders.

"Right." He stripped off his jacket. "Get his coat off, Miss Livvie. Not his trousers, I've none to spare. And don't you get wet as well. Save the hugging for dry clothes."

She pushed the jacket off his shoulders and down his arms. His attempts at helping her were so clumsy she frowned. "Stay still." She pulled his shirt out from the waistband of his trousers, then up and over his head.

"I can't swim," he said, trying to explain.

"Nobody swims in deep ocean." She draped Tommy's great-coat, several sizes too large, around his shoulders, crossing it in front rather like a straitjacket. She rubbed down his arms, inside the mummy jacket. She was looking down at her hands. Her face was wet, by her eyes. But her hair was dry.

His hair was wet, he realized, as she moved her hands up to push it away from his face.

"Your lips are blue," she said. Her hands gripped his hair at the nape. She pulled his face to hers, settled her lips on his. At first he felt nothing. Then a burn, as if she were kindling to his waterlogged fireplace.

His lips felt plenty warm now. He opened his mouth, hoping she might think his tongue in need of warming, as well.

She did. Her head tilted, as if her tongue wished to be

entirely inside him. The kindling had fully engaged his heart now. He could feel his pulse speeding up to match hers. His fingers and toes started to tingle, as if waking from frostbite.

He inhaled a ragged breath through his nose. He was sinking again. But this time, there was no panic.

"I believe he is well restored for now, Miss." Tommy's voice held a laugh. "And someone's coming up starboard."

In a flash, the warmth of her tongue, her mouth, and her hands disappeared. The tingling in his hands was changing to sharp pain. A great shiver ran up his spine and out his lungs.

"Marsh, is that you?"

"Cobbett?" Will turned his head. The scarecrow man was grinning like a skull.

"Reporters are supposed to stay out of the story, man. What were you thinking?"

Olivia waved him away. "He has no time for you."

"Perhaps he'd like my blankets? Thought so." Tommy swung their boat close enough for Olivia to collect the blankets. "There's a nice lassie." Cobbett hadn't stopped grinning. "See you in London, boy."

The bigger boat swung away. Olivia covered Will's legs with a blanket. She used the second to scruff his hair drier, then draped it over his shoulders. Propped up in the bottom of the boat, Will felt as if he were in a cocoon. One that was not quite warm enough.

"Tommy?"

"He looks ill, aye. But he's shivering, not shaking."

"That's good?"

"Good enough. We'll be home in no time." Tommy grinned. One of his front teeth was missing. "*Billy Ruffian.*"

"Who is that?" Will asked Olivia.

"The *Bellerophon*. Her nickname. More appropriate for you, Tommy thinks."

"If the shoe fits." The tree-trunk man's laugh carried across two counties, Will felt sure.

He must have dozed. Or in the blink of an eye it was dark, and they were at the docks.

Olivia jumped from the boat's seat to the dock. Will's heart lurched, but lazily. She shouldn't take such risks. Tommy threw her a rope; she caught it and tied it around a post on the dock. And another.

"Can you stand?" Tommy looked at him as if he were an infant.

"Of course," he said at his most officious.

"Well, then," the man said, lifting him by the shoulders as if he were a bag of flour.

"Wait."

"We're just going to the bench first." Tommy deposited him ungracefully on the seat. "Let me feel your feet. Can you feel this?" He rubbed the top and sides of Will's legs and feet. Will nodded. "Good. Now give me my coat back."

Tommy had to help unwind Will. "She's fish-wrapped you. Must want you to last." He got the blanket off, and half-lifting Will again, managed to get the jacket off. "Best wrap up in the blanket again."

"It smells."

"You want the lady mad at us both?"

Will wrapped the musty blanket around him as fast as he could.

"Now, on the bench, then on the dock."

Will made the leap, rather more a small step, without incident. It seemed ages ago that he had jumped from the dock, heart racing. Now he was a survivor, and his wholesale panic at the beginning of the journey seemed both well-deserved and ludicrous.

From the boat, Tommy pointed to an ancient coach pulling close to the dock. Both it and the horse looked as musty as the blanket smelled. "Only a quarter-mile," Tommy said, "though I don't envy you the journey. Still, it's hearth and hot broth at the end."

Olivia hurried back to them. "Thank you, Tommy. We'll return the blankets to you." She took Will's arm with a nicely possessive grip. They walked slowly, Will's footsteps oddly tentative, to the coach.

Her bonnet had gone missing. He much preferred her this way, hair tousled and eyes wild. What other scrapes could he get into to put her in this state again?

He could think of one.

Olivia led Will down a steep stair to the basement of the Delancey's row-house, past the coal-closet and into the kitchen. This was the warmest part of the house, especially now, near time for supper. She hoped Cook had her usual colossal pot of water on the simmer; otherwise Will might need to bathe in chicken broth.

She pulled him forward into the long, narrow cooking area. Clad in his salt-caked blanket, he looked a true vagabond hero, in the midst of the cozy city kitchen. Cook turned, the wisps of gray at her temples sticking out horizontally. Her lobstered face registered surprise, then snapped back into her familiar stentorian mode.

"He goes in the wash-room. I have two pots hot. He'll have to make do." She tilted her head, sizing him up. "We've no clothes to fit him. A man that size."

"He might fit in your clothes," said old Jaspers softly. There was a pause when no one said anything. Then Will started to huff-cough a laugh. That, more than the weak joke, set the rest of them off. Olivia could not remember when they had laughed so long, and for such a small reason. But it did feel good.

"So," Cook said, pointing to the doorway to the wash-room, at the back of the house. "There. And hand your clothes back here. We can't wash them, not with supper in the hour. But we can rinse them in cold water and iron them dry. That's your job," she said, glaring at old Jaspers. "After you carry two buckets of cold water for the bath."

"Just the trousers," Will said, teeth chattering. "I have a change for the others in my bag."

Sweat slid between Olivia's shoulders. Hard to believe Will still was cold.

"Miss Livvie. You go find that bag. And you," she pushed Will forward. "Do as you're told. Likely as not, wouldn't be in that sorry state if you did that in the first place," she muttered without rancor.

"Yes'm." Will was all contrition.

Olivia took the back stairs to the ground floor. Where would Aunt Betsy have stashed Will's bags?

The lady herself stood at the top of the stair. "What has happened?"

"He fell overboard. He is not hurt, just chilled."

"Lost his balance?"

She nodded. "Protecting me." She reached the landing and was surprised to be enveloped in a lilac-scented hug.

"Oh, Livvie. Were you hurt?" Aunt Betsy shuddered against Olivia's shoulder. "You don't know how many arguments I would get into with your father over you tom-boy ways. He never even seemed to notice." She pulled away. They shared a too-knowing glance.

"But I am fine, auntie. Nothing broken, nothing even bruised." She sighed. "Though my stomach did take quite a turn at the sight of him, toppling like a black oak into the bay."

"Your stomach?" Her aunt placed her hand over Olivia's midriff. "Or your heart?" She moved the hand up to cover that organ.

Olivia grasped the hand, then realized her gloves were wet. "Oh, I don't know."

Her aunt's mouth quirked, but her eyes held sympathy. There was a reason Aunt Betsy held everyone's secrets.

"It's impossible. I know." Olivia avoided her aunt's gaze by pretending to have trouble peeling off her gloves. "Imagine the argument with Papa, for one."

"Cross that bridge when you get to it. What are your thoughts?"

Olivia had no clear thoughts where Will was concerned. Every shimmer of hope carried the shadow of a doubt, the whisper of a caveat, the hint of joy, the fear of great disaster. She shook her head.

"I would appreciate your impressions."

"Then he will stay for dinner. And, as he has no lodging, he may stay the night. With Mr. Delancey's approval, of course." Aunt Betsy clapped her hands together.

"Mr. Delancey? That story still holds water?"

"Solid as timber and tar. His bag! Where did I toss it?"

They found it just around the corner from the door, a simple set of saddlebags. Rather than rummage through his personal effects, Olivia carried the lot downstairs and through the kitchen.

"He should be ready for you now, ducks." Cook waved at the wash-room door. Jaspers, near the door, flipped Will's trousers across the ironing board. The hot iron drew rivers of steam from the fabric as he drew it down. "Don't burn the fabric."

Jaspers jumped at the tone in Cook's voice, then drew himself erect. "I did perform the duties of valet for decades, you will recall."

"Just be sure you do recall."

Olivia stood to Jaspers's side. "Here are the rest of his clothes."

"Just take them in to him. The tub is only half-full, so he shouldn't have splashed much on the floor."

Without thinking much beyond where on the floor would stay the driest, Olivia pushed the curtain away and stepped through. The steam was not as powerful as usual, perhaps because there was not as much water.

Then she saw the naked man.

His back was to her, all muscled shoulders. His hair shone black, no more salt. His arms rested on the sides of the high tub.

She could see his knees. If she leaned forward a little more, she might see much, much more.

She dropped the bags where she stood.

At the sound, he turned his head. He grinned.

"Scrub my back?"

He took advantage of her discomfort. He was the naked one. He should be ashamed. But it was her skin that felt as if it were on fire, her hands that trembled.

"I – I brought your clothes."

He looked down at her feet. "I see. Quite obliging." His gaze met hers again. "Oblige me a shade more, would you?" He held out a hand toward her, water dripping on the floor. "The towel, there."

She followed the drops as they trickled down his arm, past his index finger, onto the floor. Then across the floor to a stool just to her left.

As she bent to pick up the towel, she heard the water roll. A rather large disturbance of the water.

She had thought her face could not get redder, but in fact it could. For a moment, she froze, in the middle of standing up straight.

"I don't wish to spill more water on the floor." His tone was conversational, except for its delivery: a whisper. "But if you wish me to step over—"

She stood quickly, spun, and thrust the towel toward him. It quickly unfolded in her hand. By the time she opened her eyes, all she could see of him was his very big chest, and his grin.

He took the towel and raised it over his head, rubbing at his hair underneath. Olivia now could see the hint of another patch of hair, starting near his navel, growing to a nest between his legs, tapering down his legs. Judging by his manhood, though, he was not quite as entranced by her presence as she was by his.

She was panting, she realized. And hot, everywhere. Without thinking, she reached out a hand.

His head popped out of the towel. He started rubbing his chest.

"Peeking?"

She started, even though she thought she could not be more startled. His grin widened.

That just made her mad. She had seen men naked before. This man was no different. She frowned.

He laughed. She crossed her arms, willing her blushes to subside. No luck.

He stepped out of the bath. Toward her.

Her breath stopped. His scent washed over her, a heady mix of her aunt's sandlewood soap and his own titillating musk. Her vision grew fuzzy. She could not look at him. She could not look away.

"You could go outside."

The tone in his voice, urgent, drew her gaze to his eyes. They were fuzzy, as well. His breath came in gasps.

She remembered the cold of his lips when they were on the boat. His lips looked warm enough now.

Red hot.

She reached out, running her hand up his shoulder.

"You should get out." He caught her hand between his shoulder and his cheek.

Instead, she stretched her thumb to rub across his lower lip.

He groaned. She stepped into his embrace, the warm, wet towel between them. He took her lips in a kiss.

But his soft pressure did not satisfy. She pressed him harder, both hands on his shoulders, squeezing. They did not give.

He teased her mouth open with his tongue. She met his joust, parrying his moves with her own. Her hands pushed past his shoulders to wrap around the back of his neck.

She opened her eyes. His were half-open, the green glimmering. She took a much-needed breath, inhaling the air from his lungs.

His hands slid between them. A small noise escaped her throat.

"Your trousers are ready," Jaspers said from behind the curtain. "I'll just leave them here on the board."

Disengaging from Will felt like spinning down a drain. He grabbed at the towel, slipping toward the floor.

Both of them were panting, as if they had swum all the way home. Olivia had never done anything like that before. But the heat in her face surely wasn't shame anymore. This felt so right. She winked at him.

A sunbeam smile crept across his face. "Right," he said, voice all business. "And my shirt, there in the bag." As she bent down to open the bag, her head almost collided with his. Pulling back at the last moment, she gasped a laugh. He swooped in, just a light kiss on her fevered lips.

She stood. "On the board." She pushed the curtain away and stepped out into the cooler air of the kitchen.

Cook's head snapped back to the pot she was stirring. Jaspers, apparently, had fled.

Olivia picked up the still-steaming trousers, then pushed aside the curtain again. Safely on the outside, she pushed the clothing toward him. He slowly stood, reaching for it. The towel fell to the floor. She forgot to let go for a moment.

He was not indifferent to her now, she could see. He

snatched the trousers, startling her into letting them loose. The curtain fell. She heard a chuckle from behind the curtain.

She turned, wiping her brow. Cook stared at her, wide-eyed, then remembered herself. All business, she gestured to the curtain with her stir-stick.

"The young man be staying to supper, then?"

TWENTY-TWO

The wretch, with the blood of so many thousands on his head, seemed to carry about with him all the coolness of that apathy which is part of his physical constitution. If he be not now placed beyond the possibility of again outraging the peace of Europe, England will certainly never again deserve to have heroes such as those who have fought, and bled, at Waterloo for this, his present overthrow.

—The Register

A t the Delancey's Plymouth home, supper started peaceably enough, but into the fish course the winds started to blow. When one of the shutters clanged about with a noise of the giants above rolling pins, Olivia jumped up to shut the rest.

"Good thing you two are safe inside." Her aunt paused in the enjoyment of her turbot. "And I must remember to thank Cook for finding these oysters. This sauce is divine."

Will knew he looked much as usual, if a little soggier. But this place was dashed odd. Or rather, magical.

In the deepening light, Olivia and her aunt grew more like sisters than first-removed relations. Both whippet long and fine-boned, both rather measured in their cadences. And both liable to say anything.

"Cook reports that you thanked her for her efforts. I believe you are the first, outside of the family, ever to do so."

"I was not sure that she wished to hear it from me."

"She nearly fainted telling it to me. You, my boy, are a favorite."

If that were all it took. Will looked at his half-finished fish. His appetite had not yet returned, but it seemed wasteful not to finish.

"You can push it onto my plate," Olivia said. "She never expects me to eat it all."

"Did you get all you needed today?" Aunt Delancey sniffed. "You news-men. In and out on one coach."

"I did. I thought." Will's appetite returned with a swell at the scent of a fine bit of mustard tinting some sweet country lamb. "But it was lost."

"I recovered it." He looked a question at Olivia, his rescuer, who unexpectedly blushed. "I had to choose between your tablet and your person, and your tablet seemed the most in danger."

Will swallowed and stared at her.

"How was I to know you did not swim? Everyone swims." At least she had the grace to look sheepish.

"Not people who don't grow up near water." Her aunt leaned conspiratorially at Will. "We don't consider the Thames in London water, do we? More sewer than sea."

Will could only nod. Shame upon shame. First to fall in the water in the first place. Then to be found out a non-swimmer.

Although allowing Olivia to minister to him had definite advantages. And that kiss. It broke more than the ice traced around his spine. She looked over-warm as well, just sitting there, beautiful, across the table. Could she be remembering the same thing?

The daughter of a baron, fishing the son of a publisher out of the drink. He thought he'd heard everything, but never that. And that kiss, a shock that stopped his shivering cold.

He wanted another. He knew he shouldn't, he knew he'd already gone too far; he should savor what she'd given him already. But he wanted more.

Did she?

After supper, Olivia opened Will's sketchbook out on the table. "This is very like the *Bellerophon*," Aunt Delancey said, pulling her chair close to Olivia's. "Though I do not remember all those numbers in the air."

"Those are the number of masts and sails, gun-ports, that sort of thing. For the final drawing."

Olivia turned the pages. Will, standing to her other side, looked at the work through her eyes. Motion, sun, a carnival atmosphere, all on those deadly waves.

"This one," she paused after turning the page, "caused all the trouble."

The lady looked true to memory, the man a bit too wide. Will frowned. "Neither is paying any attention to me, and I wish it had stayed that way."

"What happened?" Her aunt's smile already carried sympathy.

"The man saw him drawing and waved at him to stop. You did not notice him at first?" Olivia turned to look up at him, nearly brushing against his arm. Lightning jumped across the divide.

Will tore his attention from his arm to the sketch. "I did. But I thought he was on about something else. Not me."

Olivia nodded. "That made the gentleman even more agitated."

"That, and his hat flying away."

"And, I expect, the fact that we couldn't help but laugh." Olivia smiled, warm but with sparks that burned.

"So," Will said, ignoring his thrumming heart, "he ordered his boatman to ram us."

"He did not," Olivia said, slapping him lightly on the back of his hand. Interesting that she was not wearing gloves. "He merely wished to get closer to continue his argument. I think he wanted you to give him the notebook."

"He is a fool, then."

"He soon saw the error in his expectations. And that's when he picked up the oar."

"He hit you with an oar?" Olivia's aunt's voice was shrill.

"Not me. He nearly beaned Olivia."

The older lady's eyes glinted. Will realized he had forgotten the "Miss" in front of Olivia's name.

"The oar swung pell-mell, auntie." Olivia distracted her with a wave of her hand. "He was standing, bobbing really, about here." She pointed an inch away from the side of the boat in the sketch.

"But even clumsy can be dangerous."

"Exactly." Will nodded once. "So I reached out and blocked the oar, just inches from her face."

"And lost his balance, and toppled in. But slowly, so I had time to reach for his pad, falling out of his hand." Olivia patted the pad of paper. "The work was saved."

"And my niece was saved." Aunt Delancey clapped her hands together, eyes bright, mouth beaming. "Our hero."

Will hadn't thought of it that way. "My hero," Olivia said, as if tasting the words on her tongue. He could taste her pleasure.

"It was tit-for-tat," he said. No harm in generosity. "She turned around and saved my life, as well."

"Fair enough." Olivia looked down, as if she did not wish to be reminded she was brave.

And shy.

And passionate.

His opinion of her had come around wildly in the past few days. Was it only a week ago that he thought her an untouchable icicle of social royalty? Then an unusual fixture of the political scene. Then a lady with spunk trying to help a friend. Then a gorgeous woman who did not mind a pat on the behind during a ball. Then, a bothersome supplicant trying to remake him into her image of him.

Then, simply, Olivia.

When had *that* happened? Somewhere between Swizzlewit's office and the *Beacon*, during a drizzle.

That first kiss, on his own ground. He was shocked she hadn't slapped him. Their second, at her insistence, on the roaring surf. And their third, downstairs, in the mist of warm skin and steamed trousers. Pray to god it wasn't the last.

Her looks had not changed. She still had the vivid features, the perfect shape, the noble carriage. The difference was he could see deeper than her looks. She had layers upon delightful layers, some with fortified walls. But she had allowed him entrance. And damned deep.

How deep would she be willing to go?

She must know how he felt about her. How his body responded to hers.

She had blushed at his nakedness at first, but did not blush at his kiss. Or the sight of him, erect. Wanting her.

Olivia seemed to sense his thoughts. With a quick glance left toward her aunt – a warning? – she turned the pages back to his likenesses of Napoleon. "And the man of the hour?"

Aunt Delancey pulled the candelabra closer and leaned in to peer at the page. "Mr. Marsh's likeness is well-drawn. But what can the man want from us?"

"The French are thoroughly sickened of him, Bragge says. My correspondent, ma'am." Will leaned in himself, crowding Olivia. The buttons on the general's trousers were too pronounced. Although Will's own might currently look the same. "I think Napoleon believes that if he gives himself up to the mercy of the English, we would feel honor bound to give him asylum. As a prisoner of war."

"On our own soil?" The older lady's back snapped straight, her narrowing. "So he may treat over the bones of good Englishmen who lost their sons to his ambition? Never."

"I tend to agree. But the government will decide."

Olivia leaned back, catching her aunt's eye. "One paper has suggested we put him in London's zoo."

"He'd poison the exhibition." The lady passed a thin hand across her eyes.

"I see your feelings are strong, ma'am."

"I watched our boys stream through this town and out, year over year. Including my own James. And how many have returned? And those broken. That – man – is not welcome here."

Olivia reached an arm around her aunt, pulling her into an embrace. How many other mothers thought the same? Would their voices be heard when the Corsican's fate was decided? It seemed unlikely. But then again, if the government did not contain mothers, it did hold its fair share of fathers.

Aunt Delancey sniffled, but quickly set her shoulders and smoothed out her face until only the fine lines remained. She looked at Will. "You must stay here tonight."

His cock swelled, clamoring for attention, but his mind overrode it. "You are far too kind. I'll be well at the lodging-house."

"I insist. I sent Jaspers out to inquire for you. All the reputable places are filled. And I won't have someone Olivia finds fit to rescue staying the night in some perilous place."

"But Aunt Betsy." Olivia frowned. Did she not wish him to stay? Unaccountably, he felt a stab of disappointment, deep.

"Nonsense. We have plenty of beds." Betsy frowned in thought. "At least, I believe we do. And Mr. Delancey insists. He must stay."

He had not yet met the invalided Mr. Delancey. "Should I go up and introduce myself to him? Show my intentions are true?" Though Will prayed the man would not see verily true.

"Nonsense. My dear husband thinks the same as me. No need to disturb him."

"But it would be plain rude not to ask his permission to remain in his home."

The lady shook her head. "This past night was so difficult. I daresay he caught no sleep at all. No, best we leave him be."

A whisper of worry snaked through Will. His staying here would cause chatter. But if the man of the house thought it well enough, who was he to argue? Especially as there seemed little alternative, with the inns stocked brick to brick. He brushed away the unwanted whisper.

Especially as the most interesting company in Plymouth resided here.

"He can have the first-floor room," Olivia said.

Her aunt nodded. "You will arrange it?" Olivia blinked, an odd moment of surprise crossing her face. "But first, Livvie, why don't you play for us? A soothing one, please." Olivia, after a long glance at her aunt, turned toward the back of the house.

Aunt Delancey stopped to tell her man to fetch her husband's medicine to him. The old codger stared goggle-eyed at her a moment, then turned and shuffled back down the stairs. They heard the music start. It was warm as milk, sonorous and smooth. The lady sighed against Will's arm. "I do miss that when she is in London. That fall of tones and prancing of rhythm." She led him to a sofa between the fireplace and the piano.

Olivia sat in shadow, the lights placed on tables near the divans. The closed windows behind her still let in some of the wild wind outdoors, the breeze alternately lifting and releasing strands of her hair. Her face glowed, her gaze intent somewhere between the keyboard and the top of the piano. Her aunt settled in, closing her eyes, a hint of pink at the tops of her cheeks.

Will watched time pass as measured by the change of shadows from inside Olivia's face to outside. In the candlelight, she appeared a part of the human world. In moonlight, she became something spectral.

He smiled at his whimsy. Her aunt nodded to the music, now in waltz time. Somehow, Olivia managed to twine the songs together, never stopping one and starting another but rolling out and in, like the waves on the beach. This meant no time for conversation, and too much time for day-dreaming.

Though he did not know much about playing music, he could tell she had a master's skills. Aunt Delancey tilted her head toward him. "Penny for your thoughts?"

"Miss Delancey must have practiced for thousands of hours to play like this."

"Many thousands, I expect. She started as an infant, nearly." He raised an eyebrow in disbelief, and she smiled. "After she fell off the bench and cut her face, her parents pushed the keyboard to face the wall. But she cried and carried on so long they were forced to relent. Jaspers built a stepped bench she could use safely. I believe she was three years old."

"I don't think my sisters could even hold a pencil at three."

"Oh, she could not play. But she could learn the keys, hit them one by one. She would sing the rest of her tune."

"Her tune?"

"Whatever was rumbling along in her head. For those who listened, it was a good gauge of her mood."

"And you listened?"

"When I could. She is my god-daughter, and I try to see her regularly. But it is difficult sometimes, as she is always with my brother-in-law." She winced, as if a chronic ailment had just flared up.

"There is trouble at home?"

"Not for the parents."

"But Olivia?"

"I wish they had not set their hopes on Avery. I could have told them he would not follow through."

"Is she disappointed?"

"No. Not at all, I'm surprised to say." Aunt Delancey gave him an appraising glance. "But she would be long gone from that house in Grosvenor Square if she had not been required to wait until the war let out."

"She has stayed too long at home."

"Far too long." She patted his hand, then pushed up and off the sofa. "Thank you for listening to an old woman natter. I will go see to the tea. Then look in on Mr. Delancey," she added, as if an afterthought.

The butler pushed a tiny cart laden with tea things into the room. Suddenly, the dour man's face cracked into a tiny smile. As Betsy started the tea, he tottered over to behind Olivia's shoulder.

She turned to look up at him. "How about the moon one?" She nodded, and the tune somehow altered into a lullaby. The servant's grin grew so wide Will feared his well-furrowed face might crack.

Will could see the appeal. Olivia's playing seemed to draw threads of half-forgotten summer days, the wonder of a new watch on his eighth birth-day, the jolt of triumph as he bested that marquis during a debate at university. The memories seemed drawn fresh; he picked each up and examined it anew.

He had had a good life, as far as it went. If only there were someone to share it with.

As the new melody drew down, she did not pick up another. The final chords, so tranquil and true, lingered as she lifted her hands from the instrument. She turned to her aunt. "You had this tuned recently. I did not have to play all around that broken A-flat."

"Just today. While you were out touristing."

Olivia stood but did not move far from the piano. She swayed, perhaps still swimming in the music.

"Have some tea." Aunt Delancey walked to her previous position next to Will, but turned and looked at Olivia. The younger woman followed her lead. Will could not express his thanks for the dreams in the music except by very graciously accepting Olivia's proffered cup of tea. It seemed a weak return.

Unfortunately, Olivia did not seem as inclined to talk as her aunt. But just sitting beside her was somehow soothing.

Soon enough after tea, Betsy started a series of prodigious yawns. She stood and stretched in nearly unladylike way. "You'll show our guest to his room?" She nodded at Will. "I wish you a good night."

She had no idea.

TWENTY-THREE

The sea was alive with boats of every description, full of good English men and women eager to see the display. They looked more like a multitude assembled in a public square than anything else. When The Prisoner came out, the noise and gestures of so many people presented a most striking spectacle; it was, at the same time, very easy to perceive that nothing hostile was meant.

—The Beacon

Olivia had been playing for nearly twenty minutes before the panic hit. She had forgotten to stop and start, falling so easily into the playful improvisation game, finding the odd links between pieces and filling in with her own step-melodies.

She could have given her secret away. Did Will suspect she was a composer?

But he did not say anything, as they sat nearly touching, hands and mouths busy with tea cups.

Shivers of awareness replaced the fear. He sat a half a foot away from her, yet it felt as if his spirit, something spectral yet solid, enveloped her. She drank him in with her tea.

At last, there were only dregs, and Olivia was forced to rise and collect his cup. He watched her as a cat watches a spider, allowing it to spin its web only to scratch it apart as soon as it is done.

He rose on her signal, though she was not sure it was a signal. He followed her down the hall, up the stairs, and down another hall. They passed three closed doors. Olivia gestured at the first, on the left. "Aunt Betsy is here."

"In the front of the house?"

"She says she – and Mr. Delancey – don't mind the noise. It calms her." The lie gave her pause. But it was not hers to tell, and it served her aunt so well she was sure Betsy never would. It was too stifling to live as a woman alone. A woman with an invisible husband, though, had many freedoms. All Plymouth knew Mr. Delancey had fallen gravely ill during a trip abroad. None but those who lived within these doors knew that he never had returned at all. His grave lay in India.

Past two more closed doors, and on to the last, which was left open. Will followed her through the door.

"This is your room," was all she had time to say before he had closed the door and planted his mouth on hers. She did not struggle. She wanted this as much as he did. Probably more.

At last, they came up for air. "It occurred to me," he said, his hand stroking down the side of her face as if it were silk, "that I had not properly thanked you."

She lifted her chin. "Call that a thank you?"

He slid the hand behind her neck, pulling her into him. This kiss was less sweet and more demanding, his tongue teasing hers into a *pas-de-deux* that grew more familiar by the moment.

She needed to touch him, to feel him. Now. She reached for the front of his shirt, pulling it free from his trousers to find that taut midriff.

He chuckled, then gasped as her hands, still warm from tea and playing, stole across his skin.

"Didn't get enough in the bath?" He pulled the shirt completely free. She slid her hands around his back, pulling them together tighter.

He growled, nipping at her earlobe, then the divot where her collarbone met her neck.

She pressed against him, pushing the softness of her skin into the hard planes of his chest. Pushing the hard edges of her pelvis into the soft mound that was his manhood.

Will sucked in a breath, gasping. "That's enough."

She shook her head no.

He drew his thumb across her lower lip. She leaned into the touch, mouth opening slightly, drawing his finger in. Drawing him to her.

"Olivia." His voice scratched his throat. "What can you want?"

"You," she breathed over his thumb. She teased it with her tongue, then sucked. Hard.

He shuddered.

"And Mr. Delancey? What does he want?" The name meant nothing to her, so little did she react. She blinked, as if recalling a dream.

"He will not call you out, if that's what you fear. I am of age, and sound mind. He would not deny me my happiness."

"Aren't you afraid?"

"Are you going to hurt me?"

Will froze. That's what Deidre had said, but she had hurt him. Pulling his head away from kissing range, he scoured her face with his gaze. "What is the game?"

Her eyes spoke true bewilderment. She wasn't toying with him. Damn reporter's instincts. She was real.

"You have experience in this?" Doubt rolled across his words.

"Of course." He felt her hesitate, and bite her lower lip in that way he already adored. "Once. But it was just," she looked directly at him, terror and hope in her eyes, "just bodies. You are you."

"I should hope so." He pushed her against the papered wall, kissing the tip of her nose. He could drown in her generous eyes.

"No." Olivia closed her eyes, trying to stem the rush of emotions through her body. Lust, she recognized. But why pain? Why loss?

He pulled away. The air chilled the skin on her palms. Her fear grew.

"I didn't take you for a tease."

"I didn't mean that." She frowned, closed the distance between them. "Only..."

"Only?" She had his skin in her hands again. The cords twisting in her neck eased. She felt his life, his pulse, under her hands. The cords twisted in her belly tightened. She was simmering in unfamiliar places, low.

The rain had eased, but the wind still pounded the shutters, pushing moonlight into the room, pulling it out again. The candle guttered, but Will could still see the cream of Olivia's skin, the wide dark of her eyes. He traced the top of her cheek, where he'd seen the fine line earlier. "This is where you hit the piano when you were three?"

She blinked slowly. A shadow crossed her face, or a cloud scuttling across the moon. "A flaw," she said in a whisper.

"The flaw that makes the vase unique. Priceless." He cupped her strong chin in the palm of his hand. She had to know how beautiful she was. How precious.

How out of his league.

He caught his breath. He shouldn't be here. What was he thinking? He wasn't thinking. He lifted his hand.

But she caught it in her own, trapping it against her cheek as if she, too, could not bear to lose their connection. He felt her other hand against his chest, brushing up to his shoulder, behind his neck. She pulled his head, his lips to hers.

For a moment, only, he closed his eyes and let her lead. He would do the right thing and step away, but first he'd savor this moment, the wondrous soft strength of her.

Then she nipped at his lip. Startled, he opened his mouth, and she plundered it. The heady taste of her went straight to his head. He had to brace a hand against the wall behind her head to stay upright. The minx only pressed herself closer to him.

He grabbed her ass and drew her even closer. Ignoring the claxons of sensation – her breasts brushing his arm, her hips molding to his – he spun her so he could rest his back against the wall and give both of his hands to her. She already had all of his attention.

It was just in time, for she'd managed to loosen his shirt. Her hands snaked up his chest, taunting his so-sensitive nipples, grasping the taut muscles of his shoulders, kneading them.

He froze, as if a bucket of ice water had tumbled over him. He jerked his head back, breaking the kiss. The lady Deidre had mocked him for his shoulders, so obviously a working-man's.

Olivia leaned in and nipped at his collarbone. "So strong."

"You don't mind?"

She looked up, her brows arched in surprise.

"I'm not shaped like a lord." The words sounded suddenly weak, even to him. She tilted her head, making a play of considering him.

"You don't need padding to look a veritable knight in armor. Why should I mind that?" She didn't wait for his answer but started unlacing his shirt. She wasn't another Deidre. He could trust her.

And this working-man's body of his was strong enough to sweep her off her feet.

Olivia was almost too distracted exploring the sinews of Will's chest to notice when he suddenly bent at the knees. But as he stood, sweeping his hand up the sides of her legs, setting the skin aflame, she gasped.

He chuckled. "Trouble?"

"My corset."

"Tied at the bottom?" He swept his palms around her

buttocks, circling them. She pressed back into his hands, a delicious pressure. He reached the base of her spine. "Yes." The laces came loose, and the vise over her chest eased. She swayed in pleasure.

"Now it's my dress."

"Up or down?"

"Up." He pushed the fabric up from her hips, his thumbs grazing the skin of her waist. Her breasts ached in frustration as his hands passed so close. But the dress at last was off, and the underdress, and the corset, and she was free.

And busy herself. She pushed Will's shirt over his head, and was rewarded by the sight of his strong chest, lightly furred. It looked as tasty as it had felt. She flicked her tongue across one of his nipples, and his body jerked to attention. Interesting.

"So beautiful, Olivia. I would have you. Would you have me?" He ran his thumb across her lower lip. She caught it in a small bite, and let it go.

He took her mouth with his as if he were starving, and she matched him, thrust for thrust. Wanting and giving, needing and receiving, this was nothing like she'd experience before. With Avery, it had been a single string, sounded softly, a study played by a child. What Will was giving her, and what she was giving him, was two voices, a chorus, a symphony. She moaned in greedy pleasure.

"How soundly do your relations sleep?" His breath came out in gasps. She realized hers was just as ragged.

"Mr. Delancey? Like the dead."

"Good." He stepped out of his trousers and pulled her close again. Everywhere was skin on skin, burning. His manhood thrust up, and her navel lurched in response. She was wet already. She wanted more, now.

She took a half-step back, to turn toward the bed, but his hands on her hips stilled her. He cupped her ass and lifted her, settling her onto his thighs. His back was braced against the wall, but even so he must be so strong just to hold her like that.

She'd never felt so safe.

She trailed kisses up his neck, across his freshly shaved chin. Still holding tight to her with one hand, his other slipped down, into the space between her thighs that already throbbed for him. A breath of chill air from the window startled her there – she was so exposed – but the heat of his hand, cupped against her, set her right again.

She wanted more; she wanted his all. Never breaking their kiss – she wouldn't give that up for a second – she reached between them for his manhood. As she touched it, warm and hard and promising, he entered her, just a finger.

She jerked in pain, and then surprised pleasure. The callus on his fingertip scored the very sensitive skin, but somehow that increased the wondrous feeling, higher and higher.

And she had calluses, too. She passed them along his cock, and his moan brought a smile to her lips even as they kissed.

As the first exquisite shudder took her, a wave of wondrous joy, he pushed her forward. She guided him into her. Home.

H alf-awake, Olivia tried to roll over, but the gentle pressure of an arm draped across her middle stifled her. And a stirring at her back.

"No escaping," growled Will sleepily.

"Never."

"Can't sleep?"

"Thinking of Thomas. Little brother, the one who died."

"The heir." He pulled her to face him.

She spun herself sideways against him, her head resting against his shoulder. "How different we would all of us be if he'd lived. You are so fortunate to have yours."

"George?" He snorted, then settled his chin on the top of her hair.

She snuggled deeper into his embrace, her warm man-tasting blanket. His scent was strong. Her body responded, nearly awake. His body stirred, as well.

"These thoughts can't be what woke you."

"Sometimes, when I'm deep in dream, I feel so alone. I wake, more alone. Then I pile the pillow like another body. A sister."

"Not a lover?" His growl had grown into a purr.

"Perhaps." Perhaps from now on.

He ran his fingers through the tangles of her hair, tracing the curve of her ear. "Such regret. For something that may never have been. George has been no good brother to me."

"But he's your brother. He must take you in, when all your friends have deserted you." She shivered, suddenly chilled.

He rolled her onto her back, draping himself over her like a blanket. A lumpy, entirely erotic blanket. "Your friends? They are the ones you love and the ones who live for you. By choice, not duty. And by that measure, you are inestimably wealthy."

Tired of talking, she pulled his head to her embrace. Her kisses grew more insistent, and he followed her, filling some of the dark corners in her heart with his grace.

She wanted to drink him in, drown herself in him.

The warm brick of his chest, the gentle ridges of his fingertips, and the teasing jester of his tongue, all for her.

She'd never felt so much, so new. Olivia let the sensations flow over her, storing them in body and soul. She would recall them at leisure later. Now, she wanted everything.

And she wanted to give him everything in return. Her softness, her so-much-smaller hands, with their rougher fingertips. Her joy.

Though deep night, the sky outside the window an ocean of stars after the storm, Olivia felt the glow of day in her heart. Something had woken deep inside. Something permanent

Whatever tomorrow would bring, this magical man, these marvelous feelings, were hers this night. And wonderful.

Twenty-Four

The fog of battle must have addled the correspondents for the Beacon. One perceives good Englishmen cheering for the Corsican Beast; another most likely has spun a story of musical derring-do from whole cloth.

—The Register

When Will next woke, moonlight striped the coverlet, but its pink edges spoke of daybreak threatening.

Olivia stirred beside him. He felt her pulse through his palm, resting on the inside of her hip.

She must be magic. A fairy, or better yet, a sprite must have taken over the lady's body. Because a properly bred lady did not moan and groan as she did. Nor cry out for more. Nor do that thing with her tongue.

He slid his hand out from under her. She slept on her belly, face hidden by the pillow and the fall of golden hair. He lifted a strand up between his fingers, careful not to wake her. He put it to his face, inhaling the scent of it. The scent of her. For a brief, crazed moment, he cast around in his mind for some sort of implement, to cut off a lock for him to keep.

Romantic folderol. He let the hair slide out of his fingers.

He mustn't be in here when the household woke. He wasn't sure if the servants lit the fireplaces in summer, but he couldn't take a chance.

Reluctantly, he slid from under the sheets they shared. The air cooled his skin, but did not touch the heat inside. Something near his heart had softened, perhaps even melted. He had not thought it possible. But then, he had not thought it possible for a proper lady to offer him a business proposition. Or for it to reap enough reward to set him solidly in the black. Or for her to save his life.

He was picking up his trousers on when he saw his travel bag near the door. For a moment, he stood there, undecided, a foot in the air. This room had all the appearance of a lady's chamber, what little he knew of them. Two cabinets for clothing, a small bureau for hair-fixing. If he was to have slept here last night, where was she to have slept?

He pulled his smalls from the bag and started dressing properly. She stirred in the bed, and he sped up. Shoes and stockings in his hand, he tried to open the door.

Locked. When had that happened? He unlocked it, wincing at the slight click, and let himself into the hall.

Unlike most houses, which kept doors and windows open for cross-ventilation, here the doors were all shut. Not sure which could be his, Will opened the next one on the left.

It opened noiselessly, exposing a completely bare room. Wallpaper and curtains and shutters remained, but not a stick of furniture.

He closed the door and tried the next. The same. All four rooms save the ones Olivia and her relations slept in were bare. He assumed her aunt and uncle had a bed.

So where in blazes was he to have slept last night?

In Olivia's room? His face flashed red at the thought. No, she had to have planned to sleep elsewhere. She would have given up her bed to him.

He was severely tempted to go up to the attic floor, where the servants' quarters usually were. Were they as empty?

What the deuce was going on? He had heard the baron always seemed short of the ready, but this was extreme. He took the front stair down to the main floor.

Their man was carrying a pot of coffee to the dining room. Olivia's aunt was already there, reading a day-old London paper. She looked up, smiling a greeting.

"Fully recovered?"

"No aches or pains."

"All to the good." She waved him to a spot at the table, and returned to concentrating on her reading. She did not ask him where he slept, or even how he slept. So he did not need to tell her he had hardly slept at all.

He noticed the paper she was reading. Cobbett's rag. "Wouldn't expect a lady would enjoy the rantings of such as the *Register*."

"Good to hear from all countries, I find." She folded the paper into thirds. "Though he does seem rather set on calling your *Beacon* to task today."

"The *Beacon*?" She held the paper out to him. She had folded it so the large-type paragraphs in the center of the front page showed out.

BEACON DUPES ITS READERS.

Ice clenched his gut. He flicked the paper straighter to read the smaller print. The servant took the movement as a sign to pour his coffee.

Cobbett claimed he had proof that Will had pulled a hoax on an innocent London. Something about a War Veteran. Will realized he was writing about Mr. Purdy and The March.

"Who is the real composer of the March that stunned London? The *Beacon* knows, yet its proprietor is conveniently out of town and cannot answer our most innocent queries."

"Innocent my arse. Begging your pardon, ma'am." Cobbett knew exactly where Will was, since he had been here himself.

"Of course. But tell me, is it true?"

Cobbett must have ridden hell for leather to set this story in print.

No. He'd have set it before he came here.

Will was three days behind.

"I checked the story myself. Your niece confirmed it."

"Olivia is involved in this?" The tone in her aunt's voice pulled him from his third re-reading of the paragraph. But her mild expression threw him back to contemplating Cobbett's perfidy.

"I must leave at once." He couldn't leave it all to Bentley. And come to think of it, hadn't the sub-editor looked down his hawk's nose at the story himself?

"Jaspers, go and fetch Mr. Marsh's horse. It's on Cornwall Street?"

"Sawrey." Will threw the rotted paper on the table. Of all the idiotic accusations. Cobbett did not care about music. But he did care about the *Beacon*. Sinking its circulation, and buying it at cut-rate. He hadn't given up on George's deal, after all.

Lying, thieving, ingrate. Man of the people, his ass. Will gulped the coffee, nearly scalding his throat. Good thing he had taken his bags with him when he left Olivia in his bed.

Olivia. In bed. How he wished he could go up and touch her, kiss her, impress her scent on his clothes so he could carry a part of her with him home. But he could not. He must not.

And in London, there would be no such opportunity. Damn Cobbett. Will might have stayed another night, claiming he was still weak from the spill in the ocean. This was surely the only time they would have together. It was impossibly sweet, painfully short. It could not be repeated.

He closed his eyes, feeling the warm honey of her skin as it slid against his. The playful teasing of her tongue. The comfortable bundle of her backside curled into him as they slept.

"Sir?" He opened his eyes to see their ruddy cook, carrying a bit of food in a cloth. Olivia's aunt already was already on the stoop outside, talking with the man from the horse-shop. She turned and set a hand on his arm as he passed, stopping him.

"Why would another publisher attack you so?"

"It's peace – and summer. Not much to report. And when papers have no decent news to chew on, they eat one another."

"Grisly." She patted his hand, mouth opening to say more, her sharp eyes searching his. Then she shook her head, and let him go.

He took his leave of her and mounted the nag. Turning her head up the hill away from the sea, he thought again of Olivia.

How had he deserved such luck as to share a night with an angel?

But it was fool's luck. Golden, and snatched away too soon. And leaving him with nothing but the foul-tempered Cobbett to look forward to.

Damn the man.

Olivia woke to the tantalizing smell of true-roasted coffee. She rolled onto her back, stretching. Her eyes opened, shocked.

She had no clothes on.

Marvelous.

Her aunt sat at the foot of the bed, a mug of steaming brew in her hands. "Olivia, what have you done?"

She looked around the room. Her clothes were on the bench at the bureau. There was no sign of Will's.

"Where is he?"

"Gone."

Olivia's gaze flew to her aunt. Betsy sipped at the coffee. Her stormy eyes held warm compassion – and censure?

She sat up grasping her knees over the sheet. Was she disappointed in her? Olivia realized Aunt Betsy's opinion was one she really valued. Her censure would sting.

"Will you tell Papa?"

"Does he know anything about it?"

Olivia frowned, confused. "Anything about what?"

"What do you think we are talking about?"

"What are you talking about?"

Aunt Betsy waved her teacup. "The *Beacon*."

"What about the *Beacon*?"

"It's your music, isn't it?"

"The march?"

"Don't play with me."

Olivia's shoulders slumped. "They never would publish my music. If they did, Papa would never allow it."

"But they would publish a man's." Aunt Betsy gazed into her drink.

"A veteran's. And he did play it on the field, and he did play it for Wellington."

"Only, he did not write it."

"He thought it good enough to play for his comrades."

Her aunt clucked her tongue. "And he certainly did not write the second one." Oliva rested her cheek on her knees, gazing toward the window. Another beautiful summer's day in Plymouth.

"So the report is true."

"What report?" Head popping up, Olivia noticed the bit of newsprint beside her aunt at the foot of the bed.

"In the *Register*."

"Cobbett's rag?"

"Everyone seems to know the man."

"He was here yesterday."

"He's been busy." Her aunt handed her the page.

BEACON DUPES ITS READERS.

As she read the paragraphs, all the blood seemed to drain out of her. In hard type, Mr. Cobbett claimed her story was either some elaborate ratiocination or a plain bald lie. He got the few facts he cited wrong, but he had the gist of it right. The "composer" was hiding someone or something, but why must it be assumed he did it for nefarious purposes? Hadn't anyone heard of a little white lie?

She shut her eyes, then opened them. The words on the page did not change.

Her shoulders sank toward her knees, the paper crumpling between the mattress and her clenched fists. How could this happen? What could be done? Most importantly, how could she keep her name – the family name – out of circulation?

If Cobbett knew, he would tell. The man who had spent two years in prison for slandering the royals would have no scruples in naming her an accomplice to deceit. This paper was more than a day old; perhaps he had done it already.

She lifted her head and shrugged, sighing out her held breath. "It's done now."

"Olivia Maxwell Delancey." Betsy's tone shook Olivia's spine. "It most certainly is not done. Your man has high-tailed it to London, I expect to refute this slander."

"Oh no." She dropped her head back into her hands.

Her aunt's gleaming eyes seemed to bore into the top of her skull. "Tell me."

"He doesn't know it's true."

"So he will defend to the death a story that is false."

"He can't."

"You think not? He'll feel duty bound to protect this composer, won't he?"

Olivia squeezed her legs tight to her chest. She needed to think her way through this. There was always a way around difficulties. She simply needed to see it. "He should just ignore it. It's one paper's tall tale."

"He's a man, Livvie. This attack is besmirching to his honor, or some such. And have you thought of the composer?"

"He is safe. He is out of music now. He is to article with Mr. Swizzlewit." Olivia pulled her fingers through her hair. "I must return home and tell Will to do nothing."

"Why not tell him the truth?"

"The way you did last night, with your Mr. Delancey?"

Aunt Betsy's eyebrows arched into half-moons, and Olivia instantly regretted her unkind words. "I'm sorry. It's not the same at all. And besides, it's too late for that. For us."

"Why?"

"He would never talk to me again."

Her aunt patted her knee. "I cannot imagine that happening. But I can imagine his paper losing prestige, and circulation. All it has is its reputation, and as he told me this morning, peacetime is no friend to newspapers." She stood and walked to the door.

Turning back, she speared her niece with a look. "I love you, Livvie, but this is badly done. It will not be easily remedied." She closed the door behind her.

Olivia threw herself back on the pillows, erasing the indentations their heads had left, erasing another trace of him.

What had gone wrong? All Martin had to do was keep silent. The world should have moved on by now, making Martin's story old news. Why had Cobbett dredged it up?

Was it because Martin had tried to sell the work to Cobbett and been turned down?

What would Will do? He guarded the reputation of the paper. It was the most important thing in the world to him. Far more important than she.

He would challenge the claim, she was sure of it. And then Cobbett would counter his claims, and on and on. That dead horse of a story would stumble on, day after day. She groaned. The longer the story lasted, the weaker Martin would become.

What if Cobbett had spoken with him already? What if Martin had spilled everything? She would be sunk.

She pulled the pillow Will had used to her face, inhaling the fierce musk of him. She could never tell him she was the author. He would think she had lied to him. Well, she had, but it wasn't really a lie, more an easy explanation. One that had helped people. But he might not see it that way. He might refuse to see her ever again.

She did not wish to even imagine it. He must not shut her out.

She had to get back to London. She could smooth everything over, she'd done it before with her parents, with Richard, with everyone. She could do it now.

If only she knew how.

TWENTY-FIVE

With the second piece published by the masterful composer of the "Tune that Took Waterloo" already in its second reprinting, no one can deny the power – or provenance – of this talent.
　　—The Beacon

"Thank the stars you are returned," Bentley said as Will strode into the shop-front. "Have a sketch for tonight's paper?"

Having ridden straight through, barely pausing for meals, Will did not have a sketch at the ready, which only made him angrier. "I shall, and we'll run it with that third piece of music, the watery one."

"Is that wise? After what Cobbett printed?" Bentley rubbed the stubble on his jaw.

"He hasn't printed more, has he?"

"Not yet. Next is day after tomorrow, as always." His sub-editor eyed him warily. Will smacked his hand to his forehead, where a thunderstorm of a head-ache stewed. He knew Cobbett's weekly publishing schedule like he knew his own. Where was his brain?

"So the trip went well?"

Will glared at him, and Bentley's whole body flinched. "What's the leader tonight?"

"Napoleon dawdles in Plymouth Harbor?"

"England Swoons for the Corsican Monster."

Bentley nodded at the improvement. "I'll get the printers set up and wait for your copy. The only other news of note is the man in Commons. Mellon."

"What's he done now?"

"Up and died. Funeral tomorrow. You are invited, especially."

"The press is invited to a wake?"

"Not the press. Just you. It's hosted by Mellon's leader, Pettigrew."

Olivia's father. How much would his sharp eyes see? Will shuddered.

"You need not attend." Bentley smirked at him. "Although it might dispel some rumors."

Had Pettigrew already heard of his dalliance with the man's daughter? Could news travel faster than a journalist himself? He reeled. What would this do to Olivia? She lived at the whim of her father. If he put her out she'd have no one. And the Delanceys, at least the London branch, did not seem so close. He couldn't be the cause of her distress.

But hadn't she been a willing partner, as well? Why should he take on the burden of her? Because he had to. He grimaced in shock.

He loved her.

"Chief?" Bentley's quavering voice brought Will back to the present.

"What rumors?" He barked out. Damn it, when had he fallen for Olivia Delancey? It couldn't be only because she'd saved his life.

"From the Regent's affair. Mellon fell ill, and you were seen assisting him. If it was assistance."

"I killed him? Idiocy." In fact, he'd been coming to Olivia's rescue, when the rest of the imbeciles fawned over Avery's over-heated Spanish bride.

"Just so. Still, might be worthwhile to make an appearance. Who knows what Cobbett plans to print next?"

"He surely has no more to say on his present topic." He was tired of these relentless broadsides, the tit-for-tat games London publishers played with one another. Perhaps it was time to throw in the towel.

But not to Cobbett.

Bentley cleared his throat. "Should we make some response?"

"To Cobbett? Never. We don't stoop to answering slander."

Like the viper that tempted Eve, the news-man Bragge stood at the base of the steps to St. Mary-le-Bow as Martin, Merry, and her family stepped out after morning services.

Merry's whisper squeaked. "What does he want? I thought you were done with all that."

Bragge tipped his hat, an absurd piece he must have purchased in Brussels, to Mrs. Buckham and Merry. "A pleasant morning to all! Might I trouble you, Mr. Purdy, to walk with me a piece?"

Martin did not see how he could say no, especially after sitting through a sermon about duty to one's fellow man. He nodded to his companions and carefully made his way down the wide steps, favoring his gamey leg. Merry matched him, and as he reached his portly inquisitor, she slipped her arm through his. She spoke first.

"We can stroll beside the labyrinth, just in here." The men followed her into the church's good-sized garden.

Bragge pulled a worn note-book from the pocket of his fine but equally worn coat. "I have just a few questions. More in the line of points of clarification."

"Of course." Merry gestured toward a granite seat facing the circles of short bushes that formed a living labyrinth. She sat on the right, and Bragge took the edge on the left, leaving Martin to stand, as if in the dock at Chancery.

"First, Mr. Purdy, you did play the tune – the original one – at Waterloo?"

"He said he did, didn't he?" Merry drew herself up straight, less the familiar ruddy-health girl and more the thunderstorm that was her father.

Bragge gazed at her mildly. "But there is a great deal he has left unsaid. Or left for others to say."

Merry crossed her arms. "I don't know what you are on about. If you disbelieve him, stop writing about him. Even if you don't." She shook her head, and Martin realized she was near tears. His heart began its familiar pounding. He hated it when she cried, and would do all in his power if it would cause her to stop. Had she heard something shameful? Like the truth?

"Miss Buckham," Bragge plodded on. "Has someone been speaking with you?"

Fear iced his heart. "Merry?"

She wiped at her eyes. "That other one. Hair even wilder."

"Cobbett." Bragge spit the word out. Seeing that Martin didn't recognize the name, he explained, "He's with the *Register*."

"I didn't know," Merry moaned. "I thought he was your friend. He looked like you."

"Nothing like. I'm a full half a foot taller," Bragge huffed. Then he chuckled. "And wider, as well."

"But Merry, lass, what did you say?" Martin gripped at her hand as if she might blow away from him in the slightest wind.

"Nothing."

"Then there is no problem. Correct?" He looked up at Bragge.

"Depends. She may have said nothing, but answered none-theless."

Merry started sobbing in earnest. "He was so mean. Did I see Martin do this? Did I see him do that? Have I ever heard him speak of his compositions? Had I ever seen him working on an unfinished one?"

"A devil, indeed." Bragge dug into his waistcoat a moment, and then pulled out a pouch and a pipe. As Martin squatted uncomfortably to rub warmth back into Merry's hands, Bragge filled his pipe, lit it, and commenced to puffing. A few minutes of this, and Martin thought he would scream, in pain and frus-tration.

Bragge peered at him through the curls of smoke. "Martin Purdy, did you tell the truth? Cobbett claims you stole the piece from some other man who died that day on the battlefield."

"Absolutely not." The force of his denunciation fixed both Bragge's and Merry's attention on him. He tried to jump to his feet, but rather stood painfully and slowly, and started pacing in front of them. "How can he say such a thing? How could he even think of it?"

"So, not thieving." Bragge blew out a lopsided ring of smoke.

"Not and lose my pension, quick as may be." At the thought of losing even that pittance, Martin grimaced.

Merry's sobs had softened to hiccups. Her tear-clouded eyes pleaded with him. "So you did write the march."

Bragge's gaze, kindly but shrewd, finished him off.

Martin knew he could not shake the man. He held his hands out, palms up. Bragge leaned back on the bench, sighing and shaking his head. Merry gasped, gulped, and then screeched, "What can you mean?"

Martin watched the small children playing in the shrubbery, their parents idly walking nearby. He took in the drone of the bees near the tall, near-dry cornflowers planted near the church wall. He prayed to God to smite him now, amidst this peaceful warmth. He would never be so lucky.

"Merry, love," he said.

"You played the march," she interrupted. "But you did not write it. So who did? Not a soldier. Someone you knew." She looked up, as if staring at his right shoulder would draw out the answer. He saw the second she discovered it. Her pert mouth fell open, a beautiful circle. Her eyes darkened as she drank his sins in.

"Shall I hazard a guess?" Bragge, still basking in his pipe on a lovely summer's day, seemed to be unaware of the threatening storm that was Meredith Buckham.

"I've heard enough." Merry stood, forcing Bragge to his feet out of courtesy. Her frown marked lines deep into her face, as if she'd turned old woman in the space of minutes.

"Should you leave her go alone? Bragge gazed at the back of the daysilk-clad virago, already a few steps away from them. Martin limped after her. Reaching out for her arm, he succeeded in turning her to face him. He couldn't lose her now, after all he'd done to prove himself worthy. "I can explain."

"Not in front of him." She glared past him at the newsman.

"Best in front of him, my dears." Bragge tapped the tobacco in his pipe. "If you wish to come out of this sorry scandal with your reputations intact." Sitting again on the low bench, he pulled a handkerchief from his pocket and wiped at his brow.

"If any of us can."

TWENTY-SIX

Perhaps taking lessons from the Wretched Tyrant himself, the Beacon's publisher has so far compromised himself with this spun-sugar tale he has diminished our faith in his once-vaunted foreign reporting.

—The Register

Poor Jeremy Mellon could draw only a scant dozen men to his wake, in a run-down parlor off Threadneedle Street. Will paid his respects to the alabaster corpse, thinking it might be the first time the man would not have the last word on him.

"Ah, Marsh. Just the man I was looking for." The Baron Pettigrew cut a dashing line, if one in the old style, with his narrow waist, brightly hued shoulders, and long and lean face. He had not gone to seed as had many of his compatriots, starting with his regent. But perhaps it was his tendency to avoid the riotous drinking parties – and paying for them – that had kept him in the second tier of power. Everyone knew he wished a chamber appointment. Few knew why he had not obtained one. He slapped Will on his back, a reach for the slighter man.

"You are trying to butter me up? My lord."

He waved his palm at him. "You've nothing to fear from me. Unless you're bedding my wife." He poked Will in the ribs with a surprisingly sharp elbow.

If only he knew. Will nodded toward the body, in its final oaken bed. "You wish to take out an obituary?"

"No. The party can do that. I wish to sound you out. It's early days, but what are your feelings now toward the political field?"

Will groped for air, feeling as if he had been hit by a carriage. Then he was doubly shocked that the idea hadn't come to him sooner. He'd had much on his mind lately, but still.

"I lean Whig. And I would not be so easy to roll over as Mellon."

Pettigrew dismissed his argument with a flutter of his hand. "Percys are six for the ha'penny. What I need is a man who can make an argument. And who will back me the bare majority of the time."

"The paper would not come with me. It is separate, and would make separate arguments."

"I should hope so. Your paper is on the decline, if you don't mind me saying so. It is time for a change."

Will did mind his saying so. It stung, deepest because it held more than a grain of truth. Was it time to let go the reins? Bentley certainly thought so, and had said so, this past twelve-month. And Will had to admit, his thoughts had been elsewhere much of the past fortnight.

Perhaps he was, indeed, ready for a change. And here it came, on a powdered platter.

"I'll consider it." He wanted to say so much more, but the words did not match his feelings inside.

"How might I sway you?"

"I'll contact you tomorrow. Monday, latest."

"Patience is wisdom." Pettigrew scanned his face with those sharp eyes so oddly familiar now, and then nodded a dismissal and returned to three of his cronies near the window. Will sat on a bench facing the guest of honor, contemplating the life of the late Mr. Mellon. Who would have thought he man would succumb before age forty? Had he done all he wished in this life? Would Will?

He shifted, uncomfortable on the bench. His own father had died before fifty. Newspapers took it out of a man, he'd said. He'd built the *Beacon*, and nearly made it a success. But the two sedition charges – and one conviction – had taken their toll. George Marsh senior had lost his taste for publishing nearly a decade before he'd died, and the paper suffered for it.

Was Will losing his taste for it now? The latest salvo from Cobbett felt like an arrow to his chest. But he'd weathered far worse before, even months of it back when he stopped taking bribes from theatre owners. Sheriden himself had crucified him in the pages of his broadsheet for weeks. Even Bentley saw this latest tempest as business as usual; it must be Will who had changed.

Not the least of it was this fragile reconciliation with George. His brother seemed a changed man this morning when Will had gone round to the counting house. George had signed his shares in the print-shop over to Will with a flourish, and even invited him to the double wedding, on Tuesday next. "Least I can do," he said. "I know the value of your paper. What you're paying is double."

"A wedding gift. Gifts." Will shook his head at the memory. Who could have predicted that George's spoiled daughters would mend the family rift?

Would he, himself, ever have children? He pictured a girl of his own, and a boy, both with sharp blue eyes and dimpled chins. Children brought joy, he was told. He knew they were a lasting legacy, much like a newspaper.

Mellon looked to be at peace. Soon enough, Will thought, he would be the body laid out in his Sunday finery. Would people say he left precious little behind?

No.

He stood, scanning the room for Pettigrew. The man had his back to him, powder flecking his shoulders. Will waited for him to turn, then caught his eye.

"A question, Mr. Marsh?"

"A decision." He formed the word on his tongue, but needed to breathe in again to make it sound. "Yes."

"Excellent. Join me in Commons tomorrow at four. I'm to meet with a few friends and hear them out on the funding bills."

Will nodded. Despite the somber venue, he smiled.

Pettigrew snapped his fingers. "Another thing. A country squire will need to entertain from time to time. I hear your new home still needs furnishings. I might have some room-sets I can let you have. For a fraction of their original cost, of course."

Will paused. He did need furniture. And now that he had seen Pettigrew's Plymouth house, he suspected the man was devilishly short of ready cash. Was this how his cronies showed their loyalty? It wasn't illegal, at least. "To be sure," he said.

"We'll ride home together, and you can see if there's anything that suits." Pettigrew gazed at him, a glint in those silvered blue eyes. "You might also think of obtaining a bride. One who can play hostess to men talking politics. Can't begin to tell you how valuable the baroness has been." He shrugged delicately, and flicked at a speck of powder on his lapel. "In fact, a good politician can nearly always rely on advancing to the lower peerage. Quite the step up for one's marriage prospects."

Will couldn't believe his ears. His face flushed, and Pettigrew raised a brow. Did the man know about his night with Olivia? Would he approve such a match? Would she?

He hardly dared hope.

"All furnishings arrived safe and sound. You man Pettigrew doesn't shy away from comfort."

Two days after the funeral, Bragge sprawled across the new, overplush loveseat in Will's previously bare first-floor sitting room in his Berkshire home. His rheumatic mother had used only the ground-floor rooms, so those were all she'd furnished. As he spent most of his days at Printing-House Square, he hadn't needed furnished rooms here. But now it was time for Will to play lord of the manor in truth.

He crossed to the windows, now decked with burgundy curtains. Fall could not come soon enough. Though a slight breeze brought some relief, it was still bloody hot. He poured wine from a decanter on the new sideboard for the two of them and sat in his own chair, a hard pine that had come with the house. "To think my only worry in June was when would war end."

Bragge took the glass from his hand with a flourish. "What does the illustrious Pettigrew want from you today?"

"To introduce me about in Commons."

Bragge took a sip, holding the vintage on his tongue before swallowing. "Isn't the man a bit, well, oily for you?"

"I'd just be an ally, perhaps, on the floor. I wouldn't marry the man."

Bragge paused, but his question was already in Will's mind. *But what about his daughter?* Pettigrew had seemed to suggest it himself. And hadn't Will thought of it when writing the note out to buy some of the very furnishings she'd rested her sweet form upon? But his mind shied away from thinking of it. He dared not.

Or dare he? That golden smile, the face so attentive, the manner all that was lovely. And that skin, pinked in all the right places, well...

Bragge was still jabbering. "Brilliant. You need something bigger than us. We all do."

"Your wife finally gets a chance to make a home, and already you yearn to return to the vagabond life of a war correspondent?" Will's voice teased, but Bragge did not smile. He shook out his curls, such an effective weapon with the ladies, and pouted.

"In a word, yes. Bentley's breeches are in a twist over this Cobbett tempest. And yours, as well."

"And yours aren't?" Will's stomach turned. He set down his

wine. "The man makes us a laughingstock. He poaches our subscriptions."

"In fact, he does not. Bentley was ashamed to admit to me that the sales figures this week are identical – within a few dozen – to last week's. And last week's were high."

"That's because no one believes him. Yet. But he will keep pounding at us, worrying the story like a bone."

"It was a mistake to print that defense yesterday. Today."

Will groaned. They'd had this argument yesterday, at dinner, during typeset, even as the presses were running. "He's attacked us twice already. We must defend ourselves."

"Must we? We did not defend ourselves when the theatres slandered us. Remember? When we stopped taking their graft. It lasted months, that campaign."

"Six months."

"And you gained circulation."

"And a reputation. As not the sort to get taken. By theater owners or politicians."

"So *that* is the reputation you are defending."

"What is the bug up your arse?" Will downed the wine in one gulp.

"Defending yourself simply continues the argument. If we stayed silent, Cobbett would bray himself hoarse, then move on to his next screed."

"This is different."

Bragge groaned, his voice collecting volume in time. "You know how this is different?" He slapped the table with his palm. "This is different because it is, finally, absolutely, unimpeachably, unimportant."

"How can you say that?" Will jumped to his feet. Bragge rolled up to his. He put his hands on Will's shoulders, pushing him back into the chair. He picked up Will's glass and headed to the sideboard.

"We are arguing about a blessed piece of doggerel. Music!" He lifted the wine jug, then slammed it down and turned to Will. "Life and death it is not. It isn't worth spending ten seconds thinking about." Calming himself, he poured out their glasses and returned to his overstuffed perch.

"It isn't the music, and you know it." Will left the glass on the table beside him. "It is the story. If the *Beacon* can't be trusted to write an honest story, who can?"

"I hate to rain on your pretty delusions, but most readers think every story is a lie. And," he held up a hand, "they're right."

"They are not."

"We never get every detail correct. We don't fully describe every scene. We couldn't. Two hundred people in a room at Commons, we're going to describe what every last one said?"

"That is editing. Not lying."

"Depends on who gets quoted." Bragge shrugged. "We're off the topic. As your senior correspondent and your oldest friend, I feel I should tell you when I think your head is up your arse. As it is now."

"Get out, get back to town. We have an edition to put out." Will picked up his glass, only to brood into it.

"You promised me the night off if I'd marshal your new furnishings. *Voilà*. Don't damage that sterling reputation for honesty now." He burped. "Bentley says you've been a bugbear ever since Plymouth. I see why."

"Bragge." Will's patience was at its limit. Did the man never stop pushing?

"Allow me to offer a proposition. I'll go. Not today, but soon. Frankly, I cannot stand it here. Parliament is out, the royals are only good for scandal, and no one is doing anything interesting."

"We aren't a gossip rag."

"Exactly. I would argue that the news this season is in the shires. The small towns. Send us there."

"I don't have the blunt. Can't you stay happy just re-writing the copy from the borough papers?"

Bragge sighed with his whole torso, a theatrical display. "The regionals aren't reporting what truly is going on. My sources on the coaching routes say the Luddites are re-forming, the weavers are considering action, and the good folk of the villages may back them. Shire publishers aren't interested in helping revolutionaries."

"Cobbett would be all over that story, were it true."

"That man's got a bee in his bonnet, baiting you."

Bragge had a point. And he did have the best sources on the island, as well as on the continent. "Mayhap. The people fear recession?"

"And you don't? Of course they do. The other story is how poorly the veterans are treated. The War Office is cash poor, and many men have not been paid off. Will they turn into a generation of beggars and highwaymen?"

Will nodded. "You could do that story here."

"Port towns are better. We have some blunt left over from this year's correspondent's budget. And I have friends in most ports."

"Lucky man."

Bragge leaned forward, elbows on knees, hands spread wide. "Let me go find you some real stories. Something to make your paper worth printing. You can still use the back page for your musical interludes."

"We're done with music."

"It wasn't the music; it was the story," Bragge parroted back at him. "Haven't we gone to re-print on each piece?"

"Yes. And we have a lot more female readers."

"Women aren't the only ones who love music. You, yourself, attend the musicale of an evening, or so I hear." Bragge pulled out his pipe and lit it. He blew the smoke toward the open window. Across Will.

"Enough. Get out of London. Just get us good copy."

"Always. I'll beat Cobbett on his home turf." He set a smoke ring floating. "Show him how tight we can truly twist his breeches."

TWENTY-SEVEN

No longer content with his Common Man pretensions, this new Contentious Man would see nothing but evil hidden in simple sunlight.

—The Beacon

T he next afternoon, Will found the Baron Pettigrew holding court in Commons, busy even with Parliament out of session. Unfortunately, Will was not the only member of the public attending on those lords who would not close up shop for the summer.

Pettigrew sat in one of the towering window seats, the mighty August sun at his back. Will trusted it was at trick of the light and the man's powder that created that halo around his bewigged head. He waited for the gaggle of young men to thin out, and Pettigrew signaled to him to come closer.

"I trust this is a firm yes?"

Will nodded. All of a sudden, he couldn't speak, and he realized how serious a choice this was. He was turning a page in his life.

Even before he could read, he had been a newspaperman, running sheets, pulling presses, learning to set type and etchings. Nearly three decades already. And these past few years had been nothing but type, new presses, and getting the paper out.

Now he wouldn't be holed up in the wee hours of the night, hands inky, hair smelling of pulp. He could go to the theater, and stay through the second encore. He could go out to the balls after.

As a politician, he would have to.

Will loved going to the taverns and listening to other men rail about politicians, taxes, and the royal family. That wouldn't change. But now he might do something better for them than merely complain in print. He squared his shoulders and found his tongue.

"What must I to do?"

"Today, merely be agreeable. I'll squire you around. You know everyone here, but they need to make a new impression of you. A month of mourning, during which you are meeting the outlying folk. Then another event at the inn, and you are in by the early session. God willing," he added as the archbishop ambled by. The man merely shook his head at them.

"Love to dig into the man. It's my worst habit," Pettigrew said pleasantly. "Have you thought on which causes you wish to stand for? Taxes? The plight of veterans? The stamp fee for that man?"

Will turned to see to whom he referred. Cobbett, shambling as ever, hair especially electric, headed their way. He stopped directly in front of them and sketched a smart bow, drawing attention. "The two men I seek. And in conversation. Could they be cooking up another devious plot?"

"I see none of your laboring men here, Cobbett." Pettigrew's voice could frost glass.

"I merely seek comment." Cobbett drew a small note-book from a pocket of his black jacket, shiny with age. "Marsh, how did you convince Pettigrew's daughter to wallow in your dirt?"

Will blinked, stunned by the broadside. Then fear and anger started to rumble in his belly. How had the bastard discovered his night with Olivia? The man best not mention it before all this crowd, or Will would have to slay him on the spot.

"I beg your pardon?"

"No playing dumb, now. I have it all from impeccable sources."

Pettigrew laughed, a shrill staccato.

"There is no source for slander such as that," Will said stoutly, relieved the baron still seemed to consider Cobbett's play a farce. If only the others in the hall did. More and more faces turned toward them. More and more ears cocked.

"My daughter is in Plymouth," the baron said, languor signaling his boredom with this conversation.

"The Honorable Olivia Delancey is at Cheapside, my lord, at an event celebrating the engagement of the man known as the composer of the Song that Sank Waterloo."

"Tune that took." Will couldn't help interjecting.

"A march, you say?" Pettigrew sniffed. "Olivia doesn't do marches."

Alarms claxoned across Will's mind. What did he mean, she didn't do *marches*? Will's legs failed, and he sat down hard, crowding the Baron.

"But she does compose other pieces?" Cobbett looked like a terrier in heat. "Say, a thrilling piece about the sea?"

Pettigrew stopped to consider, which was all the confirmation Cobbett needed. He hopped from foot to foot. Would he cackle?

Will had to stop him, to explain somehow. "The man played the music for me," he said. "Wellington praised him. He conducted it at the Prince's celebration."

He stopped short. Olivia had played it at the celebration. She was a virtuoso pianoforte player. She invented musical connections and bridged tunes for fun. She was always at the piano.

The day turned chill. He'd been fooled again. Made a fool. Taken for a fool. More fool him.

He closed his eyes. "Damn me," he whispered.

Pettigrew, startled by Will's reaction, at last noticed Cobbett's antics, and blanched. He lifted his walking stick and poked it at the dancing man. "You will not drag our name into this."

"No need, my lord. I will merely say the *Beacon*'s publisher was duped by a lady. The shame will be all his." He turned to Will. "How do you explain your stupidity? Don't you know better than to trust anonymous sources? Especially beautiful ones? Or does every generation need to learn it again? A chip off the old block you turned out to be."

A knife-edged pain shot across Will's gut, forcing him to bend forward. But his anger was stronger, and he pushed the pain away. Lurching to his feet, he barreled toward Cobbett, only a foot away. The man, startled, hopped back, but Will's momentum was so strong they must collide.

But with all the reserves he could muster, and at the expense of a badly bitten tongue, Will pulled himself erect, stopping a bare inch away from his rival.

Cobbett flinched, but did not cede him space, though Will towered over him. "Like father, like son." Every man in the room was watching them.

He would not rise to that bait again. "This story is beneath even you, Cobbett. The man is a veteran. You would ruin his name just to poke a stick in my eye? Is not he one of your beloved working men?"

"He should have thought of that before he joined forces with you."

"He did, from what I recall. He came to you first. And you suggested my name." Will forced his mind to stop scrambling, and crossed his arms. Perhaps he could play to this crowd. "So, one might say, you yourself set me up."

"Why would I do that?" Cobbett's voice had risen an octave.

"Because my brother sought to sell the *Beacon* to you." That drew a murmur from the crowd. Will smiled to himself. "You seek to knock me down to buy my paper at cut-rate."

Cobbett turned to look at the others in the room, gauging the effect of Will's words. Softly, he said, "You may win opinion here, in this chamber of relics. But my words will reach the great multitudes not allowed in this room."

"Such bitter talk," Pettigrew said mildly. "Do all publishers scorn each other so?"

Cobbett pulled himself up to his full five foot seven, wayward hair and all. "Marsh brought it upon himself. Set yourself up as the purest of the pure, and any small blemish with do you in. To my benefit." He turned on his heel, the click-clacking of his wooden heels loud in the room as he departed.

In the blink of an eye, Will recalled his history with the lovely, duplicitous Olivia Delancey, recasting all in this new light. The music, in her hand. Selling it herself. Speaking in the place of her "wounded" compatriot. Pretending reluctance, then agreeing to a second piece. Suggesting a third. Playing it for the Regent!

And in a boat rocked by the ocean, crying when she heard it in chorus.

She had lied to his face. She'd made a complete ass of him. She had even used his body. How often had she played inexperienced miss for a man?

How dare she deceive him?

Will could not release the fists of his hands. He shoved them into his pockets, muffling the screams of his palms where the nails bit in. The baron tapped the cane on the floor once.

"Might I suggest a trip to my residence? I have the idea you might wish to speak to a certain someone there. I know I certainly do."

Will nodded. He trusted that when he did lay eyes upon her he would not throttle her like the lying tube of steam she was. But he would make his displeasure known. She would regret ever playing with him.

Was every English lady a Deidre? Of course they were. That's how they were raised, after all. The epitomes of selfishness and careless cruelty.

Did she even know what she had done to him? His tattered reputation was the least of it. She threatened the life of his paper, and all the good it could do in this blasted world.

He'd done it to himself, again. Left his walls undefended.

Allowed his hopes to fly too high. Damned the consequences. And now he would be damned by them.

Pettigrew tucked his handkerchief into his wrist sleeve. Slowly, as if life were completely calm, he rose and they made their way around the room. The baron had a word, a hint, a gentle challenge, for every man. Every man responded as if unconcerned. But by the time they reached the door, Pettigrew had another guaranteed vote for new taxes and two men rushing to their own minority whips to marshal forces against it.

And Will had an ache down deep that all the drink in London could not cure.

Twenty-Eight

The scurrilous publisher of the Beacon may cast all the aspersions he wishes, but this paper merely shines light on falsehoods and execrations. It is he who must explain himself.

—The Register

Meredith's family had invited only their closest friends to the engagement announcement tea party. Nearly one hundred souls filled the shaded yard beside the parish church. With more than two years to wait before they could be wed, Merry had wanted her festivities now.

Olivia greeted Merry's mother and father, who seemed to have already tested the punch thoroughly, but she did not see her friend.

"My girl was whispering something to Martin last I saw her. Those two, like lovebirds they are." Merry's mother, draped in butter-yellow crepe with a matching bonnet, swept her into a deep embrace. Olivia felt as if she were trapped in a linen closet with a warm minty comforter. But it felt good to be there.

"We can't thank you enough for what you've done for our Merry," she said, finally releasing her. "I know that Mr. Buckham thought our dear girl would give over, but I knew she never would. Lovey-doves, they are, each finishing the other's sentence."

"You're too kind. I did little." Olivia caught herself in the lie. She had done a great deal. But it was they who closed the deal.

"Aren't you sweet?" Merry's mother tipped Olivia's chin. "And if I'm not mistaken, you look a bit sweeter than before. Is there a lover involved?" She blushed. "I see. I wish you happy. Just as happy as my girl."

Olivia did not see the happy couple in the open yard, nor in the arching walkways that ringed it. She walked slowly in the shaded walks, passing the other guests, shopkeepers and store owners and their families. They smiled at her but did not engage her in conversation, perhaps over-conscious of their place. Later in the afternoon, flush with drink, they might not find their differences so insurmountable.

Close to the far corner at the end of the long hall, she heard Merry's voice, high and upset. The curtain of canvas must be concealing a space behind, perhaps storage for the tables and trestles. "You hurt me," Merry said.

Olivia quickly pushed the curtain aside. Merry looked unhurt, but was rather red-faced and round-eyed. Martin leaned against the cold stone wall, arms crossed, lank hair hanging past his downcast eyes. The space was bare but for the three of them. "You!" she said.

Olivia drew back, confused.

"No, come in here." Merry stepped closer to Martin, allowing Olivia space behind the curtain. The air was warm and close. "I know everything." She set her hands on her hips. "About the music. How could you?"

Olivia tried a bluff. "What music?" Behind Merry, Martin groaned.

Merry threw up a hand. "All of it! Starting with that blasted march. I hear it everywhere."

"Why are you so angry?"

"Answer my question," Merry crossed her arms.

"What does it matter?"

"You wrote." Merry turned to Martin. "And you took the credit."

Martin, pale-face, pleaded. "Merry, dearest, it didn't mean anything." She stared at him as if he were a stranger, a criminal one.

Olivia did not understand the change in her. Demanding, demeaning, angry. She had to do something, to bring back the Merry they both loved.

"It is simple." Under the full force of Merry's glare, Olivia gulped her next breath. "Mr. Marsh saw Martin playing it, as he had on the battlefield, remember? He simply assumed Martin had written it."

"And no one disabused him of this notion?"

"It made the story simpler. Easier to write and to read. The details were unimportant."

"Unimportant!"

"The story was how the song was played on the battlefield. Why go into the details of composer, especially when she isn't even the long-suffering *fiancée*."

Suddenly, Olivia could see the way Merry saw. A lover betrayed. A good friend's lies.

Merry blew out a breath and wiped her brow with her hand. "Why ever did you send it?"

"I wanted someone to enjoy it. Someone who could appreciate it." Someone besides her and the mice in the floorboards.

But to the every-practical Merry, frowning in apparent disbelief, the reason would sound pathetic. What true lady would need such approbation?

In Merry's eyes, Olivia was so much ribbon candy, ornamental unless one needed one's mail franked. She had proved a poor doorway to the *haut ton*, even though her father was in the government's vest pocket.

True, she'd served as a beard for Merry and Martin's afternoon engagements, but even that did not reflect well on her, Olivia realized. What other proper lady would allow her social inferiors to take advantage of her in that way?

Friendship to Merry meant usefulness. And Olivia had proved useful, until now. The ends were all, no matter the means. The daughter of trade, Merry would have had to fight for every rung on the social ladder, only to watch Olivia carelessly spurn her own birth-born opportunities.

A cherry pit of ice settled high in Olivia's throat. She would lose this friendship. She already had.

"You shouldn't send correspondence to men not of your family." Merry sneered at her. "None of this would have happened."

Olivia recoiled, then shot back. "If none of this had happened, you would not now be engaged."

"Happily engaged?" Martin looked up in faint hope.

Merry snorted. "How could I marry a man who lies to me?" Martin returned to hiding his face in his hands.

Olivia couldn't believe a celebration party continued mere inches away through the curtain. Here, it felt like Waterloo itself. She straightened her spine and searched for words to repair the breach.

"He did not lie to you. He is not to blame."

Merry, turned from Martin and stepped toward Olivia. It took all the strength she had not to take a step back in retreat. "And who put him up to this?" With an index finger, she poked Olivia on the breast-bone. "You. There's a reason you don't have friends in Society. Because you are no good friend yourself."

"Don't play the innocent, Meredith. You wanted me to remedy things for you, and that I did. You had no fear of saying nothing to your family when you met Martin every afternoon. You were willing to play the sister with me to get into the hospital."

"I'll not listen to more of your lies. Olivia Delancey." But she pointed at her chest again. "Fix this."

"I did my best to help you. I got you Martin. I gave you ... I gave you a piece of me." She stopped. How could she say she had given them her heart? It sounded outlandish, but it was the truth. She needed them to be happy together, even if she never could. Especially then.

Merry rolled her eyes. "It was a piece of music. Nothing."

Olivia drew back as if Merry had slapped her. Her face even felt warm.

"Merry," Martin tried to intervene, but a glance over her shoulder kept him pinned him to the wall.

"Listen to the truth, Olivia Delancey. You hid behind

Martin's skirts to get your moment in the sun. Don't argue any different. And now this Cobbett is threatening to tell all he knows to Mr. Swizzlewit. An advocate cannot have a checkered past. Martin might never get a license!"

Olivia frowned. "That's not true. Mr. Swizzlewit himself is not lily-white."

"I don't care about Mr. Swizzlestick, Mr. Half-wit, whoever. All I care about is Martin." She turned away from Olivia. "At least, the Martin I knew."

Martin reached a hand out to her. She ignored it, and he pulled it back, a tattered wing. "I am no good, Merry. You've painted me a saint. All I am is a broken man."

Though staring at him, Merry seemed not to hear him. She whispered half to herself, half to Olivia, "Lies. Who could marry a man who brings such trouble home with him?" It wasn't the lying Merry hated, it was the bother. But suddenly Olivia pictured Will standing before her in Merry's place. For him, it would be about the lies. He never would forgive her. She was an idiot to have convinced herself he would.

A publisher whose pride was reporting the truth, choosing a lover who had no qualms about lying to him.

She'd ruined everything.

The stone wall of the church seemed to tilt. She blinked quickly to regain her balance. She must remember to breathe, to stay in control of herself. She must concentrate, must find the way to explain things, to smooth everything over. To make everyone happy.

She saw none.

The pit of ice in her heart had now grown to trap her whole chest. Her lungs pinched. She had to get out of here.

She met Merry's steady gaze. "What can I do?"

"I don't know. You're the one with the imagination. Think of something."

Her thoughts were lightning, too much light and no substance. Olivia shook her head.

Merry's eyes were bright, glazed with anger and frustration. "I do know one thing. I cannot marry Martin with this threat of public lynching hanging over us. If it comes down to Martin or you, I'll throw you to that Cobbett and the rest of the wolves. The man lurks outside the shop every day now."

"I will think of something."

Merry lifted the curtain beside Olivia, exposing her to the milling crowd. "Get out."

Olivia gasped and schooled her features, presenting her Society Lady mask to any onlookers as she stepped back in the garden.

Merry followed, her face transformed by smiles. Martin trailed her, a weak attempt at a grin wavering across his lips.

Clear-sighted, pure in body and mind, Merry had no need for worries. If Olivia could not mend the rent in their lives, Merry would sew it up herself, using Olivia's shredded reputation as binding.

Calling attention to herself, Merry smiled her widest smile and clasped one of Martin's hands to her chest, over her heart. Their friends and relations raised tankards and cheers. Olivia clenched her hands into fists. Clever Merry always got what she wanted.

For Merry to succeed, to have her "pure, untainted" Martin back, Olivia must fail. But how could she come clean to Will, and then watch his face as his feelings for her changed from affection to abhorrence?

Waiting on the church steps for her carriage to pull up, she twisted her hands. It was so blasted hot today. If all her myriad attempts to help, how could this one have turned out so horribly? Why could people not solve their own problems? Why couldn't she?

How could she have been so blind to the way this all would look to Will? How could she ever explain it to him? Say, "Sorry you were a fool for championing Martin, but would you still consider spending more time – a lifetime, even – with me?" He would spit on her.

Her heart pounded so in her chest that she yearned to tear it out. Even her body would not listen to her.

He never would forgive her. Or he would, decades from now when they were both old and gray. Where was the blasted coach?

Her boy ran up to her. The coach had been called to pick up her father from Parliament. Could he call her a hack? The road shimmered in the August heat. She was two miles from home, and her piano. She set off on foot, trying to shield herself with her pathetic lady's parasol.

Why must she always be the sacrifice? Always be the one who needed to prove herself worthy? Her parents did not seem to shirk on their own needs, while she was left to fend for herself.

Well, so be it. She had been born with intelligence, and she'd dashed well use it. So she was not destined to be one of the fortunate, for whom everything fell out just so. She would make her own way. She'd done it before.

She might well lose Will's affection, but not without a fight.

She had to tell him now. He had to hear it from her first, before anyone else spun the story against her.

Taking the short-cut in the shade of the long buildings of Westminster, Olivia promised herself one thing. She would solve this puzzle if it took a week's piano playing to do it.

Will and Pettigrew were halfway through the brandy when the footman announced that Olivia had returned. Pettigrew told him to send her in.

"I'll take the lead, if you don't mind," he said. "Come stand by the fireplace."

As soon as Olivia came through the door, Will could see something already was wrong. She was patting her hair back into place, and the ribbons of her bonnet hung around her elbow. There were shadows under her eyes and faint worry lines beside them. Her shoulders slumped a bit, breaking that well-remembered line from the top of her head to the round of her lovely rump.

When she saw him, she paused mid-step. Her gaze darted to Pettigrew. "Father?"

"Close the door." The servant departed, closing the door behind him. "Olivia, it has come to my attention that you have had business dealings with this man."

Will saw the cloud of panic cross her face as she looked at him. He nearly shook his head to reassure her, but stopped himself. He had not come here to support her. He was very angry with her. And betrayed. And bloody hurt.

But it was her face that carried those emotions. "I can explain."

"No need." Pettigrew waved a hand. "I understand it all."

Confusion wounded her face with reds and whites. Will could see why. He himself did not understand much of anything. He wanted to hear her explanations, and then to condemn her. He scowled. She quickly looked away, but not before he saw the flash of pain in her eyes.

Damn her eyes. And the rest of her. "I'd like to hear an explanation," he said.

Pettigrew lifted a hand. Will could see his heartbeat pulse along his jaw, just as his daughter's did. "The floor is mine."

"Of course." Will could see the power inside the slighter man. Small wonder he held sway in Lords.

"Now, Olivia, we give you great leeway in your personal life."

She opened her mouth as if she would object to that, but looked up at her father again and closed it.

Pettigrew continued. "We ask for only one thing. That you do nothing – nothing – to besmirch the family name."

Her shoulders slumped more. Her fine hands, hidden in mauve gloves, twisted into each other. "That is what I am trying to do."

Will frowned. Wait a moment. To her father, Olivia's crime was not lying. It was not playing the paper for a fool. It was not even playing the regent for a fool. It was taking the infinitesimal chance that somehow Pettigrew's name might become connected to the story.

Suddenly, he understood why she would pass her work off as that of another. Not merely because it was "unladylike," but because it might mar his continual push for power. Pettigrew had no idea Olivia's talent was true, and even less interest. His selfishness choked her talent, and her spirit, the same way a farmer choked daffodils out of a barley field.

The baron was as blind as a miner who failed to see a vein of gold because it was snaking through a coal mine. Olivia had the wrong sort of genius, and must be punished for it. Again and again. His breath burned in anger on her behalf.

Then he remembered how angry he was with her.

"Our name is not anywhere in the story, papa," she whispered, gaze on the floor.

"Only because I ensured it, this afternoon. The man came to me in front of my peers. My peers, Olivia."

She looked up, surprised. "What passed this afternoon?"

Pettigrew shrugged. Will spoke up again, ignoring the frown Pettigrew sent his way. "Cobbett popped up at Commons and said he had the whole story."

"From whom?"

"Impeccable sources."

She frowned. "But I was together with the only impeccable sources then."

"Not every day."

"No matter," Pettigrew said. "It won't happen again."

Olivia's eyes widened in fright. "You're sending me away?"

"Of course not. It's difficult enough finding suitors for you here."

She glanced at Will, and blushed deep into the roots of her hair. "That isn't fair. I was engaged until just recently."

"And what have you done for yourself since then?

Consorted with people beneath you. Haven't been to more than two balls all year."

Olivia's mouth set. "You know why I can't attend many balls."

Why not? She was so beautiful she might outshine any collection of bred-in-bone aristos. But her nerves were showing now; she fingered the ribbons on the bonnet in her lap, the same he'd seen her wearing when she saw him at the press that first time.

And the second.

She didn't have the requisite clothing to attend many balls, he realized. Not in a crowd that considered wearing a spotless new frock to each event *de rigueur*.

Now he understood why her parents cultivated their reputation for oddity in preferring a backward, old-style fashions. It saved the outlay for the newer styles each season.

Locked in a stare-down with his daughter, Pettigrew blinked. "Immaterial," he said.

She raised an eyebrow, her jaw line pulsing almost as fast as the baron's. An angry Olivia might be someone to be reckoned with. He decided to help her along.

"I demand reparations," he said to her father.

Pettigrew turned on him, eyes shuttered.

"You want her?"

Olivia gasped.

"She has no dowry. Nothing to recommend her but her looks. Which should last. Her mother's have." Her father wiped his hands together as if washing his daughter out of his life.

Her eyes were oceans, the tears at the brim. Her lower lip trembled. She stood so still.

Will couldn't look at her anymore. He had been the brunt of many a pummeling by George and the girls, but he had never doubted his parents' affection. Their love.

It seemed Olivia had never had anything but doubts.

He pitied her. But he would not marry her. She had lied to him. He could now understand why, but that did not make it any more right. Pettigrew waved his fingers.

"Marsh, can you manage to keep our name out of this? I expect you must write something."

"A retraction, yes. I acknowledge that I was duped, by a mysterious gentleman, and not give credit where it's due?"

"Yes."

Will's own jaw set. "I could. But Cobbett will not. And I fear he has enough of the scent to ferret out the truth. Or just weave his own truth from whole cloth." His gaze turned to Olivia, then back to her father. "It would be better to acknowledge the error in the *Beacon* and be done with it."

"Never."

"You'd be open to even more criticism, accused of buying off the publisher to protect your family."

"Surely not. It is a piece of music, not legislation. It will blow over."

"As you wish. I leave it to you – or the lady – to tell the Duke of Wellington." That man thought little enough of the Press. This would only reinforce his bad opinion.

As it had Will's opinion of high-born, so-called ladies.

TWENTY-NINE

We have never and shall never suffer ourselves to be betrayed by our partialities, whatever they may be, into any expression of dissemblance or untruth. Need we put it plainer?
—The Beacon

Finally, Olivia was dismissed from that abyss of a sitting room. Papa at the fireplace, the place where he meted out every punishment. At twenty-five, she was appalled to find that seeing her father in that familiar position could bring all the old shame and wounds rushing back.

And this time Will joined him. She knew he would be angry, but he was worse. Granite was softer than the planes of his scowling face. For a moment, his mouth had seemed to soften, but those eyes that once seemed to see through her and yet find her worthy, now had turned to glass. His voice cut like ice on her burning nerves.

He'd heard Papa say those familiar, awful things. And Will

agreed with every one of them, of course. Olivia had no place in either of their lives. She had no place anywhere. Everywhere she was an imposter. A pretender.

It had always been so. But sometime over the past few years, she had lost the ability to pretend. It never had been easy, but she'd forced it into habit. And now, somehow, that habit had broken, and she wasn't sure she could rebuild it again. Fact was, she didn't wish to.

She wanted to stomp, and punch, and shriek. Loud and long. Instead she ran up the stairs and down the hall toward the sanctuary of the music room, ignoring Jaspers's calling at her back. She pushed open the door and threw herself into the room.

It was bare.

Swaying on her feet from the sudden stop, Olivia closed her eyes, disbelieving. But when she opened them again, nothing had changed.

All the air left the room. She collapsed against the wall, face turned toward where the piano should be.

"Miss Olivia." Jaspers was out of breath, too. "They took it away yesterday morning. He said these things would fetch more than the other sitting room would."

He knelt beside her. Taking her deadened hand in his, he rubbed gently, peering into her face. She couldn't bear to look at him, and turned away. The tears she had held back so long in the face of Papa's punishment flooded out.

"Leave me," she whispered.

"We'll get it back. The baron says one more push."

Always one more push. Olivia closed her eyes, resting her temple against the wall. "Go away."

Jaspers stood slowly. "I'll return in a spell." He touched the top of her head, patting it the way he used to when she was a child, tucking a stray lock behind her ear. Then, blessedly, he left.

Olivia gulped air. It did not reach her lungs. It was as if she were drowning, here on land.

Will had almost drowned. Now he would never speak to her again.

Merry had been her closest friend since Miss Manningly's finishing school. Now she would never speak to her again.

And Papa. Her one and only father would disown her before she brought scandal into the house. He had tried to trade her for Will's favor, as if that would ever work.

And the piano, her release, her confessor, her balm. Now it, too, was gone.

Olivia's head spun. It was no better when her eyes were open.

Then she remembered her music.

She scrambled to her knees, then her feet. On wobbly legs, she pushed herself toward the shelves built into the walls. She kept her scores and working-pieces stored in the space tucked under the piano bench. Surely the movers had not taken that.

But the shelves were empty. She looked frantically along the walls, in the corners.

Gone. All of it. Everything.

She dropped to the floor. Lying spread-eagle against the planking, she saw the gaping wound in the ceiling. They had even taken the chandelier. She covered her face with her hands, as emptied out as this room.

Everything about her, everything special, everything worthwhile, had been erased in a single afternoon. Like her brother, who had been born, then taken a day later. She had been born, but not taken until two-dozen years later. What was worse?

She must have dozed. Jaspers loomed over her, shaking her shoulder.

"Cook's made that tomato soup you like. It's ready in your room?"

"Why?"

Jaspers seemed confused by the question. "You must eat, miss. And I put some of your music things upstairs. To keep them safe."

Olivia sat up so quickly she nearly fainted again. Jaspers helped her to her feet and to take a few steps. Then he could not keep up with her as she raced through the door and up the back stairs. She shut the door on him.

The room smelled warmly of tomatoes. And the guitar lay on her bed, with its bag of accessories. Olivia sighed in relief. But the air choked off again when she saw her sheet music still was missing. She threw open the doors to her smaller wardrobe. The shelves sagged with books and stacks of music paper. She pulled out the top sheets; a snippet from last winter.

The final bit of starch in her spine melted. She sagged against the shelving. All her work from the spring was gone. On its way to some spinster's house, or to a family with small children. No one who would take a moment to look, really look, at the neatly tied bundles. Or the sloppily tied ones.

They would throw all of it in the trash, or, more likely, use it as kindling. The thought took the strength from her knees. She sank onto the floor.

No tears came. This was worse than tears could salve.

After a few long minutes, though, the aroma of the soup set her stomach growling. She hadn't eaten since the coaching inn early that morning. She rose, picked up the guitar and carried it to her chair. Pulling off her gloves, she stopped to drink a bit of the soup. Then she started running her fingers through the patterns Rosa had taught her. Slowly, carefully, every position, every note.

Because she had to concentrate on her fingers and the frets, it was not calming the way the piano was. So be it. She would concentrate. She would play. She would keep playing until she ceased to feel so transparent.

Or until she truly became a ghost.

Will kicked the door to his office shut, then strode to the mantel and kicked it, too. He did not kick the desk, it having fought back the last time. But he sat down hard on the chair.

How dare she? And such bald-faced lies?

It was his own fault. He knew better than to listen to a woman. A lady, so-called.

He picked up the quill. A correction. He had to write a damned correction. Like a schoolboy caught out in some hare-brained scheme, he had to write yes, Cobbett is right, I am a shill, a dupe, a buffoon. Please continue to purchase my paper.

He threw the quill down in disgust.

Just print the truth. But what was the blasted truth?

The truth was that women were as pernicious as poison ivy. It would be easy to write about how they teased you, taunted you, and then stomped all over you. How they were the meaner sex, under their frills and lovely scents and delicious tastes.

The trouble was, he could see exactly why she'd done it. Trapped like a butterfly in amber, Olivia was fixed into her only possible role, that of a beautiful object. She could not be allowed to upset the balance by having both beauty and talent, and she absolutely could not be allowed to outshine her ambitious parent or any of the men he wished to please.

If she had been typical *ton*, a Deidre, perhaps, he would have no compunction in sacrificing her petty cares to the greater goods of truth and objectivity. And if she were merely talented, he could easily have exposed her and been done with it.

But Olivia Delancey carried greatness in her. She could touch people's hearts with her music, translate their inner fears and joys into sound. Her music should be heard. It should be appreciated. Even loved.

But she should not have lied to him about it.

Will picked up the pen and tapped against the inkstand. He couldn't mention her, even as Miss D---. Too close to her father, and damned if Will didn't want a favor from that Machiavelli. Worse, he didn't want to hurt her, cause those robin's-egg blue eyes to brim with tears. Confounded idiocy. Wanting to help others, and please her father, was no excuse for deceiving him. He must keep telling himself that until he had rubbed her completely out of his good graces.

But what would he have done if she had told him the truth that day she appeared in his office? He'd like to think he would have at least listened to the music, but he knew himself better. He would have taken one look at her, with her fancy bonnet and shimmering ribbons, her hours-long hairstyle, her effect on his sub-editor, all that, and closed his mind to her without a note being sounded.

She was no fool. She'd convinced him the only way she could have, by pretending a man had done it. By lying.

He understood it completely, understood her. Perhaps, someday, he might forgive her. Someday, when the beating of his heart at last returned to normal. When his eyes stopped searching for glimpses of her, when his ears stopped angling to hear the cadences of her voice.

He leaned back and put his palms over his eyes, rubbing his fingers into his forehead. He'd already missed deadline. Tomorrow night, then, he'd run the rotted correction.

And blast the buggered lot of them. Starting with him.

Thirty

When will the truth be told? Did this mealy Army short-timer steal these ditties from a fellow soldier, wrenching the food from his widow and children? Or did he merely thieve it from some benighted composer on the Continent?
　　—The Register

After a sleepless night and an hour in the coach on a blistering August morning, Olivia was flagging as they reached the curving drive of the new-built manor that now housed her piano. The red brick square of the building looked mature, but the columns for the portico lay in a stack beside the porch. As she stepped up the entry stairs, she wondered what it would be like to live in a place so new. All her homes had been in the family for at least six generations, every corner redolent of history. But now, some of those very furnishings were starting a new life here, among all this fresh history.

She never dreamed they would sell the piano. And who

could have guessed the movers would cart away her scores? She would never have let them.

But she had not been here.

Now Olivia knew why she had been sent to Plymouth. To frighten Aunt Betsy into taking more economies, of course. And to be gone when her soul was spirited away from her home.

She did not blame her parents. They always hoped to avoid unpleasant scenes. Olivia had used that to her advantage more than a few times, most notably her tantrum over marrying a politician. But all those times added together did not come close to equaling this betrayal.

Jaspers had dug through the rat's nest of her father's desk to find the bill of sale, written out so poorly she couldn't read the name and could barely make out the ill-formed address. Must have been sold to a political crony, who would not wish a clear accounting. She prayed the address, at least, was true. She couldn't dawdle, as her father needed the coach in a few hours' time.

Jaspers had insisted she wear her wrap. "It's warm, but the dust is up." His hands rested on her shoulders a second longer than necessary. She turned to look at him, his hang-dog face even lower than usual.

"I am so sorry, miss. We all in the kitchen could hear you, and we did love to listen." He clasped her hand in his. "It were an honorable thing you did, giving it away like that, to that deserving man." He shrugged. "What else could you do?"

"You'll not tell anyone else?"

He stiffened, took his hands away. "Of course not. We've kept far worse secrets, that's for sure."

Olivia, ashamed at her sudden wave of panic, reached out

and grasped Jaspers's upper arm. She didn't want to frighten him with a more-extreme gesture.

"Thank you. Thank everyone."

"You have people here, miss. Don't you forget it."

She wilted in the sun and heat as the coachman knocked on the unroofed door of the two-storey house. In the full minute it took for the surprised housekeeper to answer it, Olivia's throat tightened as if it were circled by a noose. She touched it to be sure it wasn't.

Fortunately, the family was not at home. She explained her business to the mob-capped matron, a not-unfriendly woman who seemed to understand her muddle of words and excuses.

Leaving the coachman with the horses, she followed the sprightly matron up the hall stairs. "Quite a surprise, a piano," the woman said. "I did not know the young master to play." As they gained the landing, she turned to wink at Olivia. "But perhaps there's a young lady he fancies who does. Wouldn't that be well."

Down the hall to the back of the house, she could see the house overlooked a low, rolling hill, falling to a small brook. So peaceful.

"Aye, the mother – may she rest in peace – she loved this view, though she saw it from the floor below. She couldn't climb the stairs."

Olivia nodded politely if impatiently, the cool of the plain white and dark wood of the interior bringing her mind back to the reason she was here. Finally, they were through the door to the large parlor, and she saw her piano. For the first time in a day, her heart started beating its simple, steady pattern.

She rushed to its bench onto her knees in front of it. Taking a deep breath, she lifted the lid.

It was all there.

She propped the lid up, and rested the side of her head on the pages. She closed her eyes, thanking the heavens for blessing her benighted self by the return this treasure.

"An odd position for an artist, Miss Delancey."

Her head snapped up, dizzyingly, and she turned toward the voice.

Mr. Bragge? Before her racing heart closed off her throat entirely, she managed to croak out, "You live here?"

In the doorway she had come through, he leaned against the jamb, arms crossed.

"Come to steal something else from my boss?" He said it in a jovial tone, but his dark eyes were hard.

This was Will's house? The woman who had enjoyed the view his mother? Why would Will Marsh need a piano? Why hers? She covered her eyes with her hand to stop her head's spinning.

Of course. He was currying favor with Papa to gain that empty seat in Commons. But surely Papa knew how much the instrument meant to her. Did he intend to sell her along with it?

He'd as much as said so last night.

But he'd made a grave mistake. Will would have none of her now. He wouldn't even want the piano, her treasured and most-stalwart friend. Perhaps he would cart it up and hand it over to Mr. Bentley. Or make kindling of it. He could do what he pleased. And he certainly wouldn't wish to please her.

"Miss Delancey?"

She spread her fingers and through them. Mr. Bragge hadn't

moved, though his raised eyebrow and turned-down mouth spoke volumes. She owed him some explanation, at least.

She gestured at the piano, "This used to be mine. My family's. I had left some pages in the bench and came to retrieve them. They are of no use to anyone." She quickly pulled the pages out, stuffing them into the bag she'd brought.

"Ah, there you are wrong, my sweet lady." From his vest, loosened in the heat of the day, he pulled out a page of music with smudges and cross-outs. "If I am not mistaken, this is an early attempt at our notorious march." He waved the paper in the air, then speared her with a glance. "Am I mistaken?"

She didn't need to see the paper to be sure. "No," she whispered. Her knees shook, her hands shook, her world was shaking. With Mr. Bragge mounting a charge, Will would have to expose her, and himself. She would be shunned. No lady would associate with a professional artisan, which everyone knew meant no better than a tradesman, really.

Worse, Will would never talk to her again.

"Now there is your problem." Bragge unlocked his posture and ambled toward her. "If you wish to lie successfully, you must persist in it. Hold your head high and say only the lie, again and again. No matter the evidence, a passionate enough lie can often beat it." He handed her the page. "Especially when the evidence is as flimsy as this." She saw at a glance it wasn't even music, but some text he must be composing.

"Let's have some lemonade, shall we?" He took her elbow, bringing her to her feet, and led her to a sturdy chair by one of the tall windows. He bellowed toward the hall. Olivia could hear the skitter of feet.

Bragge sat in the seat beside her. His girth made her old loveseat look out of normal proportion.

He did not look angry now. More like an uncle sent in to heal the wound after the father had administered a beating.

"Why do you look at me like that?"

He smiled sadly. "So beautiful. And so foolish. And you nearly got away with it. More fools, us."

Neither said anything as a maid brought in a pitcher of lemonade and poured out two glasses.

"I did not set out to 'get away with it.' I just wanted to help my friends."

"That is all?" His smile told her he knew every one of her secrets.

"I did want people to hear my music. I wanted to know if it was as good as I thought it was. I wanted," she spread her hands out, "to make something of myself. Even if it had to be in secret." She bit her lower lip. "But that has all changed now."

"How?"

"Father has given away my piano. I can no longer compose."

"Dramatic enough for the stage, m'dear."

"It feels that way. Plus," she stopped.

"Plus?"

"I find it hurts even more to have squandered Will's friendship. Mr. Marsh's. He sees me, understands me."

"I think not, Miss Delancey. Nor you him. Otherwise this would not have happened."

"It happened before I knew him."

"And there was no moment since when you could have come clean?" He could turn her from comfortable to anxious in a moment.

"It was working so well."

"So. You were perfectly willing to build a – friendship – on false pretenses."

"Put it that way," she said.

"It was ill-done, however one puts it." He leaned back in the chair, twining his fingers behind his head. "But not fatal."

Bragge leaned deeper into the seat. He looked out the window for a moment. Olivia tried to read his face, ruddy with weather and cares. His gaze snapped back to hers. "How much does this matter to you?"

"A great deal?"

He frowned at her answer, watching her. Reading her.

"Everything." She had to look away, her hands crushing the top of the satchel.

"Truly?"

"I can't see that it matters." She let loose her grip. He mustn't see how important Will was to her. It was too late by far.

"Of course it does." He ran his hands through his curls, exasperation in his voice. "What are you willing to do to make things right with Will?"

Was it possible? She had to think. She took up her lemonade and sipped it. She must not harm the family. She must not bring wrong attention to herself. She must not be herself. She must not be.

He took her silence as an answer. "I see," he said ominously.

"No. It's not that," she said. "You're right." She knew she wasn't making sense, and his raised brow confirmed it.

"Refreshingly honest. Doesn't love make idiots of us all."

That stopped her. Was she in love?

Well, of course. No wonder it burned her to her soul to have disappointed him. Small wonder that everything she thought was reflected in the next thought by "Will wouldn't approve" or "What would Will think?" She needed more time to consider.

Or perhaps she'd had too much time, and simply needed to feel.

That afternoon with Will had changed her, and she'd thought it might have changed him, too. And after that night, she could not go back to sleep, pretending to be the perfect lady, even if she wished to. He spoke to her mind, her heart, her soul.

He understood her. And now he understood what she'd done to him. The why didn't matter. You do not hurt those you love, at least not on purpose. But she had.

Love. That explained the horror of seeing his disappointment, the wretchedness at his disapproval. She'd always known she might be found out, and thought she could face the scandal. What she couldn't face was the pain of broken trust and hope. A hope she'd never dreamed of when she cooked up this rancid scheme.

"Miss Delancey, won't you come back to me?" Bragge's wheedle broke into her reverie, dragging her back to the present. It felt like a long journey. "Excellent. Here's a thought: If one were interested in reconciling with the publisher of a daily journal, say, one might start by offering to bare one's breast. So to speak."

"You mean, take out a public notice?"

"Or offer to sit for a formal interview."

"Declare myself?"

"If you cannot be truthful with him, with whom can you be

truthful?" He leaned in closer, patting her knee. "Isn't it time, really, to let go this secret? It harms you, it hurts him."

"But my family."

"Who is more important? And it's possible that Will can become a part of your family."

"Papa wants him for the Commons seat."

"That, too. Come now, Miss Delancey. It's not like you to be so slow."

"I'm tired." Her lids were half-closed now. It was all too much. And what did it matter? She could not do what Bragge suggested, even if it did sound wise. The whole thing was hopeless.

Bragge rose from his chair. He gently pulled her out of the hard chair and onto the familiar loveseat. "Rest now. I must return to town, but I'll leave instructions for Mrs. Dawkins to wake you in an hour."

As she heard him leave the room, Olivia closed her eyes. But that opened her mind. She could not smell Will here, especially with the trace of Bragge's scent lingering. But she felt him in the house. His spirit somehow combined with her piano and the familiar scent of the sofa. She had slept on its cushions so many times, between bursts at the piano.

This time, she fell. Past the depth where her music flowed, past the depth where she held her lost brother. She fell so fast, and so deeply, it frightened her. Except the fear was on that higher level, and she was far lower.

As she fell, she saw a light coming closer. She entered a pure space, bright and clean, like a fog in heaven.

She was not alone; the ache of solitude had lifted. She lifted her hand to look at it. It glowed white, not clear, translucent.

She realized she felt safe here. Safe enough to ask questions? Yes.

Her parents, her friends. Merry and Martin. Mr. and Mrs. Buckham. Jaspers, both father and son. Aunt Betsy. Cook and Sarah, the maid. Will, Mr. Bentley, and Mr. Bragge, who had just been here. Even Mr. Cobbett.

None were evil, but none wanted for her what she wanted for herself.

And what was that? A career? Not exactly. A life, lived the way she wanted. Publishing music that people would buy not because it was a freakish piece of art done by a woman but because they liked it.

Living a quiet life, without worrying about other people mismanaging their funds. Sharing her days with someone who understood her and still loved her.

Someone like Will.

In the dream, tears flowed down her face. Not bitter, not angry, but full of regret. She could picture the life she had lost, and by her own hand. No room in this white room for self-deception.

Will might have understood why she had done what she did, but she had not even given him the chance. She had shut him out.

What she wouldn't give to do it all again. She would not have strayed one step from the truth. Will might not have published her name, even then. He would have taken the decision on himself. Instead, she took it from him, leaving him powerless to control the fate of his own paper, the business he had rebuilt with his own hands and heart. The only thing he could not live without.

She had failed him. And herself.

"Livvie." She felt a hand smoothing down her hair. A finger traced up the track of a tear, stemming the next one. She shuddered in a breath and opened her eyes.

Will, wild-eyed and windblown, knelt at her side. "You were sobbing in your sleep."

Sitting up slowly, she blinked to clear her vision of tears and chase the cobwebs of dream away. Then she realized he was here, his hand falling from her face and resting on the cushion.

Without thinking who else could see, she threw her arms around him. She breathed in his scent through the soft hitches in her breath.

He wrapped her loosely in his embrace. When her breathing returned to closer to normal, he let go. He held her face between his hands. "Why are you here?"

Her eyes flicked toward the piano. "I needed my music."

His face clouded. "Right." He rolled back onto his heels, about to rise.

"No." She reached for him, pulled him to sit beside her. "I didn't know it was your house."

"Rather clever of your father, wasn't it?"

"I don't understand."

"Your heart is where your instrument is."

"Not my heart, my soul. My heart is with you." Some of the storm lifted from his brow, but the sun did not reach his eyes. He didn't believe her. "You distrust your ears?"

"I don't know if I can play second fiddle to an inanimate object." He turned to her, mock concern in his eyes. "What if you find a finer instrument, and leave us both?"

"You've left already," she said, her voice flat.

He closed his eyes. She watched the emotions storm under the skin of his face. He took in a deep breath, held it for what seemed like eternity. She searched for something to say, something that would tilt the balance in her favor. Silence was all she came up with. And faith.

Finally he exhaled. "Olivia," as if her name was a benediction, "what are your intentions?"

"What must I do?"

"What do you wish to do?"

"Stay here. With you." She gripped his clasped hands, and called on all the coquettishness she'd once had as the beauty of the Season. It did not come to her call; her lips, instead of pursing prettily, merely wobbled.

"I cannot let you do it." Perhaps sadness, perhaps regret, laced his voice. "You'd ruin your reputation, and your family's. I will not ruin you, whatever you may have done to me."

"Let me make amends. I know you enjoy—" Her mouth suddenly dry, she swallowed to continue. "My body."

He gripped her hand. She winced. He turned the hand over, saw the blood where the guitar strings had drawn blisters and cracks the night before. He brought the tips to his lips. Watching her with too-somber eyes, he planted the softest of kisses on each finger tip. She shuddered. Such lost opportunity.

"I enjoy more than your body, Olivia Delancey. But you are your father's daughter. Your scheming drew harm down on my paper, not least my person."

"Your reputation."

His lips twitched almost into a smile. "It turns out my reputation can survive it. But my heart cannot. I bought this furniture thinking you would like it if you came to live with me. I thought I was being foolish, because what lady would want to marry such as I? But I find the real reason I was a fool because it is I who do not wish to marry such a lady."

She couldn't cry. She couldn't breathe. He was right to hate her. He never would forgive her.

She had to get away from here, from him. Get out of his sight, and bury herself far away and forever. She snatched her bag, filled with what she had thought was the most important thing in the world to her.

She'd been wrong about that, too.

THIRTY-ONE

The twopenny Register *seeks to create a tempest in the smallest of teapots. If its publisher can find no real news to report, perhaps he should cease publication until Parliament returns to session. It's High Season down at his farm, after all.*
　—The Beacon

The next day, Olivia rose as the church bells rang noon. Sleep had eluded her until nearly daybreak, when exhaustion won out. But as she came downstairs, ready for nothing but a quiet pot of cocoa, she saw a flurry of activity in the entry hall.

"Isn't it wonderful, Livvie." Her mother, decked out as if for her court come-out thirty years earlier, spun in a circle. The small boat perched on top of the vertical waves of her hair teetered dangerously.

Olivia eyed the wide panniers of Mama's skirts as she came closer to kiss her good morning. "What, Mama?"

"The Ministry of the Exchequer." She clasped her hands together, gaze to the ceiling. Olivia looked up. The chandelier was missing.

"Papa gained a position?"

Mama returned her gaze to Olivia. Grinning, she grasped her hands and pulled her into a swinging circle. For a moment, Olivia was a child again, playing ring-of-roses with her beautiful mama.

"At last, we can stop economizing. It was that last push that did it. I think I'll name it the pianoforte-push."

"I wish you would not."

"But dear heart, you cannot go looking like that." Her mother stopped twirling, though her wide skirt kept on for a half-circle, bumping Olivia on the hip.

"Go where?"

"The installation ceremony. We await the carriage."

"He is to be installed already?" Such a ceremony usually took weeks to plan and carry off. No one usually was in such a hurry.

"Must be today. There is some debate or officious whatnot where it would be advantageous for Pettigrew to be exchequer." She shrugged. "Isn't it marvelous!" She clapped her hands together. A shadow crossed her eyes when Olivia did not join her, but it quickly dissipated as they heard a familiar tread on the stair. Mama turned and raised her clapping hands, serenading him as he skip-stepped toward them.

From the top of his powdered gray wig to the tips of his silvered heels, the Baron Pettigrew was a monochrome marvel. Olivia wondered bitterly how much of her piano had paid for this apparition.

"Don't touch me," he said. "Powder." Mama hugged herself instead. They shared a smile so strong Olivia thought she saw the beam of light between them. Or perhaps that was the sunlight through the opening door.

As her father turned to look toward the door, their gazes met.

"Olivia. You do not wish to share this joyous day with us?"

"This is the first I am hearing of it, Papa."

"Right. You weren't to supper. You should really tell cook beforehand. Then she won't need to make three dishes."

"No need to think like that anymore," Mama took his arm, but gently, not to disturb any of his shiny ornament. "We can all have two dishes now."

"Just as you say, my love." He led her toward the door, as if they were the heads of a small country. Jaspers opened it with the daintiest of flourishes.

They paused at the threshold and looked toward each other. Mama turned back to Olivia.

"Livvie, you don't allow that woman to wait upon you?"

She looked past him to see Rosa Avery at the base of the stair. "I do, Mama. She's family."

"No relation of ours. She performs for money."

"A trained monkey," Papa said.

Rosa must have heard them, though she gave no sign. Olivia concentrated her anger at the ship sailing Mama's false hair. "She is my guest. She comes to call on me alone."

The baron glared at her. "We shall discuss this tonight." He turned back toward the door. She lifted her chin, then remembered that was what Papa always did, and lowered it again.

Rosa, curls tamed by a blood-red kerchief, waited as they

promenaded down the stairs, faces averted from her. Then she stormed up the stairs and into the hall, mouth set.

Rosa. Yet another entertainment to cancel. Another person to disappoint. Olivia followed her with heavy tread down the hall to the only remaining furnished sitting room.

"Where is your guitar?" Rosa stalked the room as if it were too small for her. Olivia realized she was taller than the pacing woman. Odd that she had not seen that earlier.

She held up her hand, trying to halt the pacing. It did do that, but caused Rosa to rush to directly in front of her instead. She grasped Olivia's wrist, turning the hand so she could see the tips of her fingers.

"Too much of the practice."

Olivia desperately wished to pull away, but even now, with all in shambles, she must not act impolitely. Not be her parents. She tried to explain. "I cannot have lessons anymore."

"Of course not." Rosa nodded. "I have come for to tell you this."

Olivia's head spun a moment. "I do not understand."

"We are going on the tour!"

"Your family is coming over?"

"We start in Plymouth, no? Three days, and they are here." She let go of Olivia's hand and clapped hers together. "Avery says you have done it all. We must thank you."

"He's all yours," Olivia said, trying to keep the irony out of her voice.

"But why are we in this room, today?" Rosa looked about her as if seeing it for the first time. "You could play for me one of your musics."

"What musics?"

"You cannot fool another composer," Rosa set her hands on her hips. "I know your style now. I can hear it in those pieces in the papers."

Olivia's heart fluttered in her throat. "Who else knows?" she whispered, her hand gently touching her collarbone.

"Do not worry," Rosa said, pulling her onto the couch, redolent of Mama's rose-water scent. "I know it must be secret. These Englishmen," she said the word as if it were an expletive, "they are so frightened, like little boys."

Olivia had not thought of the men of her acquaintance as frightened boys, but it made sense. Rosa watched her, and apparently judging when Olivia had come around to her way of thinking, plunged in again.

"You must come with us. Get out of this house."

"With you?"

"As our piano player. It would, too, be proper," she said as Olivia's brows rose. "Avery is related to you. Safe as houses."

Olivia pressed her lips together. She couldn't possibly.

But why not? To be part of a family of musicians. What she'd always wanted. Here it was, offered up on a platter.

Nothing held her here. Her parents wished her well and gone. Merry and Martin, as well. As for Will, he would be the most glad to see the back of her.

She could not bear to be in the same city as he was. It was hard enough to read the paper. Even in the morning's paper, which she'd read at four o'clock, she recognized his way of phrasing.

Every tall, well-shouldered man on the street could be him. Her heart would lurch, then see it was not him, and sink. She was heart-sore just from walking the park.

Why not run away and join, if not the circus, a pack of passionate musicians? If the fearsome Rosa thought her good enough to share with her family, what could stop them?

She nodded. "A stellar idea."

Rosa's smile, the one she usually saved for men, burst out. "Yes? I am so relieved."

"Why?"

"Avery said I could not persuade you, because my English is poor. But you did the persuading. It is so easy for me." She leapt up. "I must be getting ready. One day, and we leave. When will you meet us?"

"The day after." Olivia's face set. "I must be getting ready, as well."

She needed to pack, but first send a note to Aunt Betsy, warning her of her return.

But before all that, she must go to the offices of the *Beacon*. She had an apology to make.

She would come clean to Will. That would fix things for Merry and Martin. Her leaving the city would help fix things for her father. People would think he sent his odd, spinster daughter away to rusticate.

It also would fix things, as much as could be possible, for herself. The Plymouth house still held a piano. And Olivia's recent income would add to the pot. Perhaps they could see a show or two each week, and have beef on Sunday.

Best of all, she thought as she changed her blood-flecked white gloves for clean taupe ones, it was the musical opportunity of a lifetime. From masters of the *guitarra*, she would learn so much technique, hear so much new music. It might be another finishing school for her, except in music instead of prancing and pouring tea.

Her heart leapt at the idea, all except that small leaden anchor at its center. Nothing she could do about that, she thought as her poor, footsore errand-boy opened the door for her again. Will was as good as dead to her.

His heart certainly was.

Thirty-Two

It has been the constant trick of the Corsican Brigand whenever he has got his companions into a scrape, to leave them in it, and seek his own safety by flight. In Egypt, in the Moscow expedition, and at Waterloo, such was his conduct. Could the bleeding Beacon's perfidious publisher follow in his footsteps?

—The Register

"An eventful weekend, Mr. Purdy?" Mr. Swizzlewit seemed in his usual good cheer as Martin settled behind the spare desk. He was ever grateful to the man he replaced, Simmons, for insisting the assistants' chairs be standard height.

"In truth, sir, there is something I'd like to speak with you about."

"We'll need to clean up that grammar before you write my correspondence, my boy, but for now let's have at it." His employer walked toward him, his torso rocking side to side a bit with every step.

"Yes, well, there's been a change in my status. I thought it right to inform you."

"Got married, did you, boy? Well done. Best to do it on the cheap, be the lady amenable to the idea."

Martin cleared his throat. This couldn't be harder than that scene with Merry had been. "Rather the opposite, sir. I fear any marriage of mine is nowhere near imminent." He fingered the papers on his desk, only his for the past week, though Simmons already was on his way to Plymouth. "I fear the postponement may be permanent."

Swizzlewit leaned against the side of his desk, his armpit near the countertop. "Called it off, did you?"

"She has found a flaw with me, and if I cannot convince her it can be mended, she will call it off." He looked deep into the older man's kindly eyes. "And I'm not inclined to convince her otherwise."

"I see. Your flaw – it is related to Olivia's musical scheme?"

Martin nodded. Watching his Merry storm at poor Olivia Delancey on Saturday had opened his eyes. Merry hadn't lifted a finger to help him find work. She was tired of his tiredness, and scornful of his wounds. In her experience, she said, people picked themselves up after a decent interval – say, a week or two – and got on with their lives.

"It's simple," she had said during tea that evening when they were alone for a blessed minute or two. "Olivia lied, and you paid the price. We both did. She is no true friend."

"But we would not even be engaged without her. That tune is what has paid for my training, as well as that necklace."

Merry had grasped at the pear dangling from her neck as if she expected him to rip it away at any moment. "That may be. But did she have to do it like this?"

"How else? How would you have done it?"

"Without deception, for one." She had shivered as if playing Ophelia to the high balconies.

"Meredith Buckham. Our entire courtship was built on lies. Did you not attend on Miss Delancey under false pretences, and spend whole afternoons with me while telling your mother you were with her alone?"

"Oh that." Merry had waved a hand, dangerously near to tipping her cup on the small table beside her. "I merely left an unimportant detail out."

"Exactly what Miss Olivia has done."

"Nothing like." Merry had slapped his hand, a playful-looking gesture that stung. "And if you continue to take her side, I shall consider this engagement over. Why, Martin, you act as if you were engaged to her instead."

Had her misunderstanding been willful or genuine? Martin had feared the former, though the latter would be no good reflection on her, either. She was just a child, he saw. Nothing, no war, had ever forced her to grow up.

"Merry, we are none of us saints."

"Speak for yourself."

Martin rubbed his eyes, trying to wipe the past back into its place and return to the present. It eased his heart to talk of it to someone, even his mildly threatening pint-sized employer. "Not that I blame her, or either of them."

"Help can sometimes go so awry."

"Miss Delancey may well have done us a favor. For my part,

anyway, it's right to wait."

Swizzlewit dug into his vest and pulled out a pocket-watch. Glancing at the clock on the mantel, he altered the time on his watch and started to wind it. "Did not you tell me you lived with your in-laws?"

"That's my other trouble." Mr. Buckham would surely to see the back of him, now if not sooner.

"Simmons stayed at the rectory with his father the reverend. Won't do as well for you."

He glanced up at Martin, then back to his timepiece. "Well, it's not much done in law-circles, but many apprentices in other careers room with their masters. Mrs. Swizzlewit and I are on our own now, with the girls up and grown. We could use someone with your, ah, altitude, around our humble patch. You'd have to agree to walk Bartleby around the park from time to time."

He wasn't fired? For the first time in weeks, perhaps months, Martin felt the possibilities of this life might outweigh its detriments. "Of course, sir. I thank you."

The solicitor replaced the timepiece in his pocket and crossed his arms. "Don't mention it. Now, one of the first rules of a solicitor's work is confidentiality. We don't speak of what we see or hear unless a client wishes us to."

He pushed himself away from Martin's desk and toddled toward his office. "For example, a lady, arriving alone and unaccompanied, in ten minutes' time."

On entering Mr. Swizzlewit's offices, Olivia found Martin Purdy in place of Mr. Simmons. She nodded to him cautiously, unsure of her reception, but he jumped to his feet and bowed deeply. And then smiled.

"Mr. Purdy. At least one part of my scheme has succeeded, I see."

"Our scheme, ma'am. And I thank you." His face did not carry quite so many shadows, and he had shaved, but his hair still flopped across his brow.

"I trust Merry is well. I am sorry to have disappointed her."

"Aye, that I've done, as well. But at least we are wiser now." His lopsided smile caught her off-guard. She hadn't seen it since Napoleon escaped Elba. "And we know there is more to life than love."

She was not sure she did know that. "Do you think so?"

"No." He had to admit that, chuckling to himself. "But I don't regret what happened. Have this new place, don't I? And it showed me that Merry was in love with her picture of a man, not the real one in front of her."

"She could change."

"She may well," he said, but did not look convinced.

The solicitor waved her into the inner office, where it took only a few moments to explain what she wanted. Then she had to explain it again.

Mr. Swizzlewit gaped at her. "I can't have heard you right."

"Your ears are perfectly fine." She drew in another long breath. "I am twenty-five now, and coming into my inheritance from my grandfather."

"As well as your gift from your godparents. Both together aren't that much."

"But which, added to my recent earnings, should be enough to settle me in a small house somewhere, with two servants."

"If they are day-help."

"One servant, then. Until my music picks up."

"I cannot recommend this, Miss Olivia. As your godfather, I wish I could forbid it."

"If I remain at home, my father will take control of my funds. And we both know what that will mean."

"But things have changed now."

"Have they? We won't need to spend more to earn more, just as always?"

Mr. Swizzlewit paused, then shook his head sadly. His hair didn't reach to his collar any more. "It is a bad thing in children to know their parents too well."

"Let us begin searching for a suitable place now. I shall sound out my friends. Perhaps there is another lady in similar straits."

"Must the situation be in London? Your funds would go further in Bath. Or Plymouth. Perhaps your aunt would prefer to live in a home with furnishings, for example."

"It would be harder to sell my music from Plymouth."

"But not impossible. Especially if you had an advocate."

"Like you?"

"I handled your Mr. Marsh well enough." His smile faded in the face of her crashing frown.

"Far better than I." She clasped her hands in her lap, the sore tips of her fingers pulsing in protest.

"My dear child. Why did you hide the truth from him?"

"Oh, it all sounds so stupid when one says it aloud."

"I cannot believe it would sound that way to me. I love you, girl. I know you don't hurt people."

"How was I to know he was not like other publishers? A hold of rats, that's what people call Printers' Row."

"And you found the only eagle."

She shrugged, mostly to keep herself from crying. "You are right. I will go to Plymouth. Aunt Betsy will take me in. And her Mr. Delancey."

"He's still clanging his chains about, then?" Swizzlewit's laugh boomed as if he were a living little kettle drum.

She couldn't bear to look at him, with his loving eyes. Did she not carry enough shame as it was?

"Olivia. Might I offer one more piece of advice? Not as a godfather, merely a friend."

She chanced another look at him. He dripped pity. Quickly looking away, she nodded.

"You are so unhappy. Is it really wise to run away?"

"I cannot live with my parents any longer. They cannot even remember my birthday."

"This is not about your blessed mama and papa. You are well used to them. It is someone else. Must you run away from him?"

"He won't have me."

"Are you sure?"

Now the tears came, softly and silently. Swizzlewit leaned over his desk to hand her his handkerchief. "A publisher's wife must be equally above reproach, he said."

"But he is no longer a publisher."

"He lost the paper?" Her heart bled for him.

"Oh no. The paper is strong. We paid the last of the note this morning. And he's still publisher. But he is giving up the day-to-day operation. Mr. Bentley takes it on."

A wisp of hope, as faint as the spark from a soggy flint, rose in her chest. "Bentley?"

"And Will takes over Mr. Mellon's seat in Commons, if all goes well."

"A politician?"

"Exactly." He winked at her. "And what sort of wife does a politician need?"

One like her.

Perhaps if she could start to make amends, perhaps in a few years he would be persuaded she was truly trustworthy. It was too much to hope.

And first she had to make amends.

THIRTY-THREE

In Plymouth, Lord Keith presented the former emperor not with the passport to America he had requested, but one-way passage, no return, to the isle St. Helena. The Bellerophon is to weigh anchor and join the Northumberland, which will bear le petit tyrant away, one trusts this time for ever.

—The Beacon

N o one lounged outside the *Beacon*'s offices this time when Olivia and her little errand-boy arrived. The sky was dark, threatening a summer storm. Best to get this over with, she thought as she pushed open the door, leaving the boy again to sit on the stoop.

The bell over the door sounded in the empty room. She paced back and forth in the shadowed space, with its smells of ink and paper and few candles, before anyone appeared. It was the thin man, Mr. Bentley.

"Miss Delancey," he nodded a bow. "I regret that Mr. Marsh

is unavailable at the moment." He did not look as if he regretted it at all. His hands, resting on the big bench of a counter, made a triangle of him, with his head at the top. He didn't scowl or sneer, but something in his expression told her he disapproved of her.

"I do not require Mr. Marsh to complete this business. You will do just as well."

Now his eyebrows shot up, as if he had formed a bellows with his hands and pushed them there. He waited for her to speak.

She took a wavering breath, and started in. "I would like to take out an advertisement. I started to write it out, but I was hoping you might assist me. I'm not sure of the cost, as well." She pulled the sheet out of her bag. Another sheet came with it, lilting to the floor. He leaned over to see it, then sniffed.

"More music? Haven't we had far too much of that?"

"It's not for you. Just the advert."

Bentley read it through quickly. "This won't do."

"Should I make it longer? Shorter?"

"It should be another form altogether." He looked back up at her, measuring. "What is your purpose in writing it?"

"First, to clear Martin Purdy of any wrongdoing. He is completely innocent."

He nodded. "And?"

"And, to clear the *Beacon*, as much as I can, of all charges of collusion in this matter."

"We're not criminals, then, merely idiots?"

"Isn't that better?" she asked.

He pursed his lips. "And?"

"And." She stopped. How could she tell this man, this

stranger, that her heart, her health, depended on the good will of his employer?

He waited for her, arms and hands back in the triangle formation, her paper trapped under his left hand.

"Is not that enough?" She hated the pleading tone in her voice.

"If you say so." He did not sound convinced. But at least he pushed the page out to look over again.

Of course, as a news-man, he would expect the whole story. And wasn't telling half the truth what had gotten her in this trouble in the first place? But he was so stiff, so proper. He would judge her ill. He already had.

But was she not changing her ways to the good? How strong was she, really, if the first scarecrow of a judge made her quake to a stop?

She was weak. Too weak. The admission stung, but as the silence stretched in the dusty, dim, paper-draped office, she faced the deepest truth.

She was a coward.

Steps sounded in the hall. Mr. Bentley turned toward the sound.

"Miss Delancey!" Mr. Bragge came into view, his salt-and-pepper curls tumbling wildly. "Such a pleasant surprise."

He bustled through the space in the counter to greet her, reaching out as if to embrace her but at the last moment deciding on a firm handshake. His eyes, with their sunburst lines on the edges, drew her in. And drew her out.

"Oh, Mr. Bragge," she said in a rush. "Will hates me, and I can't bear it, and I wish to run this advert." She gestured toward Mr. Bentley, who had taken a short step back from the counter as if it had caught on fire. "And I don't know if it's the right way to write it or if it's the right things to say or anything, but if I don't do anything, I know for sure that will be wrong." She had to take a breath. "It's hopeless, isn't it?"

Mr. Bragge looked as if he were about to sneeze, or perhaps laugh. He caught himself, either way. "Dire, indeed, my dear. But it's always direst just before the dawn."

Behind the counter, Mr. Bentley groaned. "I was going to suggest to Miss Delancey that we do an interview and profile instead."

She frowned in confusion. Wasn't that what they called the story they published about Martin? "But that would not clear the paper."

Bragge thumped his palm on his chest. "The *Beacon* is no wilting flower, to be damaged by a small slippered foot's tread upon it. I believe that the estimable Mr. Bentley's idea has merit. Would you like him to do the interview?"

Bentley took another step back, hands up. "Oh no. You are by far the best interviewer."

"But I wrote the first piece. I might misunderstand again."

"Nonsense." Bentley cleared his throat. "You are the only person to do it. In the dining room. She can play the new piece she brought, as well."

Bragge shrugged. His eyes danced, and Olivia knew that Bentley had been played. And likely she had as well.

She could not object to the jolly man's manipulation. He was only doing what she had done to him first.

She prayed that his game, whatever it was, would help her, too.

Will kicked at a rat scurrying across his path and missed. Add clumsiness to the list of his failings, along with imbecility. Last night, he'd spent too much time at the house in Berkshire, mooning about after Olivia ran out on him, and nearly missed deadline. Now he couldn't even complete a head-clearing walk without clogging it up again with thoughts of her.

He could now see why it was considered inappropriate for a single man to meet a single lady not his relation in the intimacy of a sitting room. They might discover they love each other, the ultimate idiocy.

Why was he living way out there in the first place? So he could be seen in the neighborhood, and advance his station. It was one of the asinine steps in this dance to become elected. The votes would be secured at the ale-house and the dining rooms of the handful of powerful men in this county. But the appearances needed to be made for the common folk.

Will had not caught onto that until he reached university. He never understood why well-spoken men the likes of Angus Hawksbury and Miles O'Keefe had not won election after the fiery speeches they gave had stirred up the crowd. The crowd one needed to stir up did not much stir outside.

He did want this seat in Commons. He wanted to make changes in the laws, not merely complain when they were not made. To improve the living of tenant farmers, not shout out loudly when they lost their farms.

That was the problem with Cobbett. He was all bloviation, mere words. While the man might convince the rabble, the peers could put his paper down and listen to the man smoking a cigar next to them at the club. Will wanted to be that man. The persuasive one.

His words had made a difference once. Bentley had reported that a younger member of Pettigrew's crew had once read a *Beacon* editorial verbatim during a debate. "Quite effective," his laconic sub-editor had pronounced. Now Will wanted to be the one giving the speech.

First, though, he had to solve the problem with the second press. Steam leaked from somewhere, and it was smearing the print. Then, his brother. His eldest girl had married the dolt who impregnated her, but the younger's swain had bolted before the altar.

On the hot-dust streets, good, hard-working people bought and sold, carried packages, chatted with a neighbor. When a toddler lost his footing on the walking planks, Will swerved and caught him before he fell into the road. His mother retrieved him with a grateful smile.

Children. He shook his head, confusing the maid crossing the path in front of him. He had only just started thinking about having a babe, and George's children had catapulted ahead of him. Now he had the house, a safe home free from the soot and smell of Printer's Row. But he had lost the only woman he'd consider making them with.

Nearing his turn, he could smell the mulched paper and ink that meant home. The country was his future, but this silty, drafty nook would always hold a chunk of his affection. He smiled grimly, his mind chattering on. Then he frowned.

Would not Olivia Delancey still be a politically astute choice? Her father seemed keen enough on the idea of his taking her on. The man could not have been completely blind to what Olivia's piano meant to her.

And lord, did Will love her. Her too-wise-already eyes. Her sharp mind, darting to the right conclusion before her companion had warmed to his argument. How she helped him suss out George, reminding him that the words a man says may not reflect his true troubles. How she rose to his every challenge.

How she saved his life.

But she did not tell the truth. As a newsman, that was the one thing he could never accept.

She lied. To his face. To his colleagues. And she had never truly apologized for the ill she had done. She likely didn't even know she should.

He might always love her, but he could never trust her.

In a politician's wife, though, a little truth-twisting was to be expected. She had been trained up for politics, whether she would or no. She would serve her public functions admirably. But in private, she would fail.

Olivia Delancey had never said she was sorry. She manipulated people to serve her own ends. She never would change, or even see the need to change.

He closed his eyes, casting her into the closed library of his memory. University trained, he was a creature of mind, after all.

If only that powerful organ could convince his heart.

THIRTY-FOUR

Good riddance to that rapacious Corsican. Mayhap we should set aside another island to house those mischievous and mutable members of our press whose chief argument for deception is that they only repeated what their purchasers liked to hear. Alternately, we have sackcloth at the ready.

—The Register

A half-hour into the interview, Bragge had the story. This time, the woman's explanation was watertight. He could see the forks in the path where he had mistaken her, and she had willingly let him slip into error. He'd seen Purdy's expressions, but read them the wrong way: Not shy, guilty.

But he still did not have the answer to the most important question. Why?

He finished writing out a line, watching her through his eyelashes. Smudges under her eyes spoke of poor sleep. But her hair was perfect, pulled back into a neat sweep away from her high forehead. She maintained the proper façade, though anyone who knew her would see she was not happy.

She met his gaze with the same forthrightness she had met his questions. It seemed she could not untruthfully answer a direct question.

He would test that now.

"Just one more question. You have been so patient; I do appreciate it." He waited for her to acknowledge the compliment, putting her in his debt, but she did not take the bait. "I must ask. Why?"

"Why am I speaking with you?"

"No. Earlier than that. Why did you wish to give away your work?"

She pressed her palms on the table. Flecks of brown dotted the tips of one of her cream-colored gloves. She stared at them a moment, then raised her gaze to him. "I thought I was not allowed to have work, as you put it."

Releasing a hand, she tapped her temple. "Ladies cannot create." She looked away from him, down the narrow aisle made by the overlarge table to the pianoforte opposite them. "But I could. But what good did it do? Buried in my piano bench."

"So you posted it to your music teacher?"

"I sent it to the one person who might say, yes, well done, good show. One person. In private, of course."

Bragge allowed her a moment's communion with the inanimate object, then flicked his hand to draw her attention back to him. "And he made it famous."

She nodded. "He was the first to sell it, as you put it, to his mates and to Wellington. All I did was write it." She shrugged, her gaze far away. "It seemed a fair-enough trade."

"Fair enough, as far as it goes. Why come forward now?"

Her mouth set in a straight line. "Must that be in the story?"

"If you wish people to give you the benefit of the doubt."

"I don't care about that."

"You should." She was hiding something, but he wasn't sure if it was to save herself or another. It shocked him how much of the lady's story was about protecting others.

He set down his notebook and pen and showed her his palms, no note-taking, all innocence. She didn't need to know he had a masterful memory. "Why don't you tell me, and we can decide together whether it should be in the story?"

She considered him a moment. Bragge reflected her expression. Of all the women Will could have fallen in with, she had the purest motives, the cleanest aims. But she had gone about them entirely wrong.

"You often get what you want, don't you?" she said. The question told him she was his. He took care not to smile.

Boot steps in the hall drew her attention. Bragge cursed *sotto voce*. Will was back too soon.

He kicked out a foot and pushed the door nearly shut. His employer came into view through the crack of space that remained. Bragge signaled that he was doing an interview. Will nodded and headed across the hall to his office. For a moment, Bragge thought he'd miscalculated. Then Will shut his door, and Bragge's mind eased.

He turned his gaze back to the lady. She raised a brow, but he shook his head. "No one can overhear us. We often use this as an interview room."

She pushed her chair back. The specks on the glove, was that blood? He reached out, grabbing her left hand. Gasping, she pulled it back. But she didn't rise from the chair.

"You've hurt your hand?" How would a lady hurt her hand? No distractions. "Pardon me. Your story. Why the change?"

"Have you ever been in love?" Bragge did not allow the question to throw him, though he was sore-tested when she took up his writing hand in her two gloved ones. "I had not, at the time."

"You have since?"

"But I saw Merry and Martin. They were in love. Why must they be kept apart? Money, of course. Martin had none." She petted down the back of his hand as if it were a tiny lap dog.

"I had to help. How rare is love? How fragile." She winced and pulled her hand away. Bragge already missed the touch. "I would play the piano during my lesson while the two of them sat giggling at each other on the loveseat. Neither would have an ear for me for the entire hour."

"But something changed."

"Merry's father discovered them, somehow. He called Martin off, and Martin took the King's shilling that afternoon."

"A true romantic." Bragge fought the itch to pick up the pen.

"Willful." She glanced toward the door again. He couldn't let her bolt. Not yet. "And he was returned to us, broken. Even less promising as a suitor."

He leaned forward, attracting her attention again. "So you helped them yet again."

"I had to." She furrowed her brows, waved a hand as if to conjure an explanation from the air. "I cannot be who I will. I'm a lady, first and only. But I wanted to live, to love. Even if only by proxy."

He waited to see if more would come. Her brow cleared, and he thought he'd lost the moment, but then her crystalline eyes clouded, and then shimmered.

He saw her now. "You thought if you could make someone else happy, help these two people, then." He paused.

"Then I might be happy, as well." She tried to smile, her lip rising at the corner, then falling flat again. "At least as happy as I'm allowed to be."

So sweet, and so sweetly misguided. Time to push. "May I tell you what I think?"

For a moment, Bragge thought she would say no. She pulled out a handkerchief from her little bag and dabbed the corners of her eyes. Then she looked up at him again, nodding.

"I think of all the people you have deceived, you have deceived yourself the most."

She gaped at him. He was used to that.

"Answer me this: Have any of your noble sacrifices made your family any better? Made anyone happier?"

She only stared at him. He shrugged. "You think you are so special? All you daughters of high-born ladies are the same. A generation of doormats raised by a generation of selfish mothers."

"You know nothing about it." Her voice reminded him of the release-valve on the steam press, whisper-spit.

"You don't even raise your voice when you are angry. Do I lie?"

She pushed on the table to rise to her feet. "You think you know so much. Why not just write your story based on that?"

So she did have a temper. He'd guessed right. His eyes flicked toward the door. Still safe.

"Sit, sit. I jest, is all." He rose and went to the sideboard, pulling out an opened bottle of red wine. He poured a small glass for her and a larger one for himself. "Here. A toast. To making things better." As she raised her glass to those beautiful lips, he said, "For everyone."

She drank in small sips. He couldn't see her swallow. And her gaze kept darting to the piano. He had enough for his story, and then some. Time to swing his plan into action.

"Bentley says you brought another piece of music."

"My most beautiful piece."

"I quite liked the seaside one. Is it like that?"

She swirled the wine in her glass and then set it down. "Not as cheery."

"This is sad?"

"It's about loss. I lost my brother as an infant. It changed our lives."

She didn't need to say more. The heir, and a baby. He could well imagine the blow to the family. She looked to be remembering it, as well.

"Play it for me."

She balled her hands into fists.

"You do want it published, don't you?" She closed her eyes. He thought she might cry. "People deserve to hear such beauty."

She let a long breath out, rolled up to standing. He watched her round the head of the table, then pull her dark skirts around to take a seat at the piano. As she pulled her gloves off, he slid down his chair to reach for the door with his foot and push it open again.

She settled in to play.

Only a few bars into the piece, mere solo notes and simple chords, the tune had drawn tears from his dry creekbed eyes. He was transported back to a misty field, a graveyard. His mother's grave. The soft pitter-patter harmony above the somber melody painted both the happiness and the pain of the beloved, forever lost.

This was Waterloo, just as much as her march was. Only this captured the end of the day, the shattered buildings, torn earth, and broken bodies now at rest as the shroud of night blanketed them.

And this was a tune that only a woman could write, though he never would tell her so. All the despair of events out of her control gone terribly wrong. Fathers and their blessed boys returned home broken, or not at all.

Women were the foot-soldiers of civilian life, the front lines of society. War and death were trouble sure, but finite. Life went on forever.

But listening to her play, he also heard the strength of generations whose will to carry on superseded the grisly blows of battle.

Then he heard a shuffle across the hall, and smiled.

At the sound of the piano, Will lurched to his feet. He threw down the pages he hadn't been able to concentrate on, doubly frustrated.

Damn Bentley's eyes. The man had to know how Will would feel about his fooling around at the piano right now. Just as much as he'd enjoy watching the press jam as the night edition started its run.

Yet the tune he was playing across the hall was new, and dark, subtle yet swirling, powerful. Its rough contours matched the roiling of his thoughts, its overtones the regret and loss of the past few days. Had the man read his mind?

As he passed into the hall, Will suddenly couldn't take another step. He sagged against the wall, his mind overloaded with portraits from his past. His mother giggling and spinning in the kitchen wearing her new Easter finery. Her frantic eyes darting toward the door at every sound when father didn't return home after the trial. Clapping and smiling at the steps to their new home, face full in sunlight because the portico was not yet finished. Turning to stroke his cheek and say how proud she was of him. Cool hand gentle on his as he struggled to accept her fade into death.

His father, fighting laughter as he scolded Will for dropping the type box and for the first time letting loose a stream of boyish curses. Bent over the stand-up table, hand on his forehead as he struggled to reconcile the shop's ledgers. Stumbling and blinking in the cloudy sun, grayed hair past his shoulders, as he stepped out of the arch of Newgate prison. And that last night, gone to stone before Will could get back from the presses to bid him farewell.

The single notes of the music, raining down, dredged up all his losses, all his ghosts, all his buried pain. Katherine, farther afield in Virginia than a torment of a little sister should be allowed to be. Lady Deidre, whose face he couldn't recall but whose hands had once branded his skin.

Olivia.

At the thought of memories of her already being tucked away into his past, no longer a part of his present, pain bit into him. He lurched upright, brushing at his eyes with a knuckle. His visions of her came with a white-hot poker through his chest. And they didn't stop.

The soft give of her backside during the Regent's affair. How quickly her wide-eyed shock at his nakedness after the bath changed to vivid curiosity. The salt-sweet taste of her belly. The gentle sound of her murmuring music in her sleep.

From his first look at her, a diamond in a pig's sty of a tavern, he was gone. If only the pain had come then, and saved him this endless wrenching loss now.

She was consigned to his memory, but even in his mind she fought him. She would be remembered, if it killed him.

He thrust himself across the hall and deeper into that blasted music. "Bentley, get the lead out. It's nearly press time."

Then he saw her.

She had stopped playing, hands still over the keys. The last chords lingered as if on a draft, though he did not know how as there seemed to be no air in the room.

Beautifully turned out, her dark-rimmed eyes spelled her sorrow.

Of course, it had to be her music that had drawn him in. More folly. He turned his gaze, and his anger, on Bragge.

"You're letting her spin you a new tale?"

His reporter pushed back from the table, not least bit ruffled. "She tells a fine story, even when it's the truth."

"Truth," Will spat out.

"All tales are someone's truth. We all of us sift our facts to best effect, some better than others." Bragge took in Will's glare

347

and shrugged. He sketched a quick bow toward Olivia, and then he scooted out of the room. "Must go write the leading lines," he called, already down the hall.

Will turned back to Olivia. She already had one glove nearly on, taking care with the fingers.

"You are in pain?"

She stopped, staring at him. Her gaze was a steam pipe linked down the length of his spine. Then she looked down at her hand, and he could stand again. "My hand. A little."

She quickly donned the second glove and stood, not even fastening the buttons. She looked toward the door, as if gauging which direction around the table would be quicker.

He shut the door.

"Olivia. Why?"

She sank back down on the seat. Not looking at him, she started doing up the buttons on her gloves. The ones on her left hand gave her trouble. She must have bruised the tips by playing too much guitar again.

He made his way around the table toward her, not so fast as to completely frighten her but certainly not slow enough that she would think she could get away.

"Let me." He dropped to one knee before her.

She held the arm out, palm up. As he started doing up the half-dozen buttons, he felt her sob.

He kept his eyes on the buttons a half-second longer, and then looked up at her.

She still gazed at her hand, and his on top of it. Her long lashes shimmered with tears. Her mouth trembled.

He interlaced his fingers with hers, the fabric of the glove immaterial.

"Why, Livvie?"

"I'm so sorry."

He closed his eyes, pulling their locked hands up to the side of his face. "I'm sorry, too." She leaned into him, resting her cheek on the top of his head. He wrapped his free arm around her waist. For an endless moment, they breathed in this unlikely connection that felt so natural.

She sniffed and pulled away. She already had a handkerchief.

"You were talking with Bragge?"

"Telling the truth."

"Why? Why now?"

"I'm leaving." Her breath hitched on a sigh. He felt her hand grip his tightly, then loosen.

He did not let go.

"Forgive me." She stood. He did not let go her hand. "I did not wish to see you."

"Why?"

"I do not mean to go on hurting you."

"Look at me. Do I look hurt?" Her sadness ripped at his heart, but his outer layers wouldn't show it.

She looked down at him. Giving a great sniffle, she tilted her head, considering him.

"Your knees do."

She had him there. He lurched to his feet again, but as that made him tower over her he lifted her to a seat on the tabletop.

"You read me like a book, Miss Delancey."

"I told him too much."

"Bragge does that to everyone. He'll make sure you come out all right. He's half in love with you, you know."

"He's not." But her eyes took on that considering glint under the tears.

"I beg to differ. I know the signs, and he had quite a few of them."

"Signs?"

"His heart goes fluttery in her presence. In his case, that means his hands go fluttery." He flapped his fingers, drawing a wavering smile.

He pressed on. "He flushes, and he finds himself sizing up other men as potential opponents. He feels the need to best any man in the vicinity." This time her smile was true. It warmed his soul.

"I wish that were so."

"Why are you here, Olivia?"

She traced his jaw with one of her fragile fingertips. His knees nearly cracked as he fought to hold himself still, to allow her to drive this coach, wherever it may take them.

"I can't bear that you think ill of me, William Marsh. I know you can never forget, but might you forgive? Some day?" Her voice cracked on a sob.

He'd already forgiven her, perhaps even as far back as at her father's home. The Baron had no idea what his true treasure was.

"Of course," he said. "Is that all?"

She looked down again, and he saw now that he'd never lifted his hands from her waist. So much for giving her the reins. "All I can expect. But, perhaps, I can allow myself, to hope?"

He pulled her to him as if he would absorb her under his skin entirely. Through layers of clothing, his heart could hear her heart's staccato call. She hiccupped, her head brushing against his chin. He kissed the mass of sunshine curls atop her head.

She exhaled, relaxing into him, and he breathed through the burgundy overtones of wine to the essence of her. Her breaths slowed to match his.

At last, he said, "Why wait?"

Olivia's entire attention had moved from memorizing the warm cocoon of his embrace to soaking up every pulse of pressure from his lips on her crown. His kiss washed down her face and neck and reached down her spine, a healing balm.

Then her mind registered the words.

She pulled away from him, startled. Did he truly mean to allow her into his life again? It was far more than she deserved, but how could she doubt him? Will never lied.

"You heard right." His grip on her hips tightened. He leaned in to place a gentle kiss on her forehead. "Unless you'd rather keep up with the waterworks."

"But I'm a liability to the paper."

"I've quit the paper."

"Liar."

"Well, put it out to let. Bentley can be the lightning rod now. These next years will be about politics and land, and he's far better at that. My joy – here – is with the mechanics, the new presses. We've agreed I can keep tinkering all I like."

She trusted him, but could she trust herself? What if she hurt him again? She couldn't bear it. Her breath hiccupped just thinking of it.

He pulled away, as if she'd already failed him. But then he bent to kiss her temple, then each eyelid. "You're leaving London?"

"What if I hurt you again?"

"I'll heal. What's a little blood on the floor between lovers?" He paused, as if he meant to take back that last word. Instead, he drew his thumb down the edge of her ear. She shivered.

"Yes. I mean, no, not immediately. I must quit my parents' home, but not till they return from Brighton."

"Pettigrew summers with the Regent? His rise is complete. Where do you go?"

"Plymouth."

"So far?"

"It's not as dear as the city."

He traced the line of her jaw. "Calm and pink. You know, Berkshire's not so dear. There's a manor house I know needs a mistress. And a piano player."

She sighed. It was too much. "Don't."

"You won't even consider it? Must I drop to my knees?"

Sliding to the floor, his hands trailing down her sides, he managed to set nearly every nerve in her skin to sizzle. He came to a rest on his knees, hands cupping the tops of her thighs.

"But I am a liar."

"Aren't we all? I won't force you to hide yourself, and then you won't be forced to lie. You'll never feel pilloried by your good intentions again."

He saw her heart, read her soul and her black deeds, and embraced her. He listened to her, and understood, the perfect audience. She could not ask for more.

"Livvie?" He reached up to tap lightly on her temple.

"One more secret."

He hauled her down to sit on his knee, one hand under her chin. "Only one? Out with it."

She fell into those ocean-green eyes, so familiar, and as necessary to life as the breath she took in. "I love you."

He did nothing at all for a long moment. A rivulet of fear rippled across her brow. She pulled a hand away, ready to catch herself if she fell.

Then he leaned in, drawing her chin toward him. Their lips met, with the usual cacophony of sounds erupting in her mind. But this time her eyes were open, as were his, and she followed his gaze deep into his mind and heart. And saw herself, beloved.

She closed her eyes. He might be a writer, but he didn't need print to make his point.

THIRTY-FIVE

Here, then, is the full accounting of that most-beloved Tune, comprising a story of love deferred, an act of overwhelming generosity and, not least of all, a tale of a Lady.

—The Beacon

Though the heat of summer had faded into the chill of fall, the Swan's Neck ale-house during a political rally looked and smelled much the same. Only the man of the hour had changed.

Will's face ached from smiling, but the men of Berkshire seemed to prefer it to the serious look. They quaffed their drafts and peppered him with questions about the changes in the Corn Tax and what he planned to do about the growing numbers of vagrant former soldiers.

They listened to his lofty plans, though they doubted he could do much about it.

"Let him at it," a wiry farmer said. "He cannae do us worse

than the last duffer." A chorus of guffaws greeted him. Will smiled to show he didn't take it ill – and because it was true.

Pettigrew and his baroness had stood them up, but the crowd didn't appear unduly disappointed. He expected his "sponsor" would leave him with the bill as well, but he could easily afford ale for four score men, not just the four dozen here.

Livvie, still unsure of her reception in public though the story had been out now nearly a week, also was missing, most likely clattering around her parents' home nursing that blasted guitar like a baby.

As he made to step off the short stool after a brief speech, a farmer, so blond he must be a descendant of Vikings, called out, "One more question, if you will." Will stood straighter. "What think you of females who dabble in commerce?" A few men "Oyed" in support of the question.

"Many women must shift for themselves. It is an unfortunate fact of life these days. Your women work, do they not?"

"Aye. But they do not take on airs, or claim they are painters. Or artists."

Will took in a deep breath, choking down the smoke and hops in the air. These men were good men, but common laborers. They would expect their women – and their politicians – to hew to conservative values. It was bad enough he was a Whig. He should tell them what they wanted to hear.

But he could not lie, even as a politician.

"Truth is, women can do a great deal more than we give them credit for." A few men growled friendly askance. "No, hear me out. I know two great writers, women, who must hide behind anonymity to be accepted and published. And at least one great composer."

"No more anonymous." The crowd laughed.

"Aye. And punished for it, weren't she?" Will had their attention. "I believe anyone who can create music that moves the feet and stirs the soul has the right – nay, the obligation – to bring it to the attention of the world. The fault is ours if we will not recognize it."

The room went silent. Will saw his political career crumbling away. He stepped off the stool, and then sat on it.

So be it.

A boisterous, laughing cheer erupted, led by that blond giant. The men surrounding Will turned toward the kitchen door. Then they parted, allowing him to see.

Olivia, in Whig blue and buff-orange from her bicorne hat to her dark riding skirt, sauntered toward him. Her color was high, her smile big but her manner cautious. Didn't she know how much he'd missed her? Yesterday afternoon tea seemed forever ago.

Stunned, he stood.

"Mr. Marsh's words are a balm to my ears. Especially as I have composed a theme especially for him. I call it 'A Call to Service,' and you may hear it during his swearing-in. Provided, of course, he receives your vote."

The men raised their tankards to her, cheering.

She had changed, as well. She no longer hid behind her buffoon parents. He marveled as he watched her charm these men in her own, quieter way. Simply by listening to them, and paying attention, she won them over.

As she had him.

~

After the tap-room, Olivia had no wish to let go of his hand. They had walked from the inn, down the lane, and on the half-mile to Will's house remaining thus attached, and she did not see any reason they should stop now, merely because they had arrived at the entrance.

Will appeared to have other ideas.

"You must let me go."

"Why?"

"So I may lift you over the threshold."

"Barbaric."

"There must be some pomp and circumstance." He pulled her arm behind her as he gently swept her into his arms. She wondered how many boxes of type she weighed that he could hoist her so easily. "Do you wish to wait for a license?"

"A little late for that."

She tucked her head under his chin, just as insurance against crashing, as he stepped into the hall. Her heart stung, it was so full of joy.

Cobbett had crowed over his success for a day or two, and then moved on to the Regent's projected spending on his pavilion in Brighton. And while some of her mother's cronies thought less of her, a surprising number did not. She might still grace scores of parlors, if not Almack's.

Best, Will wanted to be with her. He wanted to be seen with her in public. Take her to the musicale, now that his evenings were free. He wanted her to live here, with him. And her piano.

She wriggled out of his grasp and ran up the stairs and down the hall. The instrument was still there. She touched its ruddy frame just to be sure.

Trailing her, Will leaned against the instrument, crossing his arms and frowning, but his kelpie eyes gave him away.

"I see where I stand in the pecking order."

"You know that's not true."

He winked. "Come down the hall. I want to show you something."

"I've seen that already."

"Minx. It's not my body. Something else."

Curious, she followed him. All the doors were open, three on each side, letting the September afternoon's light criss-cross the hall. He led her to the first doorway on the left. She looked inside.

Empty. "Just like home," she said, sternly ordering her shoulders to stop drooping.

"No. The opposite." She looked a question at him. "A new house. Needs a warehouse of new furniture. And someone to sit on it. And make some babies to sit on the rest."

"Be my bride, Olivia. And populate my home, our home, with little reprints of you."

"Or you," she said, her voice teasing to mask the surge of emotion she felt. Then she let the mask go. "Will, tell the truth."

"Always."

"Have you truly forgiven me? Could this work?"

"Do you doubt it?"

"I don't doubt you. But I make so many mistakes."

"We all of us stumble. But we pick ourselves up." He kissed her forehead, her cheekbone. The touch soothed the butterflies in her belly. "I will always be there to pick you up. Or to stand by while you pick yourself up."

"Why?"

"Because I love you. And I feel the love you hold for me. It fills you to the brim, like those tears." He gently flicked the tear from her lashes.

"How can you be sure?" Her voice caught.

"How can you?"

She hugged him close, breathing his perfect scent. "The same way as you."

"Just so." He swung her around, pushing her toward a center doorway. "There is one bedroom completely furnished. What do you say we make a start on that family now?"

Truth be told, that was exactly what she wanted.

Author's Note

I love to include real events in my stories, and since the action revolves around a newspaper and its publisher I needed a couple of doozies to be worthy of their attention. So imagine my delight, when reading about ships-of-the-line and other nautical footnotes, I came across the story of Napoleon's sailing to England after Waterloo. Well, English waters.

After the British government turned down the French request for a passport for Bonaparte to travel to the United States, he and his followers debated whether to ask again for a passport or to make a run for it, challenging the British blockade near Rochefort, France—or to request political asylum. Knowing that the British had a tradition of harboring political refugees, he chose the latter. He dictated a letter to the Regent:

"A victim to the factions which distract my country, and to the enmity of the greatest powers of Europe, I have terminated my political career, and I come, like Themistocles, to throw myself

upon the hospitality of the British people. I put myself under the protection of their laws; which I claim from your Royal Highness, as the most powerful, the most constant, and the most generous of my enemies.

—Rochefort 13 July 1815"

His negotiators, though, treated with Captain Maitland, who while he agreed that Bonaparte and his motley crew could come aboard under a flag of truce made no promise of asylum, and even hinted that his government might not agree that Maitland had any authority in the matter at all. The French envoys saw his declarations as overly careful and were very encouraged; and after all, Napoleon's younger brother, Lucien, had been captured by the British in 1810 and was now settled in a cozy country house near Worcester. It didn't seem to occur to them that the British might not see the conqueror of Europe in the same light.

On the morning of July 15, Napoleon and some 33 retainers, including women and children, boarded the *Bellerophon*. "I am come to throw myself on the protection of your Prince and your laws," he said to the captain. After a day of settling in, including stringing nets along the sides so the children wouldn't tumble off, they set off for England.

They arrived early on July 24, and immediately were an object of interest for the locals. Maitland had received orders not to let "anyone" off the ship, so the sailors dropped anchor deep in Brixham Harbor, chasing off the usual bread and goods merchants who'd come out in their shore boats. But they couldn't hide the news, and soon every inn was full, and people in boats and yachts came from up and down the coast to see if they could catch sight of the most famous man in the world. Two days later, the *Bellerophon* sailed for Plymouth, where it met with the same reception. A lieutenant estimated the crowd on July 27 at 10,000 people, seeing roughly a thousand vessels, each with more than 8 people aboard.

A week later, Napoleon had his answer:

"It would be inconsistent with our duty to this country, and to His Majesty's Allies, if we were to leave to General Bonaparte the means or opportunity of again disturbing the peace of Europe, and renewing the calamities of war: it is therefore unavoidable that he should be restrained in his personal liberty... The island of St Helena has been selected for his future residence..."

On August 4, the *Bellerophon* and its attendant ships weighed anchor, to rendezvous with the *Northumberland,* which would take the former emperor and a few retainers to St Helena.

The Wikipedia entry on the *Bellerophon* has a section on Napoleon's surrender, and also includes links to paintings that I used to describe the scene.

ALSO BY NICKY PENTTILA

Historical Fiction

A Note of Scandal

An Untitled Lady

The Spanish Patriot

Cooperative Realm: Frankie's Journeys

Cargo Trouble

Frankie Takes a Holiday

Frankie Takes a Dive

Frankie Finds a Dot

Frankie Takes a Bow

Frankie Finds a Home

Cooperative Realm: The Arkhide Chronicles

Hidden Planet

The Listeners

The Elders of Arkhide

Tales of Arkhide story collection

Here: Earthbound Fantasies and Futures

There: Journeys to Imagined Realms

Cosmic Weave

About the Author

Nicky Penttila writes about women who push back and the men sharp enough to keep up. Her novels have been featured by USA Today and the Historical Fiction Society. She also writes science fiction and fantasy—but ink and upheaval came first. Find more at nickypenttila.com.

www.ingramcontent.com/pod-product-compliance
Lightning Source LLC
Chambersburg PA
CBHW022349020726
47500CB00002B/183